"I can't keep you here against your will.

"Someone's bound to get hurt. That's not my intention at all."

Her insides fluttered. "Will you play any more tricks?"

"No." He said it with such honesty and compassion, but he looked so defeated standing there.

Her heart would *not* go out to him, she warned herself. "Can't you see—" she pleaded, stepping closer. "Can't you see? How am I supposed to know who to believe?"

Luke stepped closer. He lifted her hand, his unexpected touch sending a ripple cascading up her spine, and placed her palm over his heart. Then he flattened his own hand over hers. She felt the heat of his flesh beneath the cloth, the pounding of his blood.

"You're not supposed to know it, you're supposed to feel it."

She withdrew her hand, feeling as if it had been singed in a flame....

Luke's Runaway Bride

Kate Bridges

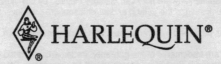

HARLEQUIN®

TORONTO • NEW YORK • LONDON
AMSTERDAM • PARIS • SYDNEY • HAMBURG
STOCKHOLM • ATHENS • TOKYO • MILAN • MADRID
PRAGUE • WARSAW • BUDAPEST • AUCKLAND

ISBN 0-373-29226-0

LUKE'S RUNAWAY BRIDE

Copyright © 2002 by Kathy Haupt

Available from Harlequin Historicals and
KATE BRIDGES

The Doctor's Homecoming #597
Luke's Runaway Bride #626

Please address questions and book requests to:
Harlequin Reader Service
U.S.: 3010 Walden Ave., P.O. Box 1325, Buffalo, NY 14269
Canadian: P.O. Box 609, Fort Erie, Ont. L2A 5X3

Dedicated to my dear friends Donna L. and Heather H.—
thank you both for your encouragement,
and your wonderful sense of humor.

Chapter One

Denver, September 1873

Tall, rugged and dangerous. Who was he?

Jenny Eriksen spotted the stranger from across the deserted street. Her pulse strummed with awareness.

Silhouetted in moonlight, the stranger walked his bay past the golden cottonwoods near the livery stable, then past the newly painted hitching posts of the corner café. A rough block of square shoulders and long legs, the man moved with muscled control. With a gun belt slung low around his hips, his Stetson tugged over his brow, he was the type of man in this wild mining town Jenny tried to avoid. Especially since the robbery in Daniel's office that afternoon.

For a moment, Jenny stopped breathing.

She had just stepped out of the crowded dance hall onto the boardwalk with her housekeeper. At first, she'd been relieved to escape the charity ball to run her delicate errand, but now Jenny wasn't so sure. In the cool night breeze, she studied the wavy black hair and somber, clean-shaven face of the stranger.

Lord, he was handsome. But what set him apart from other men was his air of isolation, of danger. His long, deliberate stride and his easy, graceful movements commanded obedience. Definitely a man who'd never interest her. She preferred…a *milder* man, who thought with his head and not his hands. A man like her wonderful Daniel, her fiancé.

The wind danced across her bare shoulders and stirred her blue velvet sleeves. Familiar piano music floating through the air eased her tension, reminding her she was safe. She yanked her peacock-feather shawl tight against her gown.

"Six months in Denver," she said, gulping perfume-scented air, "and I'm still not used to seeing strangers wearing guns."

Beside her, Olivia's satin skirts rustled. Dressed in pleated burgundy, the pretty dark woman peered up at Jenny. "At least in Boston, the men conceal them."

Stepping from the boardwalk onto the rutted path, Jenny watched the stranger disappear down an alley. She brushed him from her thoughts. Glancing up at the quarter moon, she relaxed and smiled. Tonight at the ball, Daniel had formally announced their engagement, and she wanted to waltz with excitement.

In four short months, she'd be Mrs. Daniel Kincaid. She was such a lucky woman. Wasn't it Daniel himself who'd organized this fine charity event? Such a kind, loving man. Her father was right in his arrangement, after all.

Two months wasn't a long time from first meeting to engagement, she admitted, but she shouldn't worry. She and Daniel had a solid base of companionship, and love and passion would grow from there. Marriage and children were what she'd always wanted.

Olivia adjusted her fringed wrap. "Did you tell Daniel where we're headed?"

"I tried, but he was talking to the banker and his wife, getting a big donation. I couldn't very well approach them with my bodice gaping open." With good humor, Jenny glanced down at the space where her button used to be, and pulled her shawl tighter. Her beaded bag dangled at her wrist.

"But we should tell someone—"

"If one more person sees my dress like this, I'll die of shame. Daniel's house is just around the corner. His butler couldn't leave the ball because he was serving drinks at the bar, but he told me where he keeps the sewing basket. He also gave me the key."

"Well…the fresh air's nice. My eyes are waterin' from the cigar smoke, and my nose…" Olivia, more of a sister than a housekeeper, chattered on in her usual lively manner, in a voice that had soothed Jenny since they were children.

Jenny yanked at the tight curls pinned on top of her head, wishing she'd arranged her hair in her usual beaver tail. She agreed with the elderly Windsor sisters next door—her hair was as straight and thin as a plank—but why had she allowed them to curl and powder it? Powder hadn't been used for decades!

Well, because it was the first time in two weeks, since the loss of their beloved cat, that Jenny had seen the two sisters smile. She hadn't the heart to refuse their offer.

Thank you kindly, but no. She had to practice saying those words more often.

They turned the corner, passing massive stone-and-cedar houses. Petticoats swished around their ankles. Tomorrow, Jenny would rise early. Her crate of bridal fabrics had finally arrived from the East, and she was itching to cut her wedding corset. In Boston, her late grandmother had taught her how to sew the finest undergarments—"lingerie," the French called it—and it still gave Jenny such pleasure.

Too bad she wasn't able to convince Daniel a lingerie store would be appropriate for a woman of her stature, even though it had been her dream since she was fourteen. When would he decide on the type of store he *did* consider appropriate?

Her father and brothers hadn't needed anyone's permission to plan their dreams when they'd decided as a family to move West. Why did she? Even Denver bankers had refused her loan requests, because she was a woman on her own. She still knew that newspaper clipping by heart—"Store owners needed in Denver. Plenty of opportunities for men and women"—and she ached for the challenge.

A train rumbled through the foothills, scattering her thoughts. As Olivia chattered on, Jenny glanced up through the trees.

She spotted *him* again and lightning bolted through her.

The same tall stranger. Wide shoulders and a massive frame, leaning on Daniel's porch. What did he want?

He wasn't looking at them. instead he pressed a bulky hand to his shoulder, and his suede jacket fell open. His white shirt was soaked with a spreading stain of blood.

Her heart jumped madly. Instinctively, she stepped toward him. He needed help.

But if she had a lick of sense, she'd turn around and run. As her footsteps slowed, his head came up. She heard a jingle of spurs. He gazed at her, level and bold, as if he had every right to be here. Her muscles quaked.

Apparently, Olivia hadn't noticed him. "…And so I answered, *'Oui, monsieur,'* and he was sure surprised to hear me speaking French. Couldn't imagine, he said, my folks being runaway slaves. My, it's cool—"

"Olivia," Jenny whispered, "look at the porch."

Her friend came to a stop and grimaced in dismay. "Sweet stars above! Let's get out of here."

She tugged at Jenny's sleeve, jiggling the feathers, but Jenny stayed put. If the man had wanted to attack them, he could have done it already. "He's injured. He needs help."

"Are you out of your mind? He looks dangerous! And you don't always have to be the one—"

"He must know Daniel. He must be a friend. Why else would he be on the porch?"

"Maybe he's the robber!"

Jenny swallowed, trying to control her fear, wishing Daniel had given her more details about the robbery instead of worrying he'd frighten her. "The sheriff's looking for the culprit, and the guilty man *wouldn't* be so foolish to stand right on Daniel's porch."

"We ought to run in the other direction. Bad things always come in threes, and this is the third thing today."

Jenny's gloved fingers tightened around her shawl. "That's an old wives' tale."

"You know you believe it. Ever since your shoe-lace broke this morning, you've had a run of bad luck. First the robbery, then your button. Poppin' off right in front of the entire church committee, I might add, exposin' more flesh than any of 'em has seen in the last decade. Now this." She motioned to the stranger. "Let's not get attacked by a lunatic!"

Jenny drew a clipped breath. He was much bigger than they were. "You're right, let's go back and get the men."

The stranger slumped forward, apparently in pain.

Compassion surged through her. "Are you...are you all right?" she called out.

Olivia gasped. "Jenny, don't talk to him."

He stood up, a tall dark figure in the shadows, swaying on his feet. "I'll be fine. I was...hoping for someone else. Looks like he's not coming."

Her voice wavered. "You need a doctor. Who are you?"

He staggered toward the side of the house, to the iron rings that studded the twisted cottonwood where he'd tied his horse. "I'll be heading out," he said, not bothering to give his name.

"Are you waiting for Daniel Kincaid?"

The stranger spun in her direction. He peered at her in potent silence. "Who's asking?"

Her stomach rose and fell. "I'm—I'm his fiancée. I could tell you where he is, but you really should see a doctor. Most of them are at the charity ball.

You can see the lights through the trees." She pointed. "We'll show you the way."

"We will not," Olivia squeaked.

Jenny scowled. "He might be bleeding to death."

"His *fiancée*," the man repeated, stumbling to his horse. In the streaky moonlight, Jenny caught the look of disgust that rippled across his face.

A tremble ran down her spine. Who in blazes was this man? Why was he snarling at the fact that Daniel had a fiancée? Daniel—her beloved, her protector. And hadn't she just decided, five minutes ago, she should learn to say no? Someone else could help this man. She inched back and signaled Olivia it was time to run.

She was about to spin away when the stranger placed his foot in the stirrup. Instead of swinging up, he staggered back and fell into the dirt. A moan escaped his lips.

Jenny's breath caught. The man was truly injured. As still as a boulder, he didn't rise.

She couldn't abandon a wounded man. She flung the gate open and dashed to his side.

Her friend shrieked. "We'll get beaten!"

"Hush, Olivia, he's unconscious. Come here and help me."

Jenny knelt at his side. His hat had fallen off. A breeze billowed between them, lifting black hair off the handsome curves of his face. Light glimmered from the lamppost and caught his chin. A threadlike scar ran from his left ear to beneath his jaw, as if someone had once tried to slit his throat. Jenny gasped. Controlling her shaking fingers, she lifted his shirt. The bandage around his ribs oozed fresh blood. How much pain was he in? Could she help him without endangering herself or Olivia? Living alone as he did, Daniel only required the services of one hired man, and he was at the ball. The house was empty.

Olivia's cloth boots crunched in the dirt beside her.

Jenny clawed her hands underneath his shoulders, groaning under the weight. "Help me get him into the house."

"What if he tries to have his way with us?"

"He's in no condition to attack us."

Olivia picked up a chunky rock. "Should I hit him over the head to keep him that way?"

"No. Grab his legs and help me drag him in."

In a back recess of his mind, Luke McLintock registered the faint scent of perfume. He stirred.

Regaining consciousness, but still dazed from pain, Luke slowly opened his heavy lids. Where was he? His blurry vision focused. A woman was leaning over him. One cameo button—the top one—was missing from her gown, and for a blissful, groggy moment, Luke was sure he'd died and entered the pearly gates of male heaven.

Intrigued, he stared at the glorious vision of creamy cleavage. The stickpin she'd apparently tried to fix it with still pierced one side of the gaping blue velvet, and beneath it all, her lavender lace corset—a color he'd never seen before in a corset—strained to contain her curves. He held his breath, anticipating, hoping, her cups would soon runneth over.

Then pain hammered through his right side, reminding him he wasn't in heaven. He was slumped in a leather chair, stripped from the waist up, while she wrapped gauze around his ribs. Cool air surged across his hair-matted chest. Where was he? Lying still, he eyed the room from beneath her dancing blue velvet sleeve.

Two kerosene lamps lit the well-to-do office. Cherry-wood paneling, rawhide sofa and chairs, silver-framed photographs—it contained all the trinkets an up-and-coming land developer could afford.

Daniel's house. But since the bastard wasn't home, there was no reason for Luke to stay. Besides, he had a man waiting for him at the rail station. But he'd return to haul Daniel back to Cheyenne. After what had happened between them today, Luke sure as hell would. He shifted on the plush leather. Dammit, his hands were tied behind his back!

He yanked hard on the ropes and cursed. The blonde jumped away from his heaving body, clutching a pair of silver scissors. Strands of long golden hair loosened from her upswept arrangement and tumbled over naked satin shoulders.

Luke peered up into startling blue eyes. In her mid-twenties, she had a heart-shaped face and determination in her gaze. The single dimple in her cheek fluttered, betraying her cool demeanor. He'd seen prettier women before, but something about the intelligent look in her eye held his gaze. Then her friend stepped forward, waving a gun in his face. His own Colt, for cripes sake.

"Put that thing down," he snarled.

But the woman braced herself. By the smooth way she clasped the ivory grip and cocked the hammer with her thumb, he knew she'd held a gun before. Uneasiness snaked along his spine.

The blonde drew her shoulders back and ran a

hand along her sleeve. "Don't get mad, we're trying to help you."

He shook his head to clear the fog and braced his long legs in front of him. "Then why'd you tie me up?"

"We didn't, not until..." she gulped and lowered her eyes to his chest "...not until we took your shirt off and saw those scars. We got scared."

The knife wounds were old, from saloon brawls in his younger days, and three or four from overnight stays in jail with not-so-pleasant company. He hardly noticed them anymore.

With trembling lips, the quick dark woman stepped forward. She looked a bit older than the blonde. "You like to fight, mister?"

"Used to."

"Not anymore?"

"No."

The blonde leaned in past her friend and inspected him, causing him to squirm. "Then how'd you get your latest injury?"

Daniel shot me. Luke swallowed as he stared at the flushed, upturned face. What would she say to that? His gaze dropped from her eyes to her creamy throat to the top of her scooped neckline. Heat pounded through his muscles. With a stab of disappointment, he noticed her stickpin was again in place, concealing her curves. Gazing back up at her breathless expression, he recalled she was Daniel's fiancée.

The fact that she belonged to him made Luke's teeth rattle. And telling her the truth about this injury might make matters worse. "Scraped myself on wire fencing.'' Well, the flesh wound *could* be mistaken for a scrape.

"You a drover?"

"I help out on a ranch."

"Where?"

"North of here."

Her eyes widened. "If—if we let you go, how do we know we can trust you?"

His head started to cloud. "Look, my name's Luke. If you'd really like to help me, you'll untie me." He yanked at the ropes, but they dug deeper. The sting in his side flared.

"I wouldn't pull at the ropes anymore," said the older one matter-of-factly, adjusting her bonnet. "It'll just start tearin' into your skin. Jenny's grand-dad was a sailor, direct from Sweden, then Boston. He taught her how to tie over twenty different kinds of knots. What's this one called again, Jenny?"

"The constrictor knot." A flash of amusement danced across Jenny's face. She bit it back, or had he imagined it? "The harder you pull, the more con-stricted you'll get."

Wonderful. One was good with a gun and the other good with knots. The two of them made a dangerous pair, and any man who thought otherwise was a fool. He assessed her boldly, and to his delight, she got flustered. With a huff, she smoothed the tendrils from her face and stepped beside her friend in front of the ballooning drapes.

So Daniel had picked a girl from Boston.

Well, lah-dee-dah.

It did explain the way she spoke. She fidgeted with her hands. They weren't the usual smooth hands of a privileged woman. One bulky engagement ring. A two-inch scratch on one palm, and closely bitten nails. Hands used to doing things.

Would she be as shocked as he'd been to discover *her* beloved Daniel had a five-year-old son? One he'd ignored since birth? And the only damn reason Luke was here tonight was to haul Daniel back to acknowledge his son, Adam. With the boy's mother now gone, Adam's only relative was his father.

Arguing with Daniel in his office this afternoon hadn't worked, but Luke had to solve the problem soon. What the hell was he supposed to do with a five-year-old kid? Keep him in Luke's own room above the saloon? Ridiculous.

A flash of inspiration hit him. Maybe this woman could help. When she married Daniel, then maybe she and Daniel could raise the boy together. Wouldn't that be a nice, tidy solution?

"Tell us what you're doing on Daniel's doorstep. How...how well do you know him?" Jenny's clear blue eyes, as deep as the Rio Grande, met his. His palms got clammy.

A yearning to escape this place and ride hell-bent for Cheyenne pulsed through him. "I know him well. Daniel and I grew up together. His family took me in when my father died. We used to be best friends."

Jenny's mouth sprang open in alarm. She stepped back and took a good, hard look at him. "Best friends?" Her slender neck infused with color, then her cheeks. She clutched a hand to her throat. "Oh Lord, what have we done? Are you one of the McLintock boys?" She gulped. "I mean, men?"

He nodded. "He told you about us?"

"How down-and-out you were, and how he helped your whole family get back on your feet."

Luke felt his neck flush with shame. Daniel probably made himself sound like a hero. He hadn't helped *all* of them. Luke's brothers were shipped off to another neighbor. But because Luke was only six, the youngest, he'd stayed with his ma. Scrubbing and cleaning and picking up after all the Kincaids. Wasn't that why Daniel had nicknamed him "workin' class boy"? Luke's jaw stiffened at the memory.

"I'm sorry," Jenny said, glancing down at her hands, "I didn't mean to make you sound…down and desperate."

He shrugged, pretending he didn't care, and glanced at her friend. At least she was lowering the gun.

Jenny stumbled behind him and worked at the ropes. "I'm Jenny Eriksen, and this here's Olivia Gibson, my dear friend and housekeeper. Sorry we had to resort to these tactics, but we're alone and this town's full of men who…"

The scent of her skin and faint perfume roused him. White powder floated onto his black denim pants. *Powder?*

"Sorry," she said, "it's my hair." She nervously wiped the powder off his muscled thigh. With her warm touch, he felt an awakening right down to his boots. Blushing, she slid behind him again. Her hot fingers played along his cool wrists.

The ropes slackened as she continued talking. "No wonder you came to Daniel's door. Who else would help you with your unfortunate injury but your best friend?"

Hah! His best friend was the one who'd shot him. An accident, yes, as Luke had struggled to grab the derringer from Daniel, but the recollection made his blood pound. Daniel had ordered him out of the office, shrieking at him to shut his mouth about the kid. After the bullet exploded, Luke's fury could barely be contained. He'd raged out into the street, determined to wash his hands of Daniel forever. They hadn't spoken for years, and why not keep it that way?

But once Luke had gotten back to the rail station, calmed down and bandaged his ribs, he'd realized he couldn't walk away. Dammit, he couldn't. If he did, what would happen to Adam?

Luke's last promise to Adam's mother, Maria, was that he'd do the proper thing for the boy. A man's word was everything.

"There we go," said Jenny. The knots released and Luke surged to his feet, the quick movement causing her to draw a sharp breath. He brushed against Jenny's bare shoulder with his own naked one and tried to ignore the heat that trembled between them. Light-headed, he staggered back. He hadn't lost that much blood, but due to the day's chaotic events, he hadn't eaten since breakfast.

"I didn't mean to scare you," he said. He rubbed his sore wrist, then held out a hand. "Pleased to meet you."

She reached out and their hot palms met. His stomach shuddered with the contact. She was Daniel's, Luke reminded himself. His jaw tensed. He cleared his throat, forced himself to drop her hand, and looked away.

He watched Olivia slide his gun back into its holster. First chance he got, he'd snatch it back. For some reason, a rock lay on the desktop, and she stared at it in a peculiar way.

"I suppose," said Olivia, swinging around, "if you're Daniel's—" She lowered her lashes. "I mean if you're *Mr.* Daniel's friend, I should do my duty and put together a tray of refreshments. Looks like you could use a bite to eat." The housekeeper eyed him like a cat eyeing a spider, and he twisted under the scrutiny. "Wait here, *s'il vous plaît.*"

"Much obliged." When she disappeared behind the ornately carved door, he turned to Jenny. "You two speak French?"

The mountain of curls on her head jiggled. Jenny's smile was slightly crooked, but somehow balanced her lopsided brow and single dimple, and held his attention more than it ought to. Altogether her face made a captivating composition.

"Olivia's teaching me a few words. She lost her folks when she was a baby, and just discovered they came from New Orleans." Walking to the desk, Jenny replaced the scissors. "Olivia's become enamored with everything from Louisiana. The language, Creole cooking..."

He splayed a palm over his bandaged ribs and Jenny trailed off into a sudden, uncomfortable silence. She lowered her gaze to his chest, and he saw her swallow. He couldn't help but lower his eyes to *her* bountiful assets. Her pin had come undone again, exposing creamy rounds. His heart thudded and he wondered if his wound was making him feverish, or the woman.

She flushed and snatched her dress closed. Her misty blue eyes flared. A gentleman would have looked away, her gaze seemed to accuse. Well, he sure as hell was no gentleman. But he did look away, scouring the room for his clothes while she adjusted hers.

His boots sank into the plush braided rug. He stepped to a leather wing chair and retrieved his bloodstained shirt. Pain jabbed his right side. He eyed the whiskey on the polished desk. "Mind if I take a drink?"

"Help yourself."

It slid down his throat like fire. He took another, until the pain retreated and his thoughts spun.

How could he get Daniel to follow him to Cheyenne? Even if he didn't want the boy, or stuck to his unlikely claim that Adam wasn't his, Daniel should at least do the honorable thing and sign release papers so someone else could adopt the child. The last thing Maria Ramirez had done before diphtheria took hold of her was go to the town hall and register the boy's legal father as Daniel. A month ago, after her death, the judge had told Luke nothing could be done for Adam until those release papers were signed or refuted by Daniel. If he'd only agree to see the boy...

Luke thrust an arm into his sleeve. Now suppose Jenny went to see the kid first, without Daniel.... Luke shook his head. No. Impossible. This was a delicate situation, and the last thing Luke wanted was to upset her. He needed her, the *boy* needed her, calm and rational and happily married to Daniel.

Happily married. Luke adjusted his collar. So Daniel was finally tying the knot. Well, good luck to him. Luke had never been tempted. Not with what he'd seen in his own family.

As he buttoned a cuff, Jenny leaned her supple body against the desk and tucked herself in her feather wrap. Peacock feathers and lavender corsets. What other surprises did she have under there? He tore his gaze away and smoothed his sleeves. "How's Daniel doing these days?"

"Very well. He's sponsoring the Widows and Orphans Charity Ball tonight," she said with pride, "raising money."

Luke gritted his teeth. Daniel should be looking after his own son. He hadn't even bothered to attend Maria's funeral when Luke sent the telegram. A second telegram went unanswered, too.

But Jenny was innocent, Luke told himself, and he'd try to be kind. "When's the wedding?"

"January."

"The dead of winter?"

She stumbled for words. "Spring or summer would have been nice, when the blossoms are out, but...January's fine, too." She crossed her arms defensively. "It's Daniel's slowest time of year, selling property."

"Ah, I see...." Hell, Luke didn't blame her for falling for Daniel. Six years older than him, Daniel had been his only friend in that difficult year when his father had died. Luke had grown up respecting Daniel, admiring his easy wit and mathematical skills, his ability to work hard and do his share of the farming chores, his popularity with girls. Later, Luke admired Daniel for getting himself educated in the railroad business. And hadn't Daniel even lent Luke money once, so Luke could buy his ma a penny vase, the only store-bought present she'd ever received in her hardworking, miserable life?

A voice nagged inside his brain. But wasn't Daniel also the one who'd taunted Luke with the shame of how his father had died? How his father was hanged?

Luke ran a hand through his unruly hair, and the sound of Jenny's voice broke into his thoughts. "Where do you live?"

"Wyoming Territory," he grumbled.

"Oh, Wyoming's pretty."

He tucked his shirt into his denim pants. "You been there?"

"Once, last month with my father. He's setting up the new junction outside of Cheyenne."

"Your father works for the railroad?"

She nodded and smiled. "Vice president of operations. He's working tonight. One of the trains derailed south of the Springs, and he's working to get it hitched back up. He'll be sorry he missed you."

Luke didn't care to meet her father or anyone else.

"That's how Father and Daniel met," Jenny continued in her innocent tone. "I mean, when Father was buying land for the railroad. He took out a loan with Daniel."

Luke searched the room for his jacket and warned himself to keep quiet about Daniel's business. But now that he knew where Daniel was tonight, that's where he'd head. Straight to the ball. Hell, why not settle things as planned?

Luke still had the extra rail ticket in his pocket that he'd bought for Daniel tonight. Daniel could meet Adam, make his decision. He could even catch the next day's train home, with or without the boy. There were only two trains a week between Denver and Cheyenne, and Luke had carefully thought out each possibility before he'd left.

"If you've just arrived in town, have you heard?" she asked. "There was a robbery in Daniel's office this afternoon."

Luke's gaze snapped to hers. "A robbery?" An uneasy feeling trembled through his gut. "What time was that?"

"Four o'clock."

What? He took a shaky step back. "What do you mean?"

"At four o'clock, a man robbed Daniel."

The hair at the back of Luke's neck stood on end. What was going on? *He'd* been there at four—an hour past closing, with no sign of a robber. Surely Daniel wouldn't... "What did the man take?"

Warm lamplight danced across her solemn expression. "Ten thousand dollars."

Ten thousand dollars? A lifetime of money.

Luke stared at her and gulped. He hadn't taken a cent. Was Daniel trying to set him up for a fall? Dammit! Was Daniel trying to blackmail him to keep quiet about the boy?

"Daniel said no one was harmed. He got a good look at the man, though, and gave an accurate description to the sheriff."

Luke staggered back, the news hitting him like a blow behind the knees. The sheriff was involved? Daniel planned on framing him? As hard as they'd physically fought in the past, Daniel had never pulled a stunt like this before. What kind of man had he become? Was he good enough to be a father to Adam? Was he even good enough to be a husband to this innocent Jenny, with her powdered hair and stick pin?

Luke swallowed past the rock in his throat. And where the hell did that put *him?* He'd heard about Denver's hanging judge. In this town, it'd be Daniel's mighty word against his. If Luke were caught, what would happen? Would he be hanged just like his father? He felt the blood drain from his head. Anything but that. He grabbed his jacket and his breathing came in gasps. "Did he tell you anything about the man?"

Her eyes narrowed on him. "No, he said he didn't want to frighten me." Her gaze skimmed down to his chest at the same time his hand shot up to conceal the bloodstain.

She stared at his shirt, then straight at him. The sheen in her eyes changed and he saw realization dawn. Redness crept up her neck as she stumbled backward. "You're the one—"

"It's not what you think. I didn't steal any money—"

She stared at him as if he'd crawled out of a sewer. Rage churned his veins. Inwardly, he roared. What was he supposed to do now? He couldn't go to the ball for Daniel; he'd be shot or arrested. But he also couldn't forget about the boy! Dammit! If this was Daniel's way to shut him up, it damn well wouldn't work.

A crazy thought fired through his mind and tangled with the whiskey and the pain.

Luke held her gaze, her wild eyes. Why not? Maybe she needed protecting from Daniel herself, and he'd be doing her a favor. And if Daniel was in love with her, he'd do anything to save her.

Wouldn't he? Would he tell the truth about Adam then? Would he sign the papers? Would he explain to the sheriff that he'd been mistaken about the robbery?

No, maybe Luke was imagining the worst. Surely Daniel wouldn't have…

Could Luke risk it? Hanging from the gallows like his father…

His heart drummed. Thirty-six hours. That's all he'd need her for. He'd borrow her for thirty-six hours. He'd take the most valuable thing Daniel had and force the son of a bitch into a chase. Luke would release her after Daniel caught tomorrow's train to Cheyenne and settled their affairs.

Thirty-six hours.

She stumbled backward as he stared at her with deadening calm. By the stricken look on her face, she knew she was in desperate trouble. She lunged for the gun on the desk, but she was no match for his years of fighting experience. He reached it first. Breathless, she stepped back and faced him as he leveled his weapon on her.

He sucked in a cool, shaky breath. ''You're coming with me.''

Chapter Two

"What do you mean, I'm going with you?" Jenny panted. Prickles of terror raced up her spine. Who the hell was this man and what did he intend to do with her? He swayed above her, breathing hard, his damp shirt plastered to the black hair on his powerful chest, a six-shooter pointed straight at her. What chance did she have?

Beneath her hot velvet gown, sweat beaded between her breasts. She'd never let him take her without a fight. Inch by inch, she leaned back against the desk and secretly stretched her fingertips toward the whiskey decanter. If she could reach it, she'd fling it in his face. Better yet, in his wound.

His cool gray eyes glinted, as cold as gunmetal in a snowstorm. His expression was a mask of granite. "I'm taking you to Wyoming."

The muscles in her face sank. "Why?"

His pale lips thinned. "Because it's the only way Daniel's going to listen to what I have to say."

She doubted he was any friend of Daniel's. At heart, he was just a criminal who'd stolen ten thousand dollars. When Daniel got ahold of him, he'd see to it the man paid for his crime. "Where in Wyoming are you headed?"

"Daniel will know where."

Her jaw stiffened. "I'm not going with you."

"You don't have a choice."

She stretched her arm to the point of pain until her fingers grazed cool glass. She swallowed, gripped the bottleneck hard and swung it. A river of gold liquid spewed onto his chest. Bull's-eye.

Luke sprang back and yelped, clawing at his shirt. She winced, but before he could recover, she stretched for the rock on the other side of the desk and flung it, too. He glanced up in the nick of time and, cursing her, reared out of its path before the rock could whack him on the chest. It thudded on his boot.

His mouth twisted. "Dammit, woman!"

She dashed toward the door, but a firm hand gripped the back of her dress. Strong fingers dug into her bare shoulder. He yanked her closer and she gasped when she met his blazing eyes. A swath of wavy hair fell across his forehead. His temples glistened with sweat. All she smelled was whiskey. Dear God, what would he do to her?

His face was flushed a deep ruby, but he kept his grip steady on the gun. With each tick-tock of Daniel's silver clock on the desk, her stomach quivered.

Then, with an unexpected heave, Luke tossed her away, unharmed. Dabbing at his shirt with a towel, he growled. So maybe he wouldn't hurt her. Her mind reeled, searching for another escape.

The faint sound of footsteps came from the hallway. Their startled gazes collided. *Olivia.*

Luke dove at Jenny and cupped a hand to her

mouth. She shrank back, dodged his callused palm and bit down on a finger. Hard.

"Ahhh!" He grabbed her by the shoulders and pulled her to his chest, crushing her breasts against him.

For one breathless moment they were close enough to kiss.

The shocking thought sent a current racing down her thighs. He wouldn't dare!

Emotions battled across his face. He looked like a man trapped by something he wanted to explain.

He inclined his dark head and she gasped. Would he kiss her? No…once again he slid a hot, firm hand over her lips, stifling her protest.

She stilled under the pressure. His hand carried the scent of fresh air and grass. He splayed his other hand against her bare shoulder blades and heat seeped into her skin.

He was a barbarian. A criminal.

Wasn't he?

With her soft curves flattened against his firm chest, she felt his heart drumming in unison with her own. Daniel's touch never affected her like this. Daniel's arms felt secure and comfortable. Luke's touch was anything but. How dare he!

She somehow found the courage to pound on his wounded ribs. He staggered at the light blow and she tumbled back.

His breath tore out of him in a painful gasp.

The doorknob creaked.

"Keep still," he whispered, raising his gun, "and you won't get hurt."

She stiffened. What sort of monster was he?

Olivia hummed as she stepped through the doorway, tray in hand, laden with buns, scones and jerky. Her billowing gown rustled. "Here we are, with plenty to eat...." She glanced up and her voice trailed off. Jenny met her terrified gaze with her own.

The tray toppled to the floor. Buns rolled in all directions. "I knew it was the third thing, I knew it!" Olivia bellowed, wailing as if she were being scalped. She grabbed her skirts and ran.

Luke cocked the hammer of his gun with a loud click. Olivia stopped cold. When she slowly turned around, the women stared numbly at each other. Jenny frowned fiercely, desperately wishing her friend, at least, might escape. Her breathing was harsh and rapid.

"Keep quiet," he said, "or I'll...shoot the both of you."

Trembling, Jenny stepped closer to Olivia. She shot him a hostile glare. "I'll never help a stranger again."

Luke pushed a hand through his hair and glared at her in exasperation. "Yes, you will. You can't help it." He struggled to catch his breath. "Woman, you tire me out."

She stood her ground.

Finally, he tilted his rugged face toward Olivia. "Do you have a husband, ma'am?"

Scowling, Olivia shrugged a shoulder. "No."

Jenny stepped forward. "What's that got to do—"

He raised his palm in the air and silenced her. "Just answer the question. Who do you live with?"

The worry lines around Olivia's eyes sharpened. "Jenny and her father."

Slowly, his gaze traveled to Jenny, and another qualm of fear shuddered through her. "Well, that's good," he said. "No one's going to miss you then. It'll seem natural Jenny took you with her on her trip."

Olivia slumped against her. A cold shiver whispered over Jenny. "You intend on taking us both?"

He nodded. "You can each be leverage for the other."

Her eyes narrowed. "What do you mean, leverage?"

"You'll see soon enough. If you do as I ask, *without fighting back,* then you'll return to Denver with no harm done. If you fight me, it'll take longer, but you'll still lose, and you'll get bruised along the way."

He pointed his gun toward the heavy drapes. "Now, Olivia—ma'am—pack up the food you just brought in. We'll put it in my saddlebag. Jenny, you find us some notepaper. We need to leave a message."

With skirts swishing, Olivia did as she was told. As she crouched beside the desk, reaching for the fallen jerky, she peeped up at the stranger.

Jenny watched her friend scamper to do his bidding, and humiliation seeped into her. She scooped her shawl off the floor and stepped in front of Olivia. "If it's Daniel you're after, why don't you take me and let Olivia go?"

Luke focused his intense gaze on Jenny. "You'd trade your life for your friend's?"

She shuddered. "You plan on killing me?"

"*No.* I didn't mean it like that." His forehead creased in furrows, as if he were disgusted with the thought, and in an inexplicable way, Jenny believed him. She'd attacked him with whiskey, thrown a rock at him, even bitten him, but he hadn't hit her back. She knew many men would.

She flung her shawl over her shoulders, fidgeting with the colorful feathers. Maybe he planned on getting even later, on the road. Her throat tightened. She took an abrupt step forward, smoothing the velvet at her sides. "Leave Olivia out of this. Please," she added, staring up at his stubborn face, shivering at the memory of his touch. This was what Daniel got in return for his help all those years ago? Daniel's family had helped this man get back on his feet, and in gratitude, he threatened Daniel's fiancée?

Luke inclined his windburned face. "She must mean an awful lot to you."

Her hopes rose as she stared at his stubborn features. Perhaps he had a heart, one she could appeal to. "Olivia's been with me since I was a baby. We grew up together and I consider her a sister. She's the only family I have in Denver, besides Father." Her brothers were joining them in the spring, but if the four of them were here now, they'd pound the living daylights out of him. Rightly so. He deserved a wicked beating.

Luke's eyes flickered. He looked her up and down, and she felt herself flush. "I hope Daniel appreciates your loyalty."

She blinked. What did he have against Daniel?

"Keep packing," Luke snarled to Olivia. With maddening arrogance, he turned to Jenny. "I appreciate how you feel toward your friend here, but I can't take the chance."

"What chance?"

"The chance that she'll tell everyone in town I took you at gunpoint. Daniel's more likely to follow us alone, without the law, if I keep this quiet for him."

She glared at him. "The whole town will know, anyway. It'll be Daniel himself who'll tell them."

"Oh, no, he won't."

Jenny squirmed. "Of course he will. He'll get the sheriff and they'll get a posse together. And," she added with a hot twinge of delight, "they'll string you up from the nearest tree."

His gaze was calm and cool, but a twitch of amusement pulled at his mouth. "I know you'd be in the front row to watch. But believe me, Daniel won't tell a soul."

She swayed back and gripped the desk behind her, more uncertain than ever. "Then...then my father will."

"No," he said, pulling his vest off the chair and sliding his muscled arms into it, "your father will go along with whatever twisted explanation Daniel gives him of your disappearance. I don't rightly care, as long as Daniel comes to get you." He moaned with obvious pain, and Lord forgive her, she prayed his pain would double. Then maybe they could escape.

But he seemed so sure of what he said, and this confidence, this audacity, bewildered her. "Why?"

He swung the gun toward her. "You ask too many questions. Now pull out a paper and write Daniel a note."

She stomped behind the desk. Pulling the top drawer open, she rifled through it. "I suppose you have your story all made up. What lies do you want me to write?''

''Write the truth.''

Her gaze swung to his in surprise. She watched him calmly toss his jacket over his broad shoulders. Why was he doing this?

Money, of course, she told herself with repulsion. He wanted money for their return. That's why he was kidnapping them. That's what he'd taken at Daniel's office today. He didn't have a money bag with him, she noticed with a frown, but he'd had plenty of time to stash one.

Plopping into the chair behind the desk, Jenny dipped the quill into the inkwell and began writing, mortified at her thoughts…about their heated embrace earlier, her curiosity about being kissed. She wasn't to blame. *He'd* attacked *her*. She thrust out her chin.

''My dearest Daniel,
A man who claims to be your friend, Luke McLintock, is holding a gun to my head—the same man who tried to rob you this afternoon. He says he's taking me to Wyoming, along with Olivia, says you'll know where to find us. Please find us quickly, Daniel, and if something should happen…''

She paused, then wrote ''know how much I love you.''

Guilt slithered up her spine. It was the first time either one of them had mentioned the word *love*. And she'd done it only at gunpoint. It didn't matter, she rationalized; these were tragic circumstances.

She blamed *this* cowardly man for turning her mind upside down. Well, he wouldn't get away with it. Daniel, together with her father, would send every available man and bounty hunter after them.

"All right." He yanked her off the chair with a muscled grip. "Let's go."

She'd try to stall him. Daniel and the others might already be searching. "What about my dress?"

"What about it?" His grip felt like iron. He lowered his gaze to the velvet gown, reminding her how bare her shoulders were, how much the bodice gaped without its button.

"We can't travel in these clothes. They're uncomfortable. We'd like to change."

His gaze traveled to Olivia. Her poor friend stood trembling in her burgundy satin. He eyed Jenny with suspicion. "Do you have extra clothes here?"

"Well, no. But my house is only five streets over."

He snorted. "Nice try. Forget it."

"At least let me get needle and thread for my button. Daniel's butler keeps a sewing basket in the kitchen."

"I haven't known you for very long," he said, humor tugging at his lips, "but I do know one thing." He raised a black brow and his charcoal eyes flashed, evoking another flash of fury. "If you do locate a needle, it'll only wind up stuck in my eye." His gaze skimmed her gaping dress. "I'm not letting you look for a needle. Your missing button doesn't bother me."

She felt her face blaze. She yanked her shawl around her.

His eyes grew wide with amusement. "As a mat-

ter of fact,'' he added, ''hand over the pin that's
in it.''

She gasped at the outrageous request. ''No gentleman would ask such a thing of a lady.''

''I don't rightly care.'' He raised his gun. ''Now
hand it over. *Nicely.*''

Men out West certainly weren't the same as the
men in Boston! In Boston they had manners, they
said please and thank you and they never looked
directly at your...your bosoms! Jenny felt her nostrils flare as she groped for the pin.

''Drop it,'' he commanded.

It pinged off the floorboards.

As they walked out the door, the two women in
front, Luke grabbed a hunk of bread from Olivia's
sack. He ripped at it with his teeth, like a hungry
tiger chewing on flesh. The man was truly an animal.

God, he couldn't be a friend of Daniel's.

A quarter moon lit the deserted street and houses.
Orange leaves swirled at their feet. Huddling together, the women walked ahead of Luke and his
horse. Where were they going? Jenny squeezed
Olivia's trembling arm.

Trains hissed in the railway yard behind the far
trees. They were headed in that direction. Good.
Jenny breathed faster, gulping down the scents of
damp earth and oil. They d be more visible on a
train than by horse. Other passengers might come to
their aid.

Their captor directed them around some tall pines.
A number of railway cars sat in the station. As a
result of the derailment, the trains headed south had
no place to go. But her father had told her the trains

headed north to Wyoming or east to Omaha were still running on time. This brute had obviously timed his departure well, for the Wyoming train was whistling, as if waiting for them.

In the distance, above the rumble of the steam engine and the clatter of baggage being loaded, she heard the conductor call, "Thirty minutes to departure."

They approached the train from the shadows. Glancing down the line of cars toward the platform, past the trunks and crates of vegetables, Jenny spotted a crowd. Capes and bonnets, walking canes and cowboy hats. Her muscles tightened with hope. Did she recognize any faces? They weren't in anyone's line of vision yet, but another fifty yards and she'd yell out to them.

She dodged a puddle. The train hissed and she jumped back in alarm.

A gun dug into Jenny's back and she was forced to keep walking. So help her, the first chance she got, she'd hold a gun to his head and let him know how it felt.

They passed an open boxcar stamped Union Pacific, and a short, blond man stepped out from the shadows. "Boss?"

Oh, no, thought Jenny, Luke knew him. The lithe stranger, who had a wide, flat nose and muttonchop sideburns, guided Luke's horse up a makeshift ramp. He glanced at them. "What's going on?"

"Don't ask, Tom, I'll explain later. I didn't get to Daniel, but I've got his woman and her friend. Forget about the tickets—we'll have to stay with the horses and women. We'll split them up. You take this one,'' he said, tossing a shocked Olivia into the man's arms. ''The blonde comes with me.''

Panic welled in Jenny's throat. She staggered back and screamed, as loudly as she could, at precisely the same time as the steam engine blew its whistle.

No one heard her except Luke. Her cries were muffled as he threw her into the car behind his horse. Her gown twisted up around her thighs, and her feathered shawl dropped to the tracks. Luke dove in on top of her, squashing her between the solid wooden floor and his hard muscled body. Her chest felt like it would burst.

Never in all her life had she been so mistreated, had she wished a fellow human being harm.

Before she had time to blink, he rolled off her and slid the rickety door closed behind them. Seized with dread, she watched his lean profile melt into a swirl of blackness.

Good Lord, what would he do next?

In the cool, quiet hours near midnight, Luke stared into the darkness. Now he had to face up to what he'd done.

With a mean-awful pounding in his ribs, he dragged himself to his feet. The railcar bounced and swayed beneath him. The cramp in his calf squeezed tighter and he shook it out. He'd been lying so long in one position, pinning Jenny down so she couldn't bolt and spook the horses, that his muscles needed release.

Sighing, he sought out her curvy shape on the straw. She wore the jacket he'd given her for the cool night, and she was breathing steady in a deep sleep. Fighting him at first, she'd finally simmered when he threatened to harm her friend. Empty threats, but they'd worked.

Luke's bay whinnied. Another horse, belonging to another passenger, stirred beside him. Tugging the scarred door open, Luke gazed up at purple sky and twinkling stars. A branch scraped along the train's side and he ducked his leg to avoid it. Judging by the silhouette of mountains, they were close to the territory border, had maybe even crossed it. By early morning, they'd reach Cheyenne. The next train from Denver was tomorrow, and he expected Daniel to be on it.

Thank God, Maria had told Luke the truth before she'd died. She'd lived in the boardinghouse, accepting the measly dollars Daniel sent her monthly—just enough to keep her mouth shut about the paternity of the boy, to keep her hovering above poverty.

For five years, as Maria worked the lunch hours, she'd kept the boy by her side. Luke had shooed Adam out of the way at every opportunity, never spending more than five minutes with him. Hadn't he even told Maria to try to keep Adam hidden? That having the boy around wasn't good for business? Luke burned with shame. After Maria's death, he'd taken a hard look at himself and realized he'd treated his horse better than he had the kid.

Sure, in the end, when she'd suffered that horrible sore throat from diphtheria, Luke had stepped in, taking Adam to his friends' ranch to protect the boy from getting sick. But that hadn't worked so well, either, had it? She'd died so soon, the boy hadn't had a chance to say goodbye. Luke knew what that felt like. A hole that never got filled.

Hadn't he missed the opportunity to say goodbye to his old man? He'd heard the applause from the hanging, though. He'd been sitting on the bench behind the courthouse beside his brothers, all spiffed up, their mother in her worn-out Sunday dress, begging the judge to release their pa.

Looking back on it now, he knew the hanging was inevitable. Cattle rustling, a shoot-out with the sheriff, one dead deputy... But as a sparkly eyed six-year-old kid, with two optimistic brothers and a frantically hopeful mother, they thought the judge would show leniency.

None of them had said goodbye.

Luke sighed, bone-tired of it all. Daniel's family had taken him in, saying they could use the extra hand on such a big ranch, with only one child of their own to help. For the first few years, he and Daniel were the best of friends. But as soon as Daniel's friends—especially the young women—started paying Luke attention, and Luke's abilities with horses and guns outstripped Daniel's, a rivalry grew.

Not on Luke's part. But during Luke's troubled teen years, marked by petty crimes that followed his mother's death and his brothers abandoning Cheyenne and Luke as a result—well, Daniel had gloated. The two hadn't spoken in years, not since Daniel moved to Denver.

What happened to the good person Daniel used to be? Did he deserve another chance? Would marriage to Jenny straighten him out?

She seemed like a good woman. She had guts and stamina. And out here, where men outnumbered women eight to one, the strength of men depended on the strength of their women. Once Jenny married Daniel, she'd be stepmother to Adam. She'd make a good one, too. She'd been kind enough to help Luke, hadn't she?

And how had he repaid her kindness? He stirred uneasily.

Forcing himself to look at the moving ground outside instead of the captivating woman inside, Luke ran a hand over his bandaged chest and moaned. The whiskey stains had dried. He'd been through enough fights to know his wound was light and it would heal. He was used to changing bandages all by himself, and he'd change these, too.

Her whisper pierced the quiet. "What's your real name?"

He started at the silky sound of her voice and spun around. She sat up, clutching his jacket. Her hair matted along one side of her head, full of loose straw. Moonlight shadowed the hollows of her straight nose and curved mouth. He tried not to notice how pretty she was. She was Daniel's. Luke would sooner die than cross that line of honor. He'd never chase another man's woman. *He* was not his father.

Clearing his throat, he leaned a shoulder against the rough plank wall. "I told you. I'm Luke McLintock. And I didn't steal any money. If I had, do you think I would have been standing on Daniel's porch? And do you see any bags of money?"

She frowned, glanced at the saddlebags, then eyed him with suspicion. "Tell me truthfully how you know him."

"You know already. We grew up together."

"One friend wouldn't do this to another."

He winced, then shuffled his feet. "I've been saying the same thing to myself for eight hours."

She sat up taller. Her slim waist flared to rounded hips. "Prove it to me. Tell me something only you would know." A soft tremble rippled across her mouth. She was frightened of him, and that tweaked his guilt.

"Like what?" he asked gently.

"What day of the week was he born?"

"That's easy. He says he was born to work with money. He tells everyone he was born on a Friday, the busiest banking day of the week. In mid-January."

Her eyes probed his. "When were you born?"

"Six years later, during harvest. The last week of September."

She lifted her chin. "Oh…that's next week." Her features tightened with suspicion. "What are his folks' names?"

"They *were* Lance and Ellen. They passed away years ago."

Scowling, she hugged her knees, pulling her gown around her. "Well, anyone might know that. Tell me something about yourself. How did your…your father die?"

"Daniel didn't tell you?"

She drew back. "Should he have?"

"No, I'm just surprised." After all, he thought to himself, Daniel loved to make himself sound superior. "My mother died of working too hard," he said, gritting his teeth, trying not to remember how she'd had a stroke while on her knees scrubbing floors. "And my father…" he closed his eyes for a moment and leaned back against the wall for support "...my father was hanged."

Silence.

"That can't be true," she said in a hoarse whisper.

He pressed his lips together and shrugged a shoulder, too ashamed to meet her eyes.

More silence.

"For what crime?"

"Pick one."

Straw rustled. He turned to look at her and she inched backward defensively, until she was pressing up against the slatted boards. As if she had to protect herself from him.

But didn't she? He'd taken her from her family, from all she loved.

Her lips parted. She continued to stare, measuring him with a pensive shimmer in her eyes. Her smooth skin glowed in the dim light and her messy hair tangled with the straw. He shouldn't really stare, but she had such a wild beauty. There was a softness and a strength to her that fascinated him.

"How'd you and Daniel meet?" he blurted.

For a moment, he wasn't sure she'd answer. "At a Union Pacific social," she finally said. "The Independence Day fireworks. Father arranged the introductions."

Luke found the news strangely uplifting. "You mean your father arranged the wedding?"

In a fluster, she ran her fingers through her hair. "Well, not exactly. Sort of..." She gave a little cough. "It was my decision."

"I see." Lots of fathers arranged marriages. Why did this news please Luke?

Sudden anger flashed in her eyes. "You better watch out when my father gets ahold of you."

"Daniel has a way of convincing people. I'm sure he can handle your father."

Her voice rose. "Not this time. My father will know something's wrong."

"Why?"

"Because I've never missed writing a speech for him before."

He pressed his back against the cold wall, facing her directly. "You write your father's speeches?"

She nodded and plucked at the straw near her boots.

"You're educated then. Went to college in Boston?"

"Well, not precisely. My brothers did."

"But not you?"

She furrowed her brow. "I read every one of their books."

"Why didn't you just go to school?"

"Because women don't go to college, that's why," she answered.

He paused. "But I hear they do."

Glancing down at her fingers, she twisted her engagement ring. Her voice dropped to nearly a whisper. "It's what my father always tells me."

"Oh." Luke was touched by her tender admission. "Yet he gets you to write his speeches."

"But no one knows I do." She met his eyes with such honesty, it upset his balance. "Well, except you."

"Your father sounds like a hypocrite."

Jenny's eyes sparked. "Do you always say exactly what's on your mind?"

"Mostly."

"That's why your chest is all scarred up."

He grinned with sudden humor. "That's a pretty fair deduction."

Jenny lowered her head and swallowed. "Can't you please let us go? Where is Olivia?"

"She's safe in the next car." He spun away so she wouldn't see his eyes softening. For a moment, he stared up at the stars, feeling the cool wind on his face, the wheels of the train thundering beneath his boots. Mustering strength, he turned to face her. "As soon as Daniel arrives, and I expect it'll be tomorrow, I'll release you."

She searched his face. "You promise you will?"

He prickled under her scrutiny. Suddenly the box-car seemed very small and her nearness overwhelming. "Yeah."

"Both Olivia and me?"

He nodded in reply, respecting her for her devotion to her friend. She slid a piece of straw from her hair, above her ear. The absent movement made her jacket slide open, revealing the creamy flesh of her shoulders. His pulse dipped.

"Why can't you be more like your friend? Daniel turned out so good and you turned out so bad."

Every muscle in his body tightened. "You don't know what you're talking about."

"Oh, I think I do." She coolly appraised him. "You're down on your luck. Instead of working hard to get yourself out of the hole you're in, you're stealing money. You should be ashamed of yourself."

Her comment stung. He braced his feet against

the movement of the train. "People aren't always what they appear to be. This isn't about money."

Her face became set. "Then what's it about?"

"Doing what you know is right. Truth and honor."

She shook her head. Her hair was a mass of tangles. "What do you know about those? No wonder Daniel never mentioned you much. I wouldn't be proud, either, if I had a friend like—" She stopped abruptly and averted her eyes.

An angry reply burned his lips. He didn't care what in blazes she thought of him. In about thirty-four hours, it would be settled. And then Daniel alone would have to deal with his new Boston bride.

But when she gazed back at him with confusion in her misty eyes, Luke floundered. She stirred him. He didn't want to be stirred. He didn't want to be conflicted.

"If this is about the truth," she said in a voice that reached him somewhere deep, "explain it to me. Tell me the truth, Luke."

The trusting way she said his name weakened his resolve. Should he tell her about Adam? She was engaged to be Daniel's wife, and didn't she have every right to know about the boy? She seemed strong enough to handle it.

But he had to be careful how he explained it, so she wouldn't get too upset. His own neck was on the line, and because of that, and for the sake of Adam's future, she had to remain committed and engaged to Daniel. Daniel sure as hell wouldn't drop any charges or sign any papers if Luke jeopardized the engagement.

Luke shoved back from the wall and straightened to his full height. "All right," he decided. "When we get to Cheyenne, I'd like you to meet someone, and then you'll understand."

Chapter Three

Dawn. Despite the cool, blue morning mist, sunlight twinkled through the wall boards of the boxcar, and Jenny's eyes blinked open. She shivered in the crisp air, remembering where she was.

It wasn't a dream. Her heart squeezed in anguish. She was here, a captured woman with a man she didn't know. Would today be the day she escaped?

Where was Olivia and how was she this morning? Jenny closed her eyes for a moment, then determination surged through her. She wouldn't let him win. She'd keep alert to her surroundings and lunge at the first opportunity to flee. Blazes, maybe it'd help if she were friendly.

Still wearing his sheepskin jacket buttoned to the top, she pushed herself from the straw. Was the train slowing down? It was rocking differently. While she stretched her arms to shake off her sleep, Luke sprang to his feet in the opposite corner. She started. With his cowboy boots pounding on the floor planks, his spurs jangling, he banged his fists on the wall to signal his man on the other side. A thud echoed in response.

Luke returned to his magnificent blood bay. Sunlight glistened off its red flanks. "Morning," Luke said as he saddled his mount. Was he talking to her or the stallion? She didn't answer.

Trying to ignore his masculine presence, she ran her fingers through her twisted hair, yanking on the knots. She got it into some degree of order, then flattened it on the top. Removing several of the hairpins, she did a makeshift job of tying it into a beaver tail. It would have to do.

From beneath her lashes, she couldn't resist stealing another glance at Luke. Still in his black denim pants, he'd changed his shirt and donned a knee-length leather coat. He looked almost respectable.

Watching him work, she noticed how skillful he was with animals. His movements emphasized his forceful shoulders, slim hips and muscular thighs. *Any* woman would think he and his mount were striking, standing side by side. She shouldn't feel guilty for thinking it herself, about the power and muscle in both man and beast.

The man *was* a beast, she decided. He should be shackled and chained. He *would* be once they caught him, she realized with satisfaction.

While he adjusted his saddlebags, she watched his long fingers at work. If what he told her last night about his father were true... What kind of family did he come from? No wonder he was all scarred up. It must come from breaking the law, just like his father.

Heat rushed to her cheeks. Lord, when she thought about last night in Daniel's office, when Luke had looked like he was about to kiss her—

She pushed away her disturbing thoughts. She pitied him—that's what she felt. Only pity. "Are we getting off here?"

"Yeah." Dark stubble shadowed his jaw. He needed a shave. If he'd lend her a straight blade, she'd give him a shave he'd never forget.

"Is this the Cheyenne station?"

"No, it's the stop before."

She sat taller, her voice sharp. "I thought you said we're going to Cheyenne."

"We are. But the last thing I need is two women hollering murder in the middle of the station." He worked quickly to buckle straps. "We'll go the rest of the distance by horse."

Ride a horse? By herself? She didn't know how. She'd never tried. Her throat constricted. "Am I supposed to ride the other horse?"

Luke glanced at the sorrel. "That one's not mine. I'm not a horse thief."

She jumped to her feet and brushed straw off her dress. "How honorable," she said with a shake of her head. "You steal women but not horses."

His lips quirked with humor as he finished with the lines.

"Do you find everything I say amusing?" she asked.

"Just about."

"Well, then, I'm not talking to you anymore."

"Suit yourself." A hint of a smile touched the corner of his mouth. He looked charming, and she squirmed with irritation at the thought.

Unmoved by her cold stare, he slid open the bulky door. His firm, square hand was strong and callused, like the rest of him, and no doubt he was accustomed to working hard. How could such a hardworking man be so down on his luck? Why didn't he try harder?

He'd said he was taking her to meet someone. Who? A relative? A...former girl of Daniel's? Was Luke trying to make trouble between her and Daniel?

Jenny knew Daniel was a popular man. Women had been vying for his attention at the Independence Day celebrations from the minute Jenny'd met him. He was a terrific dancer, dancing the smoothest waltz with her. Hadn't she told him so? Hadn't he smiled that gracious smile and insisted on having every dance with her, despite the other women?

No matter who Luke was taking her to see, she wouldn't let it upset her. Luke was the criminal, not Daniel.

She stepped to the open door beside Luke's tall, lean form and gazed out. Morning sunshine slanted into the boxcar, drenching her. The heat felt good. Clouds that looked like cotton candy swirled in a blue sky. Miles of golden grass, as high as her waist, rippled to the horizon. She peered ahead of the train. Tall aspens, their leaves quaking in the wind, lined a trickling creek. As the train chugged along, a herd of pronghorn antelope drinking at the water's edge scampered into the pines.

She took a deep, heady breath of pure mountain air. It was so beautiful. More beautiful than she ever could have imagined, back in Boston. The breathless grace of the Wyoming Territory filled her with a sense of awe.

Then the train screeched around a bend and she stumbled, bracing herself quickly. The sheepskin lining of Luke's jacket cushioned her arms.

Grabbing the edge of the door, Luke hung out the boxcar beside her and hollered something to his man. The wind was whistling and she couldn't hear what they said. When Luke came back, he swung up on his horse. He had to duck his head so it wouldn't hit the ceiling.

He motioned for her to mount behind him. Good Lord, he didn't really expect her to jump that high, did he?

The sound of the horse snorting and the sight of it pawing the floor made her heart pound with fear. She stepped back. Luke, wild and unshaven, looking every bit as much a beast as his sleek horse, stretched out his hand to her. She cleared her throat, about to declare that she didn't ride, when he suddenly clicked his tongue in frustration, swooped down with a muscled arm and scooped her up.

In a swirl of petticoats, she landed behind him in the hard saddle. It was one hell of a tight fit. What was she supposed to hang on to? In a panic, suddenly dizzy, she gripped his coat pocket.

Before she had time to adjust herself, the horse leaped off the boxcar. They plunged into the blazing sunrise. The wind snatched her hair. Her stomach rose and fell. "Ahhh…!"

The horse hit the ground and galloped hard. They'd made it! A thrill danced up her spine. But there was no way she was putting her arms around Luke. Instead, she tried to hold the edge of his coat, then the saddle. Anything but him. She swayed and dipped, clawing to maintain her balance.

"Sit still," he hollered.

Still? How could she keep still when she'd never sat this close to a man, in such an intimate position?

The back of his thighs felt hard and sleek along the front of hers, and she couldn't escape the salty scent of his skin. A current of excitement raced through her with every bump, every jostle of his muscles against hers. She shivered and tried to push away.

She couldn't budge. And she had to keep her legs and buttocks clenched to keep from slipping off.

They rode into a muddy clearing, crossed a line of cedars and splashed through a riverbed. As they headed down toward a grass-covered valley, Luke slowed the horse to a trot. Jenny wiped her sweaty palms on her velvet skirts and tried to loosen the stiffness in her arms. Her chest started to feel hot inside the sheepskin coat.

Ten minutes passed, then an hour. Her breathing steadied. Her hands stopped trembling. The wind tugged at her loosened hair and she found herself enjoying the sensation.

The horse swayed, and for the tenth time, her cheek brushed Luke's leather-covered shoulder. His body heat singed her cheek. His thighs rippled against hers once more, and she quivered. To take her mind off the man between her legs, she thought of Daniel.

Where was he? Did he miss her? How many men had he organized to chase after her? He'd be at the front of the pack, she envisioned, leading everyone. She couldn't imagine him with a gun, though. Did he carry one? All she ever saw him carry was that silver pocket watch and a cigar. If he never carried a gun, then who had shot Luke in the office yesterday? The guard?

And she couldn't imagine Daniel on horseback like Luke was now, roaring through the fields, leaping off the edge of a train, and just…well, just *taking* a woman he wanted. No, Daniel was a gentleman in every sense of the word, and Luke was…a hotheaded cowboy with no thought of tomorrow.

She tipped her face to the sun and let it caress her. It warmed her skin. In Boston, she never got to spend much time outdoors, or feel the wind or sun on her skin. If she were riding in Boston, she'd be forced to wear a bonnet.

Boston had stifled her—being stuck in the house at eighteen, when her grandmother had passed away. Father thought that's where proper ladies belonged, but Jenny didn't. What was wrong with getting an education?

After many fruitless arguments, Jenny had in the end cleaned and laundered and mended alongside Olivia, not because she had to but because of boredom. Soon, Jenny had started sneaking a peek at her brothers' college books on commerce and accounting. Olivia read the ones about American history. As children, Jenny and Olivia had learned to read together, taught by Jenny's grandmother.

Olivia. She hoped Olivia, who was no doubt galloping behind them, was also enjoying the fresh air, for it would give them the vigor to fight when the opportunity came.

Energized by the sun, Jenny looked up at the wide blue sky, thinking of all her reasons for coming West. Her father had his dreams of expanding the railroad, and her brothers had theirs of mining and working in pharmaceuticals. The men in her family weren't interested in listening to her, but she would show them all she had a brain and could use it in business as well as they could. Maybe better. It was at times like these, she imagined, that daughters turned to their mothers for guidance. Jenny, at two, had lost her own mother to cholera.

Ah, well. It had happened a long time ago, and Jenny preferred to look at the future. She smiled in the warm wind, reminding herself that more women owned shops in Denver than they did in Boston. More women were allowed to charge out on their own. Although the two Denver bankers she'd secretly approached for a loan had laughed at her ideas for an undergarment shop, she'd have a store yet. What exactly, she wasn't sure, but with her beloved's help she'd do it.

All she had to do was get back to him. If it weren't for *this* man, robbing her of the very freedom she cherished most...

Jenny reached out and patted the horse's red coat. The animal's hooves pounded beneath her in a steady rhythm. She glanced down at the waving grass. Their interlocked shadows, two riders atop a horse, sailed along the ground.

Why couldn't she hear the hoofbeats of the other horse? Olivia should be close behind. Shifting in the saddle, letting go of Luke's coat, Jenny craned her neck and glanced back.

She lost her balance. Panicked, she started to slide, and tried to jerk herself in the other direction.

Luke swore. She felt him grab her skirt and yank. "Hang on!"

With a loud rip, her dress tore. She slid off and hit the ground, rolling in the dirt. A rock smacked her temple. It stung. Her vision clouded. Sprawled on her back, she stayed put and tried to catch her breath.

"Whoa, boy, simmer down," she heard Luke say in the distance. Then he was by her side. "Jenny! Are you hurt?"

She felt the pressure of his hand on her shoulder. She inhaled slowly and her eyesight cleared. He was looking down at her, his dark brows creased in concern. She hadn't thought he was capable of any tenderness.

She groaned, trying to rise on an elbow. "I think I'm fine, but my head…"

He slid his hand along her back to support her. Much too close. The shadow of a beard made him look like a wild wolf. "You've got a little cut."

He brushed her forehead with gentle fingertips, then his gaze came back to hers. His dark eyes were deep, warm pools and she felt herself submerging. "You don't know how to ride," he said.

It all seemed so ridiculous—the ride, her formal gown…. "Whatever gave you that idea?"

His eyes twinkled and he smiled at her. A kind, handsome smile. Her pulse skittered. She tried to fight it. "Are you laughing at me again?"

"No," he said, ever so softly. "Why are you so stubborn? Why couldn't you hold on to me, nice and proper?"

There was nothing nice or proper about their positions on the horse. Suddenly, she became aware of how close they were sitting, how firm his arm felt around her shoulders, how fresh and manly the scent of his skin. Underneath his coat, the collar of his crisp shirt was unbuttoned, revealing a thatch of silky black hair, leading down his chest to who knew where.

He seemed to come to his senses first and jerked away. "Stay here, I'll get something for your cut."

She tried to sit up, but her right upper arm rocked with pain. She rolled back to one elbow.

Luke returned with a cloth and dabbed at her forehead. "Why didn't you tell me you can't ride?"

"I didn't have time."

He pushed his hat back. The sweat-dampened hair at his temples glistened in the sunshine. "It's my fault, I should have asked. I'm sorry."

Finally, an apology for something. He kept dabbing. "You surprise me. A polished lady from the East, dressed in velvet, wearing imported perfume...yet you sure spit tacks. You don't complain very much, do you? I mean, about sleeping in a pile of straw or at being thrown onto a horse when you don't know how to ride."

She broke their intimate gaze. The words seemed harmless, but the sincerity in his eyes... He was sitting so close she could feel the breeze whisper off his skin. How did a man like him know her perfume was imported?

How did she wind up this near to him? She squirmed away.

"Hey, come back here, it's almost cleaned up." He moved closer, poured water from his canteen onto the cloth and wiped her forehead. When he looked into her eyes again, her pulse rushed like a waterfall.

His gaze went lower, down to her quivering lips and then back up. A powerful awareness shot through her. He seemed different than he had last night. Gone was the hardened stranger and in his place was a compassionate man, rugged and appealing.

"Let me help you to your feet."

"No, it's all right..." She shouldn't allow herself to be swayed. He was her captor and she was his prisoner.

It was too late to stop him. Attempting to pull her up, he grasped her upper arms, but squeezed the sore one by mistake. She yelped.

"You're hurt." He released her. His face creased with concern as his gaze skimmed over the jacket. "Where?"

"My right arm."

"Let me check to see if it's broken."

"No, please—"

He was unbuttoning the sheepskin jacket before she could stop him, his warm hand grazing her shoulder, trailing down her bare arm. She tried to ignore his touch and the tingling sensations.

"It's not broken, thank God," he said. His charcoal-gray eyes, flecked with cinnamon-brown, glistened as he looked at her. A knot tightened in her belly.

His fingers slid from under the jacket, more of a caress than a withdrawal. His gaze slid down to her mouth.

She knew it was coming, but in her mind she whispered *No*.

She heard a shameless moan of surrender. Good grief, it was coming from her. She turned her face away so his lips couldn't meet hers. His mouth grazed her earlobe instead, sending a shudder through her body.

She thought turning away would stop him, but he

kept going, hungrily kissing her jaw, skimming his lips along her throat. She gasped. No man had ever kissed her neck before, and his warm lips were as soft as butterflies. Although untouched, her nipples ached, as if he were teasing them with feathers.

His lips tantalized her throat to the base of the hollow. In a rush of desire, she arched her neck. How would his demanding lips feel on hers?

No. This was bad. This should stop.

She tried to wrench away. He followed, not allowing a break. She gasped for air. "Please..."

How would Daniel react to seeing her here? Shame tore at her. "No. I said *no*—"

She ripped free, raised a palm and slapped him hard across the face. "I'm engaged to a man you call your *friend*."

He blinked. She watched the red stain of her handprint rise on his cheek. Who the hell did he think he was?

Regret flitted across his face. He slid the jacket closed.

With a shaky sigh, he turned away. "You have my word this won't happen again. Button up. I'll help you back on the horse. We've got miles to go."

There was no way in hell anyone was going to take advantage of Daniel Kincaid. Daniel bit off the tip of his fresh cigar and spat it into the dusty street. If he came within five feet of Luke McLintock, he guaranteed Luke wouldn't rise from the dirt for days.

Dressed in a freshly pressed worsted wool suit, silk vest, cravat and overcoat, he rubbed at the kink in his neck. Blazes, he needed a drink. He smacked his dry lips together and lit his stogy. His temples pounded from lack of sleep.

What the hell was McLintock trying to prove?

For cryin' out loud, it was just a kid they were fighting over. A Mexican. And how did anyone know for sure who the father was? Might be anyone. Hell, it might be Luke.

The only reason Daniel had paid that waitress, Maria, was because he'd been a sitting duck. It was her word against his, but she'd seemed content, and *quieter,* with two extra dollars in her pocket each month. He shouldn't have given her that.

If McLintock told Jenny anything about the boy, Daniel would deny every word.

Was he expected to give up his life for this kid?

His mouth twisted. Hellfire! If he knew Luke at all, Luke'd have the kid off his hands quicker than lightning. Luke didn't want the boy any more than he did.

Daniel gritted his teeth, chomping into the cigar. The bitter taste seeped across his tongue. Since when had Luke become so high and mighty? What had happened to the little squirt who used to follow Daniel around, mirroring his every step as if Daniel were a knight of the round table? Now Luke had proved he was no better than his lowly father.

Cripes, if the bullet had struck an inch lower, McLintock would have dropped dead…

A flash of sunlight blasted off the bank window into Daniel's eyes. Squinting, he turned the corner.

Blazes. The gun had gone off by accident. Was that why McLintock was doing this? To get even for the bullet graze? So what! McLintock had tried to grab the derringer out of his hand. So Daniel had let him have it! He wished now he'd pulled the trigger deliberately, and hadn't weakened at the last minute.

And yeah, he'd called the sheriff. McLintock needed to be thrown in jail. Anything to stop him from spreading a false rumor about the boy. Daniel's shoulders stiffened. His fury yesterday was nothing compared to how he felt today.

He reached the office door and thrust a gold key into the lock.

"Mornin', Mr. Kincaid, sir," the night guard rumbled. A former boxer from New York City, Harley Cobbs scoured the street, on the lookout for anything unusual. Daniel had hired him three years ago, the minute he'd laid eyes on Harley's face, which was as broad and gnarled as the trunk of a weathered pine. Daniel bet if you sliced his skin, you'd see the rings.

"No trouble last night, sir. The office was quiet."

Daniel turned the knob and kicked the door. He already knew that. The *trouble* had already fled town, most likely by the quickest method available—the train. Reaching Cheyenne by horseback would take two to three days. "Tell the two other men I don't need 'em anymore."

"You sure?"

"Yeah." No sense paying for extra security when it wasn't necessary. Yesterday, he'd hired additional men to protect the office. He hadn't thought of protecting Jenny, and knowing he'd been outwitted made him seethe. McLintock would pay.

Stalking into his private office, Daniel scanned his morning appointments. It was up to him to make the next move. What else could McLintock do but sit and wait for a response?

In the meantime, Daniel had to deal with Jenny's father, Nyland Eriksen. Luckily the old geezer was out of town.

What would Nyland say if he knew about the kid? Nyland wouldn't give his daughter so freely. Daniel's hands trembled as he butted out his cigar. It'd taken him ten years to get here, on the verge of the best deal this side of the Rockies, a deal with the Union Pacific. A deal with Nyland Eriksen.

Daniel deserved it. He'd scouted and surveyed land for fifteen years, using his wits and know-how to predict where the next tracks would be laid. Over yonder in that flood-prone valley, or dynamiting through the hills? As soon as Daniel was married to Jenny, Nyland promised him a permanent deal. A ten-year contract as the official scout for the railroad. Damned if Luke McLintock was going to blow this deal.

Did he think he could compete with Daniel? Did he think they were in the same league? Why, McLintock would always be nothing but a workin' class boy. Scrapin' the manure off other people's boots. Servin' them penny beer, for cripes sake, when Daniel was making deals of twenty thousand dollars a crack.

And beautiful Jenny being terrorized by the bastard...why, she was nothing more than a little kitten who needed protecting. Like all women did. Her and her silly notions of opening a store. Daniel planned on keeping her so busy with a brood of her own, she wouldn't have time to do much else. Thankfully, she could hold her own in business conversations with the mayor and the governor and anyone else Daniel entertained, and he was sure proud to show her off on his arm. Her lush body and quick mind were a delightful bonus, although being Nyland's daughter would have been enough.

"Morning, Daniel," cooed a feminine voice behind him.

He spun on his chair and peered up at Sally Bloomfield, one of his clerks. "Mornin'."

She rubbed her ruby lips together and played with a strand of her brown curls. Well now, didn't she look tempting? Her curves strained the fabric of her lace blouse, teasing him with a hint of rosy tips. Why was she wearing that blouse? She knew how much he liked it. He had an urge to lay her over the desk and take her, like he had on many occasions. But he was engaged now, and had every intention of living up to his new standards. Four weeks, and he hadn't strayed. He deserved a medal.

His stare was bold. "I told you before, address me as Mr. Kincaid."

Sally's smile faded into a pucker.

He glanced through the office window. "Go get your papers in order. I've got a client to tend to." Stiffly, he edged his tall, muscular frame around her and kept walking.

His business with the miner didn't take long. The young man was leaving when the doorbell jingled. Daniel glanced up to see who it was.

Queasiness rolled down his spine. "Did you make it in all the way from the Springs this morning, Mrs. Walters?"

The gray-haired woman straightened her bonnet. "Yep, took me nearly two hours."

"So the train derailment's been fixed?"

"Yep."

Oh, hellfire. That meant Nyland would be back in town, looking for his daughter. That changed everything. Daniel excused himself. "Harley, step into my office."

They crossed through the sunshine beating through the bars of the front windows. Daniel shoved his finger beneath his sweaty collar. His cravat was tighter than a noose. He closed the office door. "I want you to take a trip."

"Where to?" The ex-boxer curled his hand over the walnut grip of his gun.

"We're going to Cheyenne. Get two tickets for this evening's train." Daniel sputtered with indignation as he explained the situation, sticking to his story about the robbery, and adding a kidnapping-for-ransom charge. "It's a messy situation. Let's keep it quiet, so Nyland Eriksen doesn't find out."

Something in Harley seemed to come alive. His tired eyes blazed with eagerness. "Are we bringin' McLintock back?"

"No, just the two women."

"What should I do to him?"

"Stay behind a few days." Daniel crossed his arms, leaned against his desk and crossed one booted foot in front of the other. "Get him alone," he said calmly. "Then I want you to break some bones. Make him feel it."

Once again in the saddle behind Luke, Jenny tried to pull away. He'd removed his coat, and only the thin cloth of his shirt separated them. Why did he have to be the type of man a woman couldn't ignore?

He yanked her closer. "You'll fall off again. Hold tight."

"I don't want to." But she let her arms stay where he placed them, around his muscled waist. She was still shaken from her fall, and the ground below seemed awfully far down.

Her palms were slipping with sweat. A line of perspiration ran down his spine. His back muscles, under the soft cloth where she held him, grew damp, and she swallowed. Her breathing lost its rhythm every time she touched him. What was wrong with her? She wriggled away.

Why had she let him kiss her throat? Why hadn't she pulled away sooner? It was fear that made her heart pound, she told herself. She didn't fear Daniel, and that's why her heart never pounded like this when *he* kissed her.

Daniel took pains to make her feel comfortable. He never took her anywhere without the proper chaperon, and she wouldn't be caught dead with him, alone like this.

Another hour passed, but her misery didn't lessen. The sun's heat blazed through the jacket. She had a permanent squint from the glare. There was nothing but sagebrush ahead. Two speckled birds chirped from a tree they passed and a jackrabbit darted out from a shrub and slipped into a pocket of dirt.

When would she see Olivia again? Jenny scanned the rolling hills, squinting through the shimmering light, hoping to see someone. A ranch or farmhouse. Anything.

Nothing but dried grass and tumbleweeds. "How much farther?"

"We're close. Over this hill." The stallion climbed the gentle slope. Jenny poked her head around Luke's shoulder to look. Pines and aspens grew along one side of the valley. There must be a stream below. The vegetation was thicker and greener there.

She sighed. "And this is where Olivia and your man Tom are waiting?"

"Hold on now, I didn't promise they'd meet us here."

She sprang up. "*What?* Another trick? But you said—"

"I said they'd meet us in Cheyenne. And they will, in due time."

Her mouth opened in protest, then closed. Maybe he was lying about ever bringing them together. Maybe she'd have to escape on her own and come back to rescue Olivia.

They crested the hill. The green valley revealed a ranch house and stable, and he was heading straight for them. Who did the ranch belong to? Cattle grazed the fenced slopes, forty or fifty head. She spotted two horses tethered by the hitching post. Would she dare to take one?

Would the opportunity arise?

Their mount slowed as they approached the well-kept homestead. A deep green pond shimmered beside them, the reeds around it thick and as tall as people. The reeds rustled and a muddy boy jumped out, surprising her.

Luke pulled back on the reins to stop the horse.

The boy dashed to his side, holding a twisted stick. "You're home, you're home!"

Jenny reared back. Who was this child?

With shaggy black hair, he was no more than four or five. He stood barefooted, his skin bronzed the color of gold. His rumpled shirttails were laced with grime and his fingernails blackened with dirt. His smile, though, was a genuine flash of white. And, aimed straight for Luke.

Did Luke have a son? The shocking thought hit her full force.

"Adam," Luke roared from the saddle, "I can't believe how dirty one little boy can get."

A ball of emotion sprang to her throat. The man who'd kidnapped her was a father? He would go to jail for what he'd done. Who'd look after the boy while he was in jail? What kind of a father would put his own boy at risk?

A selfish one. Just like his criminal father.

She sat there, stunned.

Suddenly overcome by the dizzying heat, she squirmed on the saddle. If Luke had a son, *did he have a wife?*

And what would his wife say to *her?*

Jenny stared at the empty grounds—at the two-seater swing on the porch, the string of bedsheets hanging on the laundry line, the pretty vase of flowers in the window. A wave of nausea welled inside her as she fought to control her swirling emotions. The man who'd kissed her earlier, who'd brushed his butterfly lips along her throat, was *married?*

Chapter Four

"How many other children do you have?" Jenny asked Luke as she slid off the saddle.

Surprised, he stepped back and glanced at Adam. She thought Adam was his? Well, Luke could see how. Similar black hair, the boy's friendly greeting... Adam didn't look like Daniel. At least, Luke didn't see any resemblance. Adam looked like any little kid on any corner.

Luke met her penetrating eyes. "Adam's not my boy," he said softly. "I'm looking after him for a while. Or, should I say," he corrected himself with a warm nod to Adam, "he's looking after me?"

Adam gazed up at Luke with unabashed eagerness. Luke smiled, but shifted uneasily. Adam shouldn't get too attached to him. Yes, Luke had watched him grow up in the saloon—one of the few stable influences in his life, apart from his mother. But Adam had to learn that soon he'd be gone from here. Either gone to his father and Jenny's, or to another caring family for adoption.

Jenny inspected Luke. "Did you bring me here to meet your wife?"

She thought he was married? He stumbled back and nearly choked. Wasn't that amusing?

Why was redness creeping up her jaw? Was she feeling a tad guilty? About what? The response he'd detected in her when a *married* man had kissed her? A response he knew she'd deny.

Nervously, she pulled her jacket over her gaping gown. The wind beat color into her cheeks and whipped loose hair around her face. Even all messed up, she was prettier than a sunrise. Her pretty blue eyes fired in his direction.

"Don't worry," he teased, "I'm not married."

Flustered, she glanced away, trying to smooth her scattered blond strands away from her supple cheeks. "I'm *not* worried."

His grin became laughter. Tension lifted from his muscles and he realized he was beginning to like having her around. She amused him, if nothing else.

A gust of wind kicked up dirt. Adam rubbed his eye with a fist and shoved the hair off his brows. He stepped closer to Jenny, his brown eyes twinkling. "When I saw you ride up, your dress was blowin' in the wind and I thought you were my mama."

Luke's laughter gave way to sudden concern, and his heart constricted at the boy's next words: "You think she'll be comin' back to visit me soon, Luke? You think if someone tells Mama I lost my other front tooth, she'll want to come see me then?"

Luke's throat tightened. He squatted in the dirt, at eye level with the five-year-old. How many times had he explained to the boy that his mama wasn't coming back? "Oh, Adam."

The horse snorted and Luke glanced up. Jenny

was studying the two of them with a baffled expression.

"Adam's mother passed away four weeks ago," Luke murmured.

Her mouth opened in dismay.

"Remember, Adam?" Luke cupped the boy's narrow shoulder with his large callused palm. "Remember, your mama's in heaven?"

The boy shrugged. Pulling away from Luke, he clamped his mouth tight, glanced down at his stick and started tracing circles in the cracked earth.

Luke worried most when the boy got quiet like this. He wished he could erase Adam's pain, but there didn't seem to be much he could do. Suddenly remembering Jenny was watching them, he straightened to full height, towering over her.

Her face mellowed, all soft curves and dewy lips. "I'm sorry.... How difficult for Adam. Does he have a father?"

Luke's gut clenched. "His father doesn't live around here. I'm...I'm trying to contact him."

He wasn't about to discuss the problem in front of Adam. Luke was glad now he hadn't mentioned Daniel's name to the boy. Until Luke knew for certain what Daniel intended on doing, it was best not to raise the boy's hopes. Maria hadn't told Adam much about his father, either. She'd made him sound like an adventurer, a man who'd gone off to seek a fortune for his family. If things went the way Luke planned, the boy's life would be settled soon.

And now that Jenny had met Adam, first chance Luke got with her alone, he'd tell her the truth.

She swallowed. "Why did you bring me here?"

"You need to meet some people." He motioned to the house. "Daniel's relatives."

She stepped back in dismay. "Daniel's relatives?" Her gaze shot to the house. "I didn't know he had living family." Flushed, she glanced back at Luke. "It doesn't matter. What I'd like to do is leave."

"After you meet them, I promise you will. They're nice folks." He held his breath and waited for her reply. It was up to her now, what direction he'd take from here.

She lifted her chin. "Tell me one good reason why I shouldn't holler bloody murder right now."

"Because you might be sorry later. You might embarrass yourself in front of Daniel's relations." He inclined his head. His voice was low. "Take a look at the boy. He won't hurt you. You're not in danger. And as of now, I'm giving you back your freedom."

She frowned in confusion. "I'm free to go?"

He nodded. His decision came as a surprise to himself, but it seemed like the right thing to do to gain her trust.

"And Olivia?"

"She'll be free to go as well."

They both peered at Adam. He was hopping in the dirt, jumping over the circles he'd drawn. He found a toad to chase and, for the moment, seemed to forget about his troubles.

Walking a few steps closer, Luke nudged him. "This time *I* forgot my manners. Adam, I'd like to introduce you to Miss Jenny."

Luke turned and watched her rigid stance, her

stone wall of protection, crumble. "Pleased to meet you, Adam."

Luke *knew* it wasn't in her to be cruel to a child, and the tightness in his chest subsided. For the moment, she was distracted by the boy, and maybe the thought of meeting Daniel's family. Her future family.

Slowly, the boy shook her hand. "Ma'am." He turned and, with a shy smile that he was trying to hide, whispered something inaudible into Luke's knees.

"No whispering now, it's not polite. Speak up."

The round face peered at Jenny. When her eyes sparkled back, Luke knew he'd passed the first hurdle.

Adam leaned around Luke's knees and whispered to her. "You look like you could use somethin' to drink. Would you like a glass of cider? I helped Daisy press the apples."

The muscles in Luke's neck stiffened as he awaited her decision. Jenny paled, looked toward the house, gulped, then turned back to the boy. "That'd be very nice."

A rush of pride filled Luke at how the boy had handled himself. It was important that these two people get along. More important than Jenny could ever guess. The day she married Daniel, she'd become Adam's stepmother.

The boy squinted. "How'd you get that cut on your head? And rip your dress?"

Luke playfully tossed his wide hat onto the boy's head. "She fell off my horse. Now don't go asking nosy questions. Most people don't like it, especially women." The sooner the boy learned that fact, the better off he'd be.

Grinning with delight, Adam adjusted the oversize hat on his head. "I never met no one who fell off a tame horse before."

In a self-conscious gesture, Jenny raised her fingertips to her brow and swept them across the bruised area.

"Luke!" someone hollered. "Hello!" Two grayhaired folks had come out on the porch and now hurried toward them.

Jenny reeled back in surprise.

Lord almighty, you'd have thought Luke had gone for two weeks instead of two days. No one came running to greet him at the saloon when he returned from being away. It felt strange, but brought a grin to his lips.

Nathaniel reached Jenny's side first. He smiled, baring tobacco-stained teeth beneath his waxed mustache. His overalls were freshly pressed, the only man Luke had ever seen with ironed creases down the front of his denims. His plaid shirt smelled strongly of bayberry soap. He was a man well cared for by a woman who'd loved him for forty years.

Clutching the skirts of her faded brown housedress against the swirling wind, Daisy wove her arm through Nathaniel's elbow. She smoothed her gray bun and peered at Jenny. The wrinkles on her sunbeaten face deepened when she smiled.

Feeling protective, Luke stepped beside Jenny. Her eyes widened and she looked as if she was still struggling with her decision whether to stay or run.

"Jenny," Luke said, pressing a palm to the small of her back, "this is Daisy and her husband, Nathaniel Hill. They're Daniel's aunt and uncle, three times removed.''

''Daniel's aunt and uncle?'' she said, taken aback.

Nathaniel held out his hand. ''Well, we're more like cousins, I suppose. But because of the age difference, he used to call us aunt and uncle when he was small. It's on his mother's side, three cousins back. Howdy, young miss.''

Nervously, she moistened her dry lips and placed her hand in Nathaniel's. Luke knew she'd be surprised. He didn't think Daniel had told her about his only living kin. It would have meant admitting to a connection to Cheyenne, and the possibility of running into Adam.

Luke was counting on Daisy and Nathaniel to draw her into the house and make her feel welcome. They also didn't know that Daniel was Adam's father. Luke didn't want to raise anyone's hopes until he knew Daniel's plans.

And for Luke's plan to work right now, Jenny had to stay. But this time, there was no point in forcing her. He couldn't force her to *like* Adam. Besides, if there was a hint any one of these people here might get hurt, including Jenny, he'd call the whole thing off and send her home. He'd deal with Daniel on his own.

Adam entwined himself around Nathaniel's faded britches, peeking out from behind a baggy thigh. Nathaniel chuckled and pulled the boy's ears. The two looked mighty relaxed together, Luke observed, unlike how he himself usually felt with the boy. Why was that? Why did he feel uncomfortable with a kid?

"Jenny fell off a horse," said Adam, jumping on Nathaniel's chunky boots.

"A horse—"

"Are you all right, dear?" asked Daisy, stepping to Jenny's side and studying the cut with tender concern. Luke was now glad he'd changed his shirt, so they wouldn't question him.

Jenny rubbed her forehead. "I'm fine."

Nathaniel scratched his gray mustache. "How do you know Daniel?"

All eyes turned to Jenny. Her mouth opened but she couldn't seem to get the words out.

"They're engaged," Luke interjected. "She'll soon be his wife." Saying the words out loud made his heart kick.

Jenny slid her flustered gaze to his.

"I know I told you to expect just Daniel," Luke continued, "but turns out they're both coming for a visit. Daniel couldn't make it right away. He'll be following tomorrow." Guilt slithered up his spine at how he'd twisted the truth.

Would she speak up and tell them? Or were her feelings too jumbled? Was she too embarrassed, too curious about Daniel's family to speak up?

The sun seemed suddenly hot. A trickle of sweat ran down his temple.

Her upper lip beaded with perspiration. She opened her mouth as if to say something, making his heart pound faster, then she abruptly changed her mind.

He inhaled a big lungful of air.

"Well, it's a real pleasure to meet you," said Nathaniel. "We haven't seen Daniel in quite a while, but we're tickled you came to see us. Welcome, welcome, little lady.''

Jenny scanned the yard again, looking toward the stables, then at the line of laundry drying in the heat, and the swing Luke had tied in the apple tree last week.

"Well, let's go inside," said Nathaniel, "get out of this hot sun and get acquainted in there. Gosh, you're just in time for lunch."

"Come on in, honey," said Daisy, wiping her hands on her apron. "It'll be nice to share a conversation with another woman. Nothing but men around here." She straightened the hairpin in her bun. "Fancy that, Luke comin' back with you. How was your train ride? A few years back, we used to ride on wooden benches, but now I hear they have padded leather seats. Did you ride on those, Luke, in first class?"

First class? Leather seats? They'd slept in a boxcar with the animals! Wasn't that kind of funny? He glanced at Jenny, but she wasn't smiling. Her stare was downright unfriendly. The little hairs at the base of his neck stood up. "Not exactly."

Nathaniel stepped to the horse at the water trough. "I'll help with the saddlebags."

While he did that, Luke, knowing how much Adam liked horses, asked the boy to walk his stallion to the stables. The boy nodded enthusiastically.

Jenny stepped to Luke's side. Through gritted teeth, she whispered, "I'd like to talk with you."

"Later," he whispered back, retrieving his hat from Adam's head. With a skip, Adam led the horse away.

She could barely bridle the thunder in her voice.

"It's not fair to fool Daniel's family. I won't go along with it."

"You *are* going along with it."

She pressed her lips together in annoyance, bristled and grabbed her skirts.

Nathaniel scratched his head. "I've got Luke's saddlebag, but where are your bags, Miss Jenny?"

Luke sprang forward. "There was a mishap at the rail station," he blurted, feeling the heat of Jenny's gaze on his face. "Unfortunately, her bags were left behind." It *was* the truth. Her bags *had been* left behind.

"Oh, what horrible luck," said Daisy. "I hope they were labeled with your name."

Luke met Jenny's drilling gaze and he squirmed. Daisy must have noticed the pointed looks passing between them. "I guess they weren't. Well, don't you fret, my dear, they're only clothes. Thank goodness *you* weren't left behind."

Yes, thank goodness, thought Luke, humor causing his lips to twitch. Now that was funny; even Jenny had to admit it. Gazing down at her, expecting to see that pretty lopsided smile of hers, he became the victim of another frosty glare.

Clearing his throat with an anxious cough, he tugged at the brim of his hat. "Maybe you could lend her some clothes, Daisy, while she's visiting."

"Well, I'd be happy to. Don't have anything real fancy, though, I'll warn you now." She studied Jenny's ball gown as she shooed her up onto the porch. "Nothin' like what you're wearing. And I have to tell you..."

Jenny hesitated. "Yes?"

"Us folks around here, we're a little different

from you city folks.'' The kind old woman glanced at the billowing dress and the muddy cloth boots, concern pulling at her wrinkled cheeks. ''We don't usually get so dressed up to go visiting.''

Jenny colored fiercely, puckered her lips ever so slightly and turned in Luke's direction. He withered on the spot.

With a firm hand on Jenny's shoulder, Daisy led her across the porch. Jenny moved to the other side of Daisy, as far away from Luke as possible.

He shook his head.

He knew he'd pay for it later, but at least Jenny hadn't left yet.

Wearing a clean, faded blouse and skirt, but feeling a jumbled mass of emotions, Jenny studied Luke across the pine table.

She was trying to understand him and the reason he'd brought her here. He was a man of opposites. How could a person who'd so forcefully snatched her from her home sit so comfortably among these pleasant folks?

What in tarnation was she supposed to do now? Luke had completely stumped her by releasing her from captivity and dumping her on her future family. And he'd assured her Olivia was safe, too.

Daisy was clearing the dishes with a loud clatter. They'd left the porch door propped open during the meal, and a fresh breeze curled through the room. Jenny sipped her coffee and nervously looked around. The interior of the house was lit with sunshine and furnished with colorful fabrics and quilts. A round iron stove sat in a corner of the kitchen.

Avoiding Jenny's gaze for the umpteenth time,

Luke strode to the pie safe and pulled out a pecan pie. Its fresh-baked fragrance wafted through the air as he set it on the table. Adam passed out plates and forks.

"Don't use those everyday things," hollered Daisy from the counter. "Nathaniel, reach up there on the top shelf of the sideboard and grab me them special plates, the pretty blue ones we won at the fair."

Standing at the head of the table, Luke began to cut the pie. He had changed into fresh clothes and pulled a comb through his hair, but he hadn't shaved his two days' growth of black whiskers. The contradiction gave him a rugged, masculine appearance which Jenny was having difficulty ignoring. She bristled with irritation.

Why were Luke and Daniel fighting?

And why hadn't *Daniel* told her he had living relatives? He'd given her the impression he had no one.

Wasn't she worthy of being told?

Her lashes swept downward. She was still debating whether to tell the older folks about the real manner in which she'd been brought here, and her own hesitation confused her. What was holding her back?

The fact that the older couple might not believe her? Would they think she was a little touched? Try as she might, she couldn't seem to find the right words to express how their beloved Luke, this man they fawned over, had taken her against her will. And if they did believe her, what would her admission cost?

It would throw a shadow on her upcoming wedding.

What would that do to Daniel and his relationship with these people? She'd have a better chance of knowing what to do if she knew what in blazes the two men were fighting about.

She studied the stubborn line of Luke's jaw as he dished up the pie, looking for clues. His thoughtful silence gave her none. He winced with a sudden movement, and clutched his side. His ribs were sore. Why hadn't he mentioned his injury to anyone here? Why hadn't she?

Recovering, he passed her the first piece of pie. With a dark intensity in his mischievous eyes, he seemed to be studying her just as closely as she was him. She shot him an angry glare.

Their fingertips brushed beneath the plate and she shuddered. Quickly dropping the plate to the table, she was suffocated with the memory of their kiss. Engaged to one man, and being kissed by the other. Even now, her throat burned where his lips had brushed it.

She squirmed on the chair and sat up straighter. All right, she rationalized, it wasn't a kiss on the mouth but a kiss on the neck. It wasn't anything, really.

Oh, yes, it was.

It had been more erotic than a kiss on the mouth. That was the most sensual response she'd ever had to any suitor. Flushing, she toyed with the blue gingham napkin in her lap, refolding it for the third time.

With a gap-toothed smile, Adam stepped to her side. The boy had cleaned up for lunchtime, washed his hands and slicked back his hair. It made him look young and vulnerable. Her heart went out to him at losing his mother. Although her own vague memories of losing her mother to cholera were those

of a two-year-old child, she knew what it felt like
to yearn for a mother's embrace. She begrudgingly
admitted that Luke was very kind to look after
Adam while he tried to reach the boy's father.

"Here's a fork for your pie, Miss Jenny."

"Thank you."

Jenny watched Adam pass cutlery to Luke. The
boy was so eager for Luke's attention and praise.
Luke seemed to be trying his best, but didn't always
notice the lad. During the meal, he'd helped Adam
cut his steak into smaller pieces, but hadn't mentioned the untouched peas and greens Adam left behind. Jenny stifled her own urge to remind Luke to
take more notice. It wasn't her place. It wasn't her
concern.

Where was Adam's father at a time like this?
How had the child's mother died? She had a list of
questions for Luke.

But the longer she waited to ask, the more complicated it was becoming. Daisy had already asked
a dozen prickly questions concerning Jenny's upcoming wedding day and preparations, about her
family in Boston, about how she'd first met Daniel.

Through it all, Luke hadn't said a word. Hadn't
offered a smidgen of support. He'd carefully listened
to her every answer, as if she were here to entertain
him!

Well, she was here against her will.

So was Olivia. The thought of Olivia penned up
somewhere with a complete stranger while Jenny
was enjoying a slice of pie made her stomach churn.
Where was her friend?

Jenny pulled her shoulders back and wriggled on
the hard seat. Why not ask him? She dug into her

pie and swallowed. "Where's Olivia spending the afternoon?" she asked brightly.

Luke snapped to attention. That was more like it.

Daisy poured out more coffee. "Olivia? Who's Olivia?"

Jenny smiled at Luke as she tilted the cup to her lips and sipped. How would he get out of this one?

"A friend of Jenny's," he answered calmly, studying her with that smug look of his, pulling out a chair and sitting down. "They're going to do some sight-seeing together."

Sight-seeing? Huh! "Your friend Tom *took* her," said Jenny, raising her brows, "but I didn't get a chance to ask where exactly they were galloping off to."

"He took her to town. Travis is going to look after her."

"Travis? He's such a nice fella," said Nathaniel, gulping his coffee. "Always busier than a hornet, but he's nice."

"Where in town and who is Travis?"

Luke leveled his twinkling gray eyes at her, then in an annoying display of confidence, he winked. "Travis is my right-hand man, and he's making her comfortable at the saloon."

Saloon? She slumped back in her seat. A saloon was no place for a lady. Jenny had heard all about saloons. They were full of drinkers and fighters and gamblers and painted women.

"What saloon?" she demanded.

"*My* saloon."

Stunned for a second, she stared at his dark features. When a grin tugged at his mouth, her anger rose to a new level. "You own a saloon?"

He nodded.

It figured. He probably spent every evening away from home, drinking and gambling and God only knew what else.

"I live there, too."

He lived there? Good grief. Didn't he have a regular home? A house with rooms, with chickens in the yard, a dog in the back, a front door his visitors could knock on? Olivia must be frightened out of her skin. This man's gall was maddening. Even more maddening was the fact that Jenny just sat there, staring at him, tongue-tied.

"How could you take my friend to a saloon?" she croaked. "What kind of place is that for a lady?"

The clatter of forks stopped. The others finally noticed something was amiss between the two of them.

All eyes turned to Luke. His lips thinned. "Have you ever been to a saloon?"

Jenny's fingers fluttered to her throat. "Of course not."

"You might be surprised what's inside."

"I think not," she said, clucking with disapproval.

Eyes locked with hers, he shook his head slightly. "You're so quick to judge. I've met a lot of uppity folks in my time—"

She gasped. He was calling *her* uppity? He had the nerve to attack *her* character?

"I know how you feel," Daisy interjected, glancing from one stubborn face to the other. "About saloons, I mean. I've never set foot in one, other than that one time at Luke's. It's a pretty intimidating place for a woman, you gotta admit, Luke."

Nathaniel broke in. "You know, Cheyenne's a

big town. It's got over two dozen saloons and they're not all alike.''

"Two dozen!" Jenny gasped.

Daisy sat down beside Jenny. "That's right, the town's got over ten thousand people, and there's three levels of saloons, something for everyone—''

"Oh, we've never been to the seedier ones," Nathaniel interrupted his wife. The two of them were tripping over each other to sing the praises of Cheyenne's saloons. "No one in town goes to those. They're for the drifters who come through. You know—the rail laborers and scruffy drovers. Those are the dangerous saloons you gotta avoid. There was a knifing just last week.''

Daisy patted Jenny's arm. "And then on the top end, you've got the highfalutin saloons, for all those rich cattle barons from Texas. Lord almighty! Some of those people take their summers in England, they've got so much money. They bring in opera companies for entertainment, and singers from New York City and Buffalo Bill Cody—''

"Unbelievable," said Nathaniel. "But we avoid those, too. Regular folks don't like to dress up just to have a beer." The old man sat back with pride. "Luke's saloon is in the middle. It caters to local residents mainly, just regular, hardworking folks. He doesn't have operas yet," Nathaniel snickered, "but on the other hand, he doesn't allow painted ladies, either.''

As the older couple continued their discussion, Jenny found her composure. Daisy and Nathaniel, God bless them, were only trying to calm her.

And she'd get out of this situation sooner if she didn't anger Luke. She glanced at the tiny boy peering over the table, sitting faithfully beside Luke, and her curiosity stirred.

All she wanted to do was find Olivia and return to Denver. She'd ask Daniel what this was all about, and he'd explain it to her until it made sense. "Maybe I should see the saloon myself." She met Luke's gaze. "Would you take me to see my friend? Daisy and Nathaniel, you—you'll join us, won't you?"

Daisy rose to stack the coffee cups, and Jenny jumped to help her. "It's a lovely idea, really," said the older woman. "But I've got to tend to Adam, and I promised to bring a dozen eggs to Mrs. Mathews next door."

"And I've got a ranch to run," added Nathaniel, wiping his mouth. He reached for a toothpick. "But once Daniel arrives, I promise we'll make the time and join you all for dinner. Maybe even in the saloon."

Jenny sagged with disappointment.

Luke stood up and walked to the door. His face had lost its harshness. "If you'd like to go to the saloon," he said, removing his hat from its peg, "I'll take you."

He was being charming again, and that was when she distrusted him most. At least when he was mad, she knew how to read him. Her eyes narrowed. "You'd take me now?"

"If you like," he answered, in that easygoing manner that made him so appealing, that made her insides so jumbled. "You could stay overnight with Olivia there, if that'd make you feel more comfortable. We've got hotel rooms on the upper floor."

Oh, heavens yes, she couldn't think of anything better. Spending the night in a crass saloon... Stalling, she slid the coffee cups into the soapy water in the basin.

"I expect the saloon's where Daniel will show up first," Luke added. "His train arrives in the morning, around eleven."

Did Luke actually think she'd keep her mouth shut and wait patiently for Daniel to arrive? Luke thought so damn highly of himself. Never mind Daniel's arrival. If she met up with Olivia, they'd escape out that saloon door so fast.... "If I go with you, you wouldn't force...take me anywhere else, would you?"

Daisy laughed. "Where on earth would he take you?"

Where? The back of a boxcar. Down an alley with a gun pointed between her shoulder blades. Thrown onto a horse. "Let me help Daisy with the dishes, and I'll—I'll think about it."

"Don't be silly, I'll finish the dishes," Daisy said with a nod to the door. "Let Luke show you the rest of the ranch. Go on. No guest of ours is gonna do any dishes."

Jenny was not going anywhere alone with him. She crouched down beside Adam. "Will you come with us for a walk?"

"Okay," he said, skipping out to the porch, making Jenny feel safer. "I could show you the new foal."

"Yeah," added Luke, stepping into the sunshine and tugging on the brim of his hat. "Come protect Jenny," he said softly beside her shoulder, causing her pulse to ripple. "Tell me, it is me you don't trust, or yourself?"

Stepping back, she gaped at him. "I've never met a man with such arrogance."

"You're changing the subject." He smiled a devilish grin and her stomach fluttered. He hollered into the yard, "Wait up, Adam, we're coming." Luke focused his smoky gaze back on her. "After you." He swept the air in a mocking gesture of chivalry. He was anything but chivalrous. He was a scoundrel.

She crossed her arms and trailed behind the boy, down the grassy path to the stables. "I don't know why you're bothering to show me around. I don't plan on staying."

"Did Daniel ever tell you about this ranch?"

"No. Why should he?"

"Because this is where he grew up. Where we both grew up."

She stared up at Luke in surprise.

"When his folks passed on, Daisy and Nathaniel bought it from him. They were trying to help him raise capital for his surveying business. They paid a pretty penny for it, but at least Daniel got what he needed."

His sarcasm wasn't lost on her.

Another thing Daniel had kept from her. She glanced up at the hills. Why hadn't Daniel told her about any of this? "Why did you bring me here?"

"Before I tell you, I want to give you something."

She had to run to keep up with his long strides. "I'm tired of these games. What's this all about?"

They stepped into the stable. He slipped into one of the empty stalls, reaching for something tucked high between the boards. He came back with something in his hand, something she couldn't see. "I'm going to give you something so you'll believe I'm telling you the truth. I want you to trust me."

"If you can make that happen, you're a magician."

"Call it magic, then." Extending his hand, he unfolded his palm, offering a shiny little pistol.

She swallowed and stared up at him. He was serious.

"Go ahead. Take it. It's loaded, so be careful. You can use it on me, or you can listen to what I have to say."

Her heart began to drum. She glanced at the boy. Adam was preoccupied with a mare and foal, out of earshot.

She grabbed the gun, stepped back and pointed it at Luke. "You're so damn cocky. What makes you think I won't pull the trigger?"

His gaze dropped to the barrel. He gulped and his eyes glinted. "I'm betting you won't. I'm betting you're a listening type of woman."

"You're the most arrogant, conceited—"

"It's about Adam." Luke glanced earnestly toward the boy, who was climbing to the top of the boards. "That's why I brought you here. That's why Daniel and I are fighting."

She looked at the boy, then back at Luke. He didn't make sense. "What are you talking about?"

Luke looked her square in the eyes and calmly said, "Adam's father, the one he's been waiting for, the one we've all been waiting for, is Daniel."

Chapter Five

Jenny's mouth felt as dry as dust. She stared into Luke's clear dark eyes. His expression stilled, and she felt the color drain from her face. A voice of alarm whispered in the back of her mind. It couldn't be. Adam was not Daniel's son. Luke was mistaken.

"I'm sorry, I shouldn't have blurted it out like that," Luke said, his black-clad figure towering over her. "I should have warned you."

Stunned by his accusation, Jenny blinked. She absently watched the light bounce off an unruly lock of hair that touched his collar.

Her arms grew weak. She looked down at the gun in her hands. Lowering it, she stepped away and slumped against the rough boards for support. Her long skirt fluttered around her ankles.

Slowly, her gaze sought the quiet little boy. A dozen yards away, sitting in a pile of straw, his face barely visible behind his unkempt hair, Adam stroked the foal's white muzzle.

Daniel's son?

She shook her head. "It's not true."

"It *is*."

She watched Adam whisper something to the colt with the sweet affection only a five-year-old could give. *Her* Daniel could never desert this child. Gooseflesh rose on her arms.

Luke turned his face away from her to the heart-warming picture of boy and animal. A streak of sadness touched his composed features. "It's hard to believe."

"He doesn't look like Daniel. He could be anyone's boy."

"Maria said he was, and I believe her."

Maria. A real woman with a real name.

"Maria Ramirez was twenty-one when she started working in my saloon." He slid a hand into his pocket. "She'd come straight from Mexico. She could barely speak English, and was about as innocent as that foal over there. When Daniel started coming around every lunch hour to have her serve him meals and drinks, I warned him to stay away. She was very naive when it came to men. I thought he listened, because I never saw them together after that, but I guess I was wrong."

Jenny's lips tightened with sympathy. That situation would be horrible for any woman to go through alone. And poor Adam! With his mother gone, he needed a father now more than ever.

But Jenny couldn't allow herself to believe Daniel was responsible, because if she did…

Rebellious emotions flared in her chest. *Luke* was the criminal, not Daniel. Luke was the one who couldn't be trusted. "Daniel wouldn't keep this from me." Running a moist palm along her skirt, she tried to regain her balance, tried to deny the accusation. "He would have told me."

"Told you what? That he's a fool? That he deserted the woman and the boy?"

Suddenly woozy, she backed away.

"Listen, I'm sorry you had to find out this way. And half of me doesn't know whether I should be telling you. But I figure you've got a right to know the truth." He draped his arms over the stall, leaned against the boards and continued watching Adam. "Don't use Daniel's silence as proof he's not the father. He's kept a lot from you. Did he tell you about this ranch? Or about Daisy and Nathaniel?" He hooked his boot onto the bottom board. "Or much about me?"

She struggled for air. There had to be a reasonable explanation. "He—he hasn't had time. We've only been courting a couple of months. Half the time, he's been out of town scouting for the railroad."

Jenny watched the boy shovel dirty straw from under the horses. He disappeared with it out the stable doors, and she and Luke were alone. "I'm sure he planned on telling me about this ranch—about everything—before the wedding. He...he hasn't had time."

Luke swung around and gripped her by the shoulders. The heat of his palms burned through her blouse into her skin. "How much time does a man need?"

She struggled beneath his grip, overwhelmed by his bulk and his touch and his accusations. Why was he so full of animosity? Why would he make up this lie?

She ripped out of his grasp and tumbled backward, still holding the gun. "What's this really about? You've been consumed with rage since the moment I met you. *Why?* Are you trying to ruin Daniel? Are you…are you jealous of your friend's success?''

He swiped the back of his hand across his mouth. His eyes narrowed in disgust. ''That's ridiculous.''

''I see the flash of lightning in your eyes every time you talk about him. Why? He's built up a fine business, a place in society. He's engaged to be married—''

With a sharp intake of breath, Luke stepped toward her. The thunderous look on his face stopped her from going further. ''You think I'm jealous he's engaged?''

She held her ground. She would never back down from this man. ''You kidnapped me, remember? What am I supposed to think? And you've…you've tried to kiss me every time we're alone. You might have Daisy and Nathaniel fooled, but you can't fool me.'' Her voice rose. ''Of course you're trying to break us up, telling me this story about the boy. You're crazy—''

''*No!*''

''You're trying to keep me from the man I love!''

His eyes grew fierce. ''This has nothing to do with you and Daniel.'' A chill clung to his words. ''I hope you *marry him tomorrow.*''

Clenching her teeth, she sputtered, ''I've heard enough.'' She spun on her heel, whirling to escape.

''Oh, no, you haven't.'' He grabbed her arm, twisting her to face him, inches from his face.

''Leave me alone,'' she warned, struggling to break free. How dare he touch her!

''What I care about is the boy, and you're staying in Cheyenne until we settle this.''

Her breath burned in her throat. Then, realizing she still held the gun, she planted it against his chest and cocked the trigger. In response, he dropped his hand from her arm. Inclining his head, he stepped back nice and easy. That was more like it.

She swallowed. "Don't you ever touch me again, do you understand?"

Hiking up her skirts, she pivoted to flee, but he grabbed her by the waist.

"Let me go!" She kicked him hard in the shin.

"Owww," he hollered, stumbling back.

Glancing down at the gun in her hand, she gave a humorless laugh. "I almost believed this gun was loaded. I almost trusted you—"

"No, don t!"

She squeezed the trigger just as he leaped for her hand. A bullet zinged through the air. The sound of splintering wood echoed above their heads. Horses neighed. Her body crashed against the boards. Luke slammed against her, both of them breathing hard.

The gun *was* loaded.

He hadn't lied to her about that.

Stunned, she gazed up into his face. He peered down at her and taking a deep breath, stepped away.

Untangling her limbs from his, she dropped the gun from shaking fingers to the straw below. Her heart was beating like a runaway horse. What was she doing here, so far from home, and so alone?

What did Luke want from her? Even if she wanted to, how could she help Adam? What could she possibly do if his real father couldn't be found?

The mare circled in its stall. Adam came running through the stable door. "What's wrong? What's wrong?"

"Nothing, Adam." Red-faced, Luke beat the dust from his pants. Keeping his eyes fixed on her, he bent down and scooped up the gun. He straightened and rubbed his hand over the boy's head. "I was showing Jenny a gun and it went off by accident, that's all."

They peered up at the shredded hole between the roof rafters. She shrank back, mortified. Someone could have been shot. She gulped. Did she do that? What was happening to her? What kind of effect did this man have on her?

"The gun went off by accident?" Adam scratched his head, his eyes filled with doubt. "You never—"

"It went off in Jenny's hands." Luke headed toward the nervous animal. "I'll let the horses out into the front pasture. Why don't you go to the house and tell Daisy and Nathaniel what happened? I'm sure they heard the gunshot. They'll be worried."

Jenny watched as Adam nodded. The poor innocent boy, trapped in the middle of all this. Lord, how could anyone walk away from a child?

And he was so young and tender, having just lost his mother. He desperately needed a father. Daniel would never, ever desert his own son. Would he?

But why hadn't he told her about any of these people?

Adam mumbled to himself as he walked past her. "Fallin' off tame horses, shootin' off guns by accident…"

Her cheeks grew hot.

"Go on now, Adam." Luke patted the mare to soothe it. It simmered down. Glancing over the horse's withers at Jenny, he shook his head. "I don't know why, but I always seem to lose my head around you. I should have kept my cool.''

She didn't care for any of his explanations. What she wanted was for him to hitch a horse and buggy, because she was leaving the ranch.

She didn't want to be pulled into anyone's problems. As heartsick as she was for Adam, there was nothing she could do for him. Mostly, she wanted to be rid of this place and this man, and all his dirty accusations. Daniel would explain everything to her until it all fell into place.

But something in Luke's gaze nibbled at her conscience. His eyes, almost black, shimmered in the light.

His jaw tightened. ''Adam is a fine boy. One a father should be proud to acknowledge.''

She glanced down at her hands and played with her fingers. ''You never told Adam about your…your suspicions?''

''You can call them suspicions if you like, but they're facts. No, I never told him. Not yet. But I'm not the only one in town who knows, and there's no way I can keep it a secret forever. Sooner or later, the boy will hear the rumors. I prefer he hear the truth from me—from us.''

When she didn't comment, he continued. ''Daniel is legally registered as Adam's father.''

Jenny started. ''Who registered the boy? Daniel?''

''Maria.''

Jenny paused. ''So it's down to her word against his.''

''He's been paying Maria two dollars a month since Adam's birth. Not much money—it was more of an insult than a help. If he's not the father, why do you think he did that?''

Jenny didn't want to hear any more, but she pulled herself together. "I don't know. Did you ask him?"

Luke nodded. "He says he felt sorry for her."

"Oh." It was possible that's all it was. Jenny hadn't asked Luke the obvious question yet. "What does Daniel say about your allegation that he's the father?"

"He insists the kid is mine."

Jenny's mouth dropped open. Oh, of course; she hadn't thought of that. Maybe Luke was the one who was trying to shirk his responsibilities.

His mouth twisted. "In order for the kid to be mine, you know what had to have happened, don't you?"

She stepped back, feeling suddenly hot in the musky air of the stables.

"Well, it never happened." Luke scanned her face, as if he were well aware that she was judging him. "Although it may not seem like it, Daniel and I used to be close once. I used to respect him a great deal. If he'd just come and meet Adam, things would fall into place. Maybe seeing the kid would drag Daniel back to his senses." Luke looked away, gulped and turned back. "Maybe marrying you would, too. And then you could raise the boy together."

Jenny started. She hadn't even thought that far ahead. But if it were true, if the boy were Daniel's, what then?

No, it wasn't possible Daniel could have fooled her so completely. She was a good judge of character. "I don't know what you want from me, but...but I can't help you." She squared her shoulders, pressed her heels into the dirt. "You think I'd believe you over a fine, upstanding citizen like Daniel? While he was giving a charity ball for widows and orphans, you were assaulting two women. A man like Daniel, who's concerned about orphans, wouldn't...wouldn't desert his own son."

Luke's jaw quivered.

"Maybe there's something Daniel and I could do for Adam," she said. "Maybe when I get back to Denver, we could arrange for the widows and orphans organization to find him a proper home."

Luke flinched at her words.

"When I get back, I'd...I'd be happy to help in any way I could. I know the head of the orphanage, a friend of mine, Mrs. Peters."

He shook his head in disbelief.

Her chest rose and fell. She rubbed her face with her hands and groaned. "Please, let me leave now. Daniel will explain everything to me. I'll ask him. He'll tell me the truth. Please, just take me to see Olivia."

Luke pulled off his black hat and played with the brim. Dark locks fell across his forehead. "All right," he finally said, wiping beads of perspiration from his brow. "I tried my best. I can't keep you here against your will." He glanced up at the hole in the rafters. "You're too spirited, and someone's bound to get hurt. That's not my intention at all."

Her insides fluttered. "Will you play any more tricks?"

"No." He said it with such honesty and compassion that her throat tightened. But he looked so defeated, standing there with his hat in his hand.

Her heart would *not* go out to him, she warned herself. "Can't you see," she pleaded, stepping closer, "how confusing this is? How am I supposed to know who to believe?"

Luke stepped closer. He lifted her hand, his unexpected touch sending a ripple cascading down her spine, and placed her palm over his heart. Then he flattened his own hand over hers. She felt the heat of his flesh beneath the cloth, the pounding of his blood. She felt the passion in his words, his stance, his gaze.

"You're not supposed to know it, you're supposed to feel it."

She withdrew her hand, feeling as if it had been singed in a flame.

"I don't understand how you can ride down the main street of town," Jenny said, sitting in the buckboard beside Luke. The setting sun drifted behind the Laramie Mountains as they wove their way along the busy street. "Aren't you concerned the sheriff might arrest you?"

Luke sighed and glanced at her. She apparently expected an answer. The circles under her eyes were deeper than they'd been this morning. Her lack of sleep was catching up to her. Daisy's faded, heavy shawl wrapped around her shoulders seemed to accentuate just how young and pretty she was. And hardheaded.

She was fooling herself about Daniel. She only saw what she wanted to see. Luke witnessed it all the time. People liked to delude themselves—hell, it was part of the joy of living. Some people's delusions were quite grand here in the West. "Why would the sheriff arrest me?"

"For stealing ten thousand dollars."

Luke scoffed. "Imaginary money." He flicked the reins. "Tell me something. Don't you think it's odd that Daniel just gave the sheriff a description of me? Why didn't he give my name and place of residence?"

He watched the confusion wrinkle her brow and he suddenly felt sorry for her.

"See?" he said, softly. "There was no theft. It was just an attempt on Daniel's part to keep me out of Denver. Away from you and anyone else who might discover the truth. The sheriff in this town isn't after me."

She sighed. A look of sadness passed over her features, quickly replaced by one of stubbornness.

They stared ahead. The horse's plodding hoofbeats echoed off the pine buildings. Their buckboard squeaked past the Cheyenne rail station and the rackety crowd shuffling on the platform. Two men zigzagged across the street, making their way from Annie's Café to the guns and ammunition depot. On Friday nights the town came alive with shoppers, diners and strollers.

Luke took a deep breath. His town. His people.

The mercantile loomed to their right, and they turned the corner. He stole another look at Jenny.

The vulnerability in her eyes tore at him, made him want to protect her. Did she need protecting from Daniel? Or could she hold her own? He smiled softly to himself. He did admire her fiery nature.

With her hands clasped in her lap, she stared

ahead. Her lips had stopped trembling, but were set firmly. Barely a word had escaped her on the thirty-minute ride, but what did he expect? She was going back to Denver, and there wasn't a damn thing he could think of saying to stop her.

He might as well face it. From here on in, he was on his own in helping Adam.

He was on his own.

He flicked the reins.

He'd been so damn sure all he had to do was tell her the truth and she'd believe him. Wrong. Well, at least he'd tried. Tomorrow morning, when the train rolled in from Denver, he'd try once more. He'd ask them nicely, both Daniel and Jenny, to spend some time with the boy.

A quiver of emotion wove its way through his chest. Maybe he was suffering from his own delusions.

Did he have a hope in hell of getting Daniel and Adam together? Would Daniel make a good father, anyway? Or was it best just to ask him to sign release papers?

What would happen to Adam? How and where should Luke start looking for an adoptive family, if it came to that?

Is this what people had done for Luke—trying to find him and his brothers and mother a home when his father had died and left them with nothing? Is this what it felt like, trying to do your best for an orphaned boy, knowing that taking him away from all he knew and loved would probably be the worst thing for him?

At least Luke had had his ma. He couldn't imagine what it'd feel like, as a kid, to be completely alone, like Adam was.

No. Luke wouldn't allow himself to feel defeated. Until he came face-to-face with Daniel tomorrow and Daniel said otherwise, there was still hope. Maybe Jenny would sleep on it, and her position would soften, too. Maybe.

His body swayed with the rhythm of the buggy. A burning desire for sleep crept into his muscles. God, he was tired.

The pain in his ribs jabbed again. He grimaced and ran a hand over his bandages. What he needed was a cold beer. That'd help his ribs.

Hell, Jenny could use one, too. A good stiff drink to settle her. Couldn't hurt. He'd like to see her smile again. That warm smile that made him catch his breath, the one she'd given him after she'd fallen off the horse, right before he'd kissed her. He had to stop thinking about that kiss. She was Daniel's.

Hell, she might be Daniel's, but there was no harm in showing her *his* saloon. It was a matter of personal pride. He would put the McLintock charm to work, the one most women found hard to resist.

From half a block away, he peered at his saloon—a two-story building, one of the oldest permanent structures in Cheyenne. Two hotel patrons sat on the balcony, fanning themselves, observing the street from under the awning overhang. On the side stairs, a young couple holding hands made their way down to the alley.

Adjacent to the saloon was a smaller building, one he'd been renting for years. It housed his kitchen and supply pantry. The cook and his wife lived in the two rooms above it, and when Maria couldn't find a sitter, she'd lay Adam down for naps in a room off the kitchen. Luke had opened one of the walls and connected the building to his saloon with a hallway. Soon he'd have enough money to buy the building.

When he was a boy, most of these buildings had been tents. The town had started out as a rowdy frontier town, then had exploded in growth. The neighboring shops now boomed with business. Every investor from here to the Atlantic wanted to get in on the economic surge. It filled Luke with pride to be part of it.

"What are they doing over there?" asked Jenny, motioning to a crowd gathered at the side of the road. A dozen people were lined up behind a wagon, where a man was selling clothing out of the back.

"Oh, that's Harris. He's selling new gowns. Direct from Paris, France. They come in once a year."

Jenny craned her neck as they passed. In the crowd, a flock of arms tugged at a yellow dress. "He's selling French gowns at the side of the road? Why? Don't you have stores?"

"Most stuff like that sells before it gets to any stores." He looked ahead and nodded to two of his men, who stood at the saloon doors—Beuford James and Travis Brown.

"Is that your saloon?"

"Yeah."

Jenny came to full alert, as if she were a soldier going into battle and she'd just glimpsed the enemy across the river. Lord, she was suspicious of him. Could he blame her? She leaned forward in the fading light. Her loose, tangled hair glistened like spun gold.

The hooting from inside grew louder, the lights brighter as they neared. Luke's trained ear picked up amiable noise—music, laughter, raised voices, but no serious ruckus. He'd learned years ago that it paid to keep two men at the doors on Friday nights. It was payday for many workers, and some of them went a little wild.

They pulled up to the boardwalk, underneath the large, burnished wood sign, Luke's Saloon. Luke jumped off the buckboard, ignoring the dull ache in his ribs. He helped Jenny down to the street. As he picked up the traveling bag Daisy had packed for her, Jenny scurried away, a flurry of arms and legs.

"Evenin', ma'am," said Travis, tipping his hat as she walked by. His bushy black mustache covered much of his dark-skinned, smiling face. She nodded with suspicion and kept walking.

Luke stepped beside his men. "Howdy Beuford, Travis."

Jenny stopped and spun around to face Travis. She searched his face and stiffened. "You're Travis. You're the man who's looking after my friend."

"Ma'am," he said again, sheepishly, tipping his cowboy hat. "Pleasure to, ahh, meet you."

"Huh! A pleasure indeed," she snarled. "What have you done with Olivia? If you've harmed her in any way—"

"No ma'am, she's not harmed."

"Shame on you. *Both* of you." She shot Travis an icy look, then turned her frosty glare to Luke. Lord, she could make herself look mean when she wanted to.

A prickly heat tingled up his neck. He was more than a little embarrassed. What could he say after the way he'd treated her and Olivia? He'd acted shamelessly, but he still intended to let them go. She stood there staring at him, and all he could do was raise his palms in the air, as if he were declaring a surrender. No use fighting with the gal.

She flung the fringe of her shawl over her shoulder and stepped within inches of Travis. "How could you go along with this man? Your mother should take a switch to your bottom."

Travis's bushy dark mustache wiggled as he smiled. "Been a long time since my ma switched my bottom, ma'am."

"Don't you 'ma'am' me. Where is she?"

"She's in there someplace. Last I saw her, she was at the card tables. No," he corrected himself, "she was grabbing a sandwich in the kitchen."

Jenny huffed past him, like a queen bee about to sting her drones. She stopped when she got to the saloon doors. She stood there on tiptoe, peering over the doors, then glaring over her shoulder at Luke, silently ordering him to accompany her.

Travis tapped him on the shoulder. "Better watch out," he warned. "Olivia's madder than hell. I'm glad you're taking her off my hands."

Luke gulped and tried to steady his nerves. Adjusting his hat, he headed toward Jenny.

Loud voices bellowed from the opening. With a sudden clatter and hollering of obscenities, two men burst through the doors. In a panic, Luke dove for Jenny, but the men's bodies still managed to collide with hers. They accidentally pushed her into the street.

Helpless, Luke watched as, with a horrified shriek, Jenny landed in the dirt on her rump.

Chapter Six

He was going to pay for this one, Luke thought, gazing at the heap of upturned petticoats and finely trimmed, blue cloth boots.

Speechless but apparently unhurt, Jenny rolled upright. With cheeks as red as cherries, she opened her mouth, then clamped it tight. Luke grasped her by her arm and dragged her out of the way before she got tangled up with more bodies.

Beuford hauled one of the men to his feet, and Travis grabbed the other, giving the bigger one a kick in the pants before sending him down the street. "Get outta here!"

"Give us back our guns."

"You know the rules. Come back tomorrow, when you're sober."

Jenny's mouth puckered as if she'd downed a shot of tequila. "What kind of a place is this?"

"It's not Boston," Luke said brightly, hoping to lighten her mood.

"It certainly isn't." She glanced at the wanted posters nailed to the wall and sniffed with displeasure.

He bit back a reply. Did she have to be so uppity? Did everything from her world have to smell like fresh-baked pumpkin pie and everything from his like week-old manure?

Well, she needed to relax. He'd get a smile from her tonight if he had to wring it out of her.

She peered over the doors again. "Is it…is it safe to go in?"

He stiffened at the insult. Didn't she know he could protect her from any man? From any fight? From anything? Besides, he owned this place!

"Oh, for cryin' out loud," he said, shoving the doors wide and stepping inside, "you're with *me*."

They entered the saloon. With Jenny standing two feet away, Luke pulled in a deep breath of air and crossed his arms. Familiar, comforting scents wrapped around him—a combination of cigar smoke, spilled booze and tanned leather. He breathed better just being here. The tinkling piano keys in the background and the rowdy murmurs and shouts made his blood pump.

How could Jenny dislike this place?

Suspended from the ceiling rafters on eight massive wagon wheels, kerosene lamps flickered high above the tables and cast a rich glow on the boisterous crowd below. An archway separated two rooms—one room for the drinking tables and bar, one for the dining tables, gambling tables and the stage.

Lamplight danced off the polished oak bar close to where Luke and Jenny stood. Five bartenders worked behind it, filling shot glasses and beer steins as fast as their hands would allow. The mirrored panels behind them reflected their smooth, easy movements and seemed to double the saloon's energetic atmosphere.

Some of the regulars spotted Luke and waved. He raised his black felt hat in friendly greeting and scanned the crowd. About a hundred men were here tonight. Apart from the barmaids waiting for their drinks to be poured, and the dancing girls preparing behind the stage curtain, just a handful of women occupied the saloon.

No sign of black curls. No Olivia.

"Luke!" said a friendly voice. "Have a drink with us!"

"Later," he shouted back.

"Then come have one with us!" shouted the dentist.

"Later," Luke repeated with an impersonal nod, knowing full well he had no intention of drinking with the dentist tonight. The doc ran after anything respectable in skirts, and no doubt he'd noticed the beautiful woman standing beside Luke as soon as Jenny stepped through the door. The fact irked Luke more than he cared to admit, and unable to control himself, he lowered a firm hand to Jenny's waist.

She spurned his touch and he withdrew. Why did she suspect his every move? She was under his protection tonight. Sliding off his gun belt, he checked it behind the bar. He peered through the archway to the dining area, where the piano player began another lively tune.

Lola would soon climb onto the stage to sing. Chairs shuffled and squeaked as people maneuvered for the best view, but there was no sign of Olivia.

Luke glanced up the stairs to the balcony. The doors along the hallway were shut tight. "She's probably around the corner, through the archway,'' he said, dipping his head to Jenny's ear so she could hear him, low enough to breathe in the fresh scent of her skin. He let himself linger there for a moment longer.

Her breath caught and she clutched nervously at her shawl. She looked awkward as hell. How long would it take before she shed the ridiculous shawl? It was hotter than blazes in here with all the people. He liked her better in feathers. And that little lavender corset.

Jenny stared at the sign above the bar.

Luke's Rules
1. All guns checked behind the bar.
2. No discussing politics, race or religion.
3. Discuss women at your own risk.

Someone shoved a glass of ale into his hand and he gladly took it, fully aware of Jenny's disapproving look. "Don't be so convinced that this is a rotten place. People are having a good time." He took a swig of his drink, welcoming the familiar bite on his tongue.

"And the better time they have, the bigger your pocketbook gets."

Wiping his mouth with his shirtsleeve, he refused to be drawn into an argument. Tonight he intended to show her the marvels of this interesting place. "You know what you need?" he drawled, inclining his head to look her up and down. "You need to lighten up. Laugh a little. Daniel's got your laces tightened so much, I'm afraid they might bust."

She gasped. "And do you know what you need?" Her silky voice held a challenge.

He quirked a brow and leaned forward in mock interest.

She threw up her hands in disgust. "Oh, never mind."

Uppity, uppity, uppity. He rolled his eyes. Despite himself, he bit back a grin. "Let's weave our way through."

Whirling around, she lifted her skirt and squeezed among the tables. He followed, trying not to notice her swaying behind, trying not to think of what he needed. He knew what he needed. What he hadn't had in a while. He sucked down another mouthful of ale, trying to appease his thirst.

Jenny's heavy shawl brushed against tough old Mr. Winslowe, who was seated at his usual table. Without looking up, the white-haired gent grabbed her arm. "Get me another gin sling, would ya, miss?" he hollered, mistaking her for a waitress.

She snatched her arm from his grasp. "Oh, go get it yourself," she snapped. "Can't you see the girls are busy?"

His companions laughed, and Winslowe, eyelids half closed, turned his head in Luke's direction. "Who's doing your hirin' these days, Lucas?"

"She doesn't work here," Luke answered with a slow grin.

"Don't hire her," Winslowe advised through the gales of laughter. "She'll be bad for business."

With a toss of her head, Jenny straightened her shoulders and kept walking, her trim waist and rounded hips calling out to Luke. That sashay of hers just wouldn't let him go.

Luke caught up to her. "Winslowe enjoys sparring. You'll give him something to write about in his column."

She frowned and craned her neck. "Oh, he's a writer?"

Luke found pleasure in her surprise. Even more when she bit her lip, trying to hide it. "He's the publisher of our paper. Winslowe comes here to get the latest news, and he never has more than two drinks. So you see, we're not all drunks."

A pink tide crept up her cheeks. In rebellion, she flung her shawl over her shoulder. He moved his broad shoulder to avoid getting whipped. With her stuffy blouse buttoned to the throat, and her skirt dragging on the floor, she must be hot, but damn, she was stubborn. What would it take for her to remove the ratty shawl? Or to admit these people weren't much different from her own? And what, in God's name, would it take for her to relax?

Several men turned their heads to gawk at Jenny. Another rose to greet her. Didn't they realize she was with him? Well, not really *with* him, but they didn't know that.

Luke sighed in exasperation and squeezed through. "This man here," he said, patting the shoulder of a young man in a crisp blue shirt and suede-fringed jacket, who rose to greet her, "this man's not a drunk, either."

Jenny squirmed. Luke watched her stiffly shake Thomas's hand. Then, in a sudden burst of friendliness, she leaned close to Thomas's freckly face. "Please ignore Luke's rudeness. The man has the manners of an ox—"

Luke cleared his throat. "Say hello to Reverend Thomas."

Her face turned crimson. "Reverend?"

Thomas nodded good-naturedly and shook Jenny's hand again. "Just call me Thomas, Miss…?"

"Jenny," she croaked.

He took a step closer. "And you're from…?"

Luke pulled her along by her puffy sleeve. "We're in a bind, Thomas. We're looking for someone."

"Won't you join the hymn singing in my church tent on Sunday?"

"She won't be here," Luke answered, tugging her closer. Thomas had a fascinating effect on women—they were drawn to him like magnets to a pole—and hadn't he told Luke just last week he was looking for a wife? Well, there was no sense in letting Thomas spend time with Jenny. She was already engaged and under Luke's protection. Luke bent his dark head and whispered close to her temple. "Are you convinced yet? We're not all drunks."

Flushing, she clamped her lips together and shook her head. Her blond beaver tail shook.

Ahead, the dentist squeezed into their path. Luke muttered under his breath. It hadn't taken long to get cornered. Franklin skimmed a hand through his parted red hair and gazed down at Jenny. A strange desire to compete hit Luke square in the chest.

"Luke, please introduce me to your friend," Franklin crooned in his English accent. The rogue was wearing an expensive three-piece suit, and the chain dangling from his pocket watch twinkled in the lamplight.

Luke cupped his hand on Jenny's warm shoulder, attempting to lay a claim, but instead, causing her to surge forward. Why did she always flinch when he touched her? "Miss Jenny Eriksen, I'd like you to meet Dr. Franklin Windsor."

Luke watched helplessly as Franklin, ever the gentleman, took her hand and pressed his lips to it. "Pleased to meet you, my dear."

When Jenny smiled and fluttered her lashes, Luke rolled his eyes. Why did this Englishman always have such a feverish effect on women? It was just his accent that kept females listening. It wasn't as if Franklin had anything better to say than the rest of them, and if anyone paid close attention, they'd notice he was so long-winded, it took him twice as long to say it.

Luke reached for her other hand and whisked her on through the crowd. "We've got no problems with our teeth, Doc."

Franklin raised his brows at the obvious getaway.

Out of earshot, Jenny asked brightly, "He's a dentist?"

Luke nodded, irritated with the spark in her eyes. "They say he's pretty bad. Can't tell one tooth from another. And when he's got you trapped, lying in his fancy pull-down chair with your feet stuck higher than your head, *blazes* the man can talk. At least that's what I hear."

Jenny laughed. Luke stopped, pleasantly surprised at the warm sound of her laughter. She was unaware of the captivating picture she made, her dimple fluttering, her skin glowing. Still holding her hand, he became aware of the heat pulsing in her fingertips. The twinkle in her eyes and the pink stain in her cheeks made his heart skip.

Suddenly flustered, she dropped her hand from his. It left a coldness in his palm. She stared at him with clear blue eyes ringed with chocolate lashes. What was that mysterious glimmer? *Amusement?* Yes, it was; she was laughing at him. As if he was no better than the others who were vying for her attention! Dammit, he was better than all of them. *He* could control himself. He was well aware she'd soon be another man's wife.

He spun away from her charming smile.

She searched the crowd ahead of her, wiping her palms on her skirt as if she were erasing his touch. "Where's Olivia?"

He tugged at his hat, trying to regain his composure. "She's around here someplace."

They reached the archway and stepped around the corner, and sure enough, there she was. Sitting at a packed table, close to the kitchen door. Concentrating on her fistful of cards, Olivia was dressed in borrowed clothes, her low-cut, red satin dress revealing plenty more than Jenny's old blouse and skirt.

Jenny raced through the chairs toward her. "Olivia!"

Spotting her, Olivia shot to her feet. The wooden, slat-back chair toppled over, smacking the pine floor. "Jenny!"

The women dashed into each other's arms, hugging and crying. In between their sobs and tears, they glared at Luke, making his guts heave. He'd never meant to harm them. What he'd done, he'd done for the boy. Apparently for nothing.

Lola walked onstage. As she spoke with the piano player, the excited chatter of the eager crowd rose in pitch.

Glancing around the table, Luke nodded to the others, saying hello to the young Slavic man and his wife. One of the few married women who ventured into the saloon, she enjoyed a bit of cards and entertainment on Friday nights. God bless her.

"How are you feeling?" Jenny asked, stepping back to look at her friend. "Did they hurt you?"

Luke sighed. Did she really believe they'd harm Olivia?

"You gonna finish the hand, Miss Olivia, or are you foldin'?" The old stagecoach driver peered over his cards.

Olivia tugged at the waistline of her red dress. "Oh, why, yes. Hold on a minute," she replied. "Jenny, I've got a great hand." Her voice dropped to a whisper, meant only for Jenny, but Luke heard it, too. "I thought if I win some money, when we caught up to each other we could use it to escape."

Jenny's mouth dropped open in dismay. "Good...good thinking. But we'll be leaving tomorrow, on the noon train with Daniel. We're free to go," she whispered back.

"Really? No more keeping quiet? No more leverage?" Olivia swayed.

Jenny glanced at the half-empty glass on the table. "Have they been forcing you to drink?" She spoke a little louder than she intended.

People chuckled. Olivia blushed. "No. They offered me some refreshment, is all." Her lips quivered suddenly. "I missed you," she wailed as Travis stepped up beside them.

Travis and Luke balked at the women's harsh glances.

"Oh, you poor thing," said Jenny, comforting her friend.

Olivia rocked on her feet and wiped her nose.

"You're upset. Sit down a minute."

It looked to Luke as if Olivia's condition had more to do with the drink in front of her than her circumstances. When he glanced at Travis, the man replied, "It was the only way I could keep her from blasting a hole through my head. Offering her a brandy toddy and the cards."

"How do you know how to gamble?" Jenny asked Olivia.

Olivia sniffed. "The Windsor sisters taught me twenty-one." She fanned out her cards. "I'll take another."

The piano playing got louder, drawing all eyes to the stage. Lola introduced herself to the cheering crowd, and people hollered for Luke and his group to sit down.

What could they do but sit?

"First thing tomorrow," Jenny whispered into his ear, causing his pulse to race. "We're leaving first thing tomorrow."

Luke wedged himself into the chair next to her, just as Travis slid beside Olivia. The movement magnified the pain in Luke's side. When his sleeve brushed Jenny's, she snatched her arm away, as if his touch were poison.

With a sigh of frustration, he concentrated on the show.

Dressed in her usual slinky costume, a flesh-colored body stocking that looked almost transparent over her corset, topped with pleated satin skirts, Lola crooned out a number. Her voice was low and silky, hypnotic magic that eased your tired soul. She was a crowd pleaser, her forty-year-old figure plump and curvaceous.

"Oh, my Lord, a burlesque show," Jenny croaked.

"It's not burlesque," said Luke.

"It is, too. Look what she's wearing. Her bodice is barely visible."

"I like it."

Jenny flushed and glanced away, snatching her arm back from his again. "Well, you would. But it's lewd."

"She's got a great voice. I'll bet better than anything you've ever heard in Boston." But even as he said the words, Luke was imagining Jenny in Lola's scant costume—

"Drinks, anyone?" asked the barmaid.

Luke peered into round Italian eyes. Mona, a short buxom woman, prematurely graying from the four children she was raising alone, gave Jenny the once-over. Then she cast a maddening glance in Luke's direction, as if questioning his motives.

Luke fumbled to sit straighter. "Mona, I'd like you to meet Jenny. She's Daniel's fiancée."

"Well, whaddya know." Mona laughed. "But she's here with you tonight." He felt his neck grow warm. What did Mona know, anyway? "Pleased to meet you, sweetheart. What'll you have?"

"Nothing, thank you."

Luke ordered a round of ale for the table, and

Olivia had a mint julep. He ordered one for Jenny, too, but when it came she let it sit there, untouched. Over the next half hour, as the singing continued, Jenny seemed to resign herself to the fact that she was staying put tonight.

He knew there was nothing he could do about her leaving in the morning, but there was plenty he could do to help her unwind. Nothing wrong with her enjoying herself, was there?

He took another swig of ale. The more he drank, the better his ribs felt. "You sure you won't try a mint julep?"

"I'll have some tea, if you have it, please."

"You're kidding."

"Tea and honey soothes my stomach," she justified. She sniffed again, a habit she'd picked up since entering his saloon, and it was beginning to bother him.

"I thought people from Boston didn't like tea."

"Very funny. What else do you know about people from Boston?" Her voice held a note of humor.

Not much, but I'd like to. A slow, easy smile tugged at his lips. She blushed and he guzzled another mouthful of ale. *Stop it. She's Daniel's. With any luck, it'll still work out between her, Daniel and Adam.*

While Lola took a break, the card game resumed, and the level of noise and conversation in the saloon exploded. Jenny's tea arrived. The cook brought out a jar of liquid honey, and Luke sensed Jenny was finally beginning to relax.

Leaning back in her chair, Jenny sipped her tea. She sighed and studied people at the bar. "You have such a different mix of people here, all these different cultures.''

Luke followed her gaze to the five bartenders. One of them was dark-skinned—Travis's younger brother—and another was Luke's most trusted friend, Lee, an Asian man with cropped black hair and an easy smile. ''Lee's the best bartender. He can pour twice as fast as the rest of them, and he has a real nice way of listening to the customers.''

She pushed her blond tendrils from her face. ''How did he come to work here?''

''We met in jail. He saved me from the thief who slit my throat and left me for dead, and—''

''Oh,'' she gulped.

It had been a turning point in his life, the day Lee found him in the gutter. It was the day Luke had hit rock bottom and he'd decided he was through with fighting.

''And?'' she prompted him.

''And in return, I brought in the men who burned down Lee's house.''

''Oh,'' she said again, clutching her shawl. She *must* be hot. He noticed beads of moisture along her upper lip. ''I think it's all rather...rather—'' she swallowed ''—*exciting*.''

Exciting? Well, now, didn't that beat all. He was getting someplace, chipping through her crusty veneer. He leaned back in his seat and crossed his booted feet. Exciting was good.

She began to warm up toward him. When he ordered a round of beef stew for the table, at first Jenny resisted, then buttered a slice of sourdough bread and dug in. Something about her hearty appetite made him weak at the knees. All that slurping.

She started asking about people in the saloon, and he began telling her where they were from.

"Really?" she said, reaching for another slice of bread and butter and jam. "The banker's from California? And his wife is from South America?"

With dismay that turned to bemusement, Luke watched her accidentally dip one sleeve, then the other, into her bowl of stew. He glanced at her mint julep. It was almost gone. So she'd decided to try it. And the drink was making her clumsy.

"You sure you don't want some?" she said, smacking her lips and licking her fingers.

A drop of gravy slid down her blouse and his gaze followed it, down her buttoned collar, over the swell of her breasts. His pulse danced with excitement. When his eyes flashed up to meet hers, her color deepened. The unspoken implication electrified the air. *Would he like some? Yes, he would.*

The banjo strummed near the stage, ending the spell. Lola was getting ready to sing again.

Olivia swayed around in her seat to speak to Jenny. Still breathless from her conversation with Luke, Jenny leaned back. Her fingers caught on the tablecloth, and to everyone's surprise, she pulled the cloth with her and everything on top of it.

Luke dove to help. He grabbed the spilled teacup, but was unable to catch the honey jar. It rolled over the edge, straight toward Jenny's lap. "Look out!"

"Ahh...!" She yelped, jumping to her feet. Too late. Honey dripped over Daisy's tired old skirt, the knitted shawl, the prim line of buttons down Jenny's blouse.

The room came to a standstill.

Luke leaned back on his heels and surveyed her

from head to toe. At least she'd be rid of that stupid shawl. His mouth quirked up at the corner, then despite his best efforts, he began to laugh.

Her mouth fell open and she glared at him.

"You've got to admit it's funny. I've been trying to get you to loosen up all night."

Jenny's eyes sparkled with mischief. She swayed, ever so slightly. "Loosen up?" She reached for Olivia's mint julep and stepped toward him.

"Don't you dare," he breathed. "If you know what's good for you, you'll put the drink down."

"You're right—seeing you fight for your life is funny."

"Put it down," he said slowly, as the hushed crowd watched.

She looked like she was about to relent, reaching for the table, but at the last second, her heel caught on the wet floor and in a flash of legs and arms, she came sliding straight at him. The drink landed in his lap.

He gasped at the blast of coldness. He looked down at his pants with as much dignity as he could muster. Cool liquid trickled down his thighs.

Watching his expression darken, she cupped a hand over her mouth to squelch a laugh.

"You did that on purpose."

"No," she said, moving back, "I didn't."

"Yes, you did." Someone had to teach this gal a lesson.

"I'm sorry," she said through her laughter, "you look so ridiculous." She caught Olivia's eye, but Olivia wasn't smiling. Jenny gulped. Her shawl fell to the floor.

He stepped closer.

Glancing around the room at the crowd of fascinated faces watching her, Jenny shrank back. Perspiration popped out on her brow. She stumbled backward around the table as Luke strode deliberately toward her.

"You better run, doll," Lola hollered from the stage, a ripple of mirth in her voice.

Jenny looked around in desperation and threw an empty chair in his path. "Don't you come near me!"

"You did that on purpose. Come here and admit it." Luke was gaining on her and she grew frantic.

Then, somehow, he got blocked between two chairs and she smiled as if she were safe. "You're nothing but a brute."

"I'll show you brute." If it was a chase she wanted, a chase she'd get. He lunged up onto a table. The crowd gasped, then laughed, removing their steins and glasses.

"Stop right there!" she hollered.

"I won't," he yelled, determined to catch her.

People seated nearby cleared their drinks off the tables and he jumped onto one. His spurs jangled. He hopped onto another table, then another, then finally the table closest to Jenny. He jumped down in front of her, grabbed her by her sticky waist and flung her over his shoulder. She screamed. He deflected her flailing arms and kicks. He heard laughter from the crowd. Lots of it, as he hauled her up the stairs.

She wouldn't get away this time.

"You show her, Luke!" they cheered.

Luke turned and grinned. He clenched a fist in the air, as if he'd just won a boxing match.

He lost his footing on the stairs. He was a little tipsy himself. "Whoa...."

"Ooo...." the crowd responded.

Jenny twisted and kicked. "Put me down! That's enough!"

Luke regained his balance and the crowd clapped. He removed his hat to take a bow. He turned on the stairs, wobbly, then caught himself and lurched up the remaining steps.

"Whoa," Luke muttered, stumbling down the hall to his room. He yanked on the knob and crashed through the door, dropping Jenny onto the big iron bed.

"You know you're covered with honey?" he asked, inches from her face.

It started as a whisper of a smile on her lips. Then that low rumble caught at the back of her throat.

Husky and warm, it filled the empty corners of the room. He laughed with her, and it touched a lonely place in him no one had touched in years. He used to laugh like this with his brothers, as a child, pulling pranks and causing trouble. He let Jenny and her laughter take him, and for a moment, allowed himself to forget about the problems that weighed upon his shoulders.

Chapter Seven

Sprawled on the bed, covered with sticky honey, Jenny peered up at Luke.

She was beginning to think she'd never stop laughing. It erased the tension in her muscles, slowly and gently, until she felt like a melted ball of beeswax.

Her eyes stung with exhaustion. She'd hardly slept in two days. She wasn't sure if it was the weariness in her bones making her laugh, or the alcohol, or the sight of Luke trying to remain tough, but instead, looking drowned and beaten. His hair was smeared with honey. His crotch was soaked with booze, and three sprigs of mint leaves were glued to his button fly. She burst into more gales.

"It sure takes an army to make you laugh." Tossing his hat in the corner, he stumbled past the shaded window, either a little tipsy, or just as exhausted as she.

He lit the oil lamp, and the sparse furnishings glowed—an iron bed, a bedside dresser, a chest of drawers and two slat-back chairs by the door. Oh my, she thought, looking around at the few things, he lived here? He didn't own much.

Turning back toward her, he gave in to her smile. "Turn around and don't look." He began unbuckling his belt.

Her smile faded. She bolted upright. "What are you doing?"

He staggered back, trying to focus on the belt holes. "I'm taking off my pants."

What? "Oh, no, you're not. You're not thinking straight."

"A man doesn't have to think straight to know his pants are wet."

"You're keeping your pants on," she ordered like a drill sergeant, "you hear me?"

He paused. "This is my room and I'm changing. Your turn's next. I promise I won't peek."

Panic seized her. What in tarnation was she doing here, alone with a man in his room?

He rubbed his ribs through his shirt and winced. The tender gesture caught her off guard. He must be sore. He'd been two days on his feet, wounded and tired. The drinking had helped his pain, but what he needed most was rest.

Stumbling to the edge of the bed, he sat and tugged off his boots. The mattress creaked and jostled beneath him, then her. When he undid his shirt buttons, she snapped to attention.

She dashed to the door, turned the glass knob and peered out at the saloon below. Lola stood poised to sing. Olivia and Travis were gone. Several people glanced up at her, tittering and pointing. "Come on out, Miss Jenny, we won't do you no harm. We'll put you up on stage and you can sing with Lola!"

Her heart clamored. She slammed the door.

"What's the matter now?" He'd removed his shirt and stood there. She gulped. Shirtless. Rippling muscles. Hairy. Bandaged.

"If you take off your wet skirt," he said, sliding off his belt, "I'll get someone to wash these clothes."

Was he crazy? Remove her clothing? Time to leave.

She raced to the door, yanked it open once more and ran down the stairs. She didn't get far. The crowd was good at its word. Two young men lunged at her to lift her to the stage. Three horrifying minutes later, she freed herself and raced back up the stairs. She bolted through Luke's door.

"Stop right there," Luke thundered, reeling around with a drawn gun.

Her cheeks burned with fire.

Luke was stark blazing naked.

Standing in the middle of the room, he was trying to hold on to the gun while pulling the bedsheet over his lower half. "You again?" His face flushed. "I thought you left."

She gulped like an idiot. "The crowd is chasing me."

In the semidarkness, she stared at his striking figure.

So this was what a man looked like. She couldn't catch her breath. Heat rushed through her, down her thighs and legs. She turned away and shut her eyes, but the image was burned into her mind. He was all muscles and tanned skin, right down to his white... She couldn't think of the proper word. His white...well, his white behind.

He was stark blazing naked, and the only thing standing between her and his privates was a thin cotton sheet.

She swallowed rapidly. How did she get into this mess? The thoughts racing through her mind were not those of a lady engaged to someone else.

Ready to escape, she spun to the door. But where to? She couldn't run out the door; a lynch mob was waiting for her. And from two flights up, she couldn't escape out the window, because there was no balcony on this side of the building.

Feeling light-headed, she took several deep breaths. She grabbed a chair, placed it facing the door and plunked down with her back to Luke. She put her head between her knees to stop her dizziness. Honey was spreading everywhere. She didn't care.

"What in blazes are you doing?"

"I'm...I'm sitting right here until Lola's finished singing and...and the coast is clear."

"That'll be awhile, and I can't stand up any longer." He stifled a yawn. "You must be tired, too." Another wave of panic assailed her when she heard him blow out the lamp and lift the window shade. What was he doing? Moonlight filled the room. "No sense wasting a good bed. Come here and get some sleep."

Her muscles tensed. "You go ahead without me."

"Don't make me come and get you."

Her heart jumped. "Don't you dare."

"I'm going to count to ten and then, ready or not, I'm coming. *One.*"

She couldn't breathe. Her mind raced, searching for a way to divert him.

"*Two.*"

"I'm not tired."

"Three."

Did she detect humor in his tone? Was he kidding with her, or was he serious? "The bed's...the bed's not big enough for both of us."

"We'll figure something out. *Four.*"

Drops of perspiration beaded at her hairline. "But you're not wearing anything."

"I won't tell anyone. You should take your clothes off, too, before you get the whole room covered in honey."

"Never."

"Five!"

"For God's sake, I'm engaged. Have you no decency?"

"Indecent people need rest, too. We need it more than anyone else."

Flee. She had to flee. What she wouldn't give for a stick of dynamite. She'd fling it down the stairs and clear the widest darn path anyone had ever seen.

Sitting rigid, still with her head between her knees, she was terrified she'd feel his arms around her at any moment. But in her traitorous mind, the maddening image pounding through it was one of a very handsome, kissable, *naked* man putting his arms around her and tugging her into his bed.

Oh, she didn't deserve to breathe.

The bed creaked and her stomach tossed. She prayed he was only rolling over. She knew it was wrong of her to hope so, but she hoped his ribs were too sore to move.

He moaned softly. *"Six."*

Fall asleep, please fall asleep. She didn't move. Before she had time to swallow, she heard his bare feet on the plank floor. She yelped. "You're only at number six! You said ten!"

He ignored her protest. As naked as Mother Nature had created him, as irresistible as any man she'd ever known, he bent to scoop her up.

She vaulted to the door, clawed the knob and dashed down the hallway, screaming the words she knew would clear the biggest path. "Fire! Fire! Fire!"

She didn't stop running until she found Olivia in the kitchen, and by that time, the rowdy crowd had calmed down enough to realize there was no fire. Only when Jenny was in the solitude of Olivia's room, scrubbed clean, lying in bed and gazing up at the rafters, did she allow herself to think of Luke again. A naked man with his gun drawn. A sillier sight she'd never seen.

She fell asleep with a smile on her lips, dreaming of Luke and every line and contour of his naked body.

Her warm dreams turned to sobering visions of Daniel arriving in the morning. What would she say to him? And what would he say to her?

"Do you see anything yet?" Olivia asked the next morning, dressed in a borrowed, brown muslin day dress, standing on the tracks beside Jenny. The telegraph office loomed behind her.

Jenny teetered on the edge of the wooden platform, peering into the blue horizon, looking for any sign of a train. "Not yet, but we're early." She tilted her face to the brilliant morning sun. She was waiting for her beloved.

Daniel was coming to rescue her today.

A few people milled about the stationhouse, and two farmers with a crate of clucking chickens said howdy.

As she strolled the platform, Jenny adjusted her blouse—Daisy's blouse, this one just as worn at the elbows, with the same chipped, mismatched buttons. Jenny had promised she'd return it when she got back to Denver. She passed the time by watching passengers board the train that had arrived from Omaha earlier and was now heading to San Francisco.

Soon this charade would be over, and Jenny would confirm what she'd known all along. That a mistake had been made, that Daniel was not Adam's father. She didn't know who or where Adam's real father was, but just thinking of the man trying to shirk his responsibilities caused her stomach to become upset.

Did Adam cry himself to sleep when he thought of his mama? What would happen to him? Where would he live?

Maybe someone would adopt him. Someone nice.

Jenny groaned. Was she putting her own needs in front of the boy's? Did she just want Daniel all for herself? Was that why she hoped Daniel wasn't Adam's father?

Looking at the wispy clouds, she sent up a silent little prayer, asking that, by some miracle, Adam's real father would hear of Maria's death and step forward on his own accord to claim his son.

Yes, she thought, smiling in the mellow chinook wind, that might happen. With Luke's help it might.

Luke. Turning away from the platform, she paced

in the other direction. Why did his strong, muscular presence always send her pulse racing?

Her escapade last night had been witnessed by a hundred people. Her face grew hot with the memory. Thank God she never had to lay eyes on any of them again. She'd never forgive him for what he'd put her and Olivia through. How could he claim to be any friend of Daniel's?

Father always said a good wife put her faith in her husband, and that's what Jenny would do. Today, she'd learn the truth from Daniel himself, and this blasted mess would clear.

And *she'd* return to the crate of bridal fabrics sitting in her front hall. All that beautiful monogrammed hosiery. Her white silk wedding stockings, the thighs already embroidered with her impending initials, Mrs. D. K.

She brightened at the thought.

Olivia stepped beside her, returning the smile with one of her own. "Sure was a crazy night last night."

"I wonder if every evening's like that at the saloon."

"I doubt it. I think you gave a certain spontaneity to the place, all that commotion about fire."

Jenny giggled. The saloon was a lot different than she'd imagined. Her family had always attended Boston outings like the orchestra and opera, but never in such a mixed crowd of people and cultures. The level of tolerance and acceptance in Luke's saloon was much broader than anything she'd ever experienced, and she felt as if some dormant energy inside her had burst to life.

She hoped she'd see this side of Denver, too. Why didn't Daniel take her to places where she could meet more hardworking, ordinary people? People who reminded her of her hardworking grandparents. She'd ask him first chance she got.

A thought nibbled at her. The saloon had been packed last night. The money had flowed thick and fast. Luke was not as down on his luck as she'd first suspected. This kidnapping was not a plea for money. She swallowed and refused to think about it.

"Did you notice what the women were wearin' last night?" asked Olivia. "The ones in the audience, I mean. Why, no one in Boston has worn a hooped crinoline for five years."

"Um-hmm."

"And we both know that bright colors are the rage in Europe. The dresses here are so dark and gloomy. No wonder the women snap up the Parisian dresses sold in the street."

"Um-hmm."

"Did you see the size of their bonnets? They shield the entire face, which I suppose is fine for daylight, but in the evenin', well, they're simply outdated. I much prefer the smaller, stylish ones adorned with a feather."

"Women lead a hard life here, farming and ranching. They don't have much more than catalog stores to shop in, same as Denver. Certainly nowhere near the choice we had in Boston. It takes awhile for new styles to reach them."

Olivia scratched her chin. "What's wrong with a woman wanting pretty things? Especially if she's working hard?"

"Nothing."

"You're the one who said it when we first arrived

in Denver. You said if the women are happy, it'll keep the men happier. Don't the men know that?"

The ground rumbled. Jenny scanned the tracks and her eyes settled on the horizon, at the long train puffing steam. Both women yelped with delight. Daniel was coming.

Someone brushed Jenny's elbow. She looked up.

Luke. Dressed in a crisp white shirt. Freshly shaved, with slicked back hair. His massive shoulders blocked the sun.

Her heart pounded. "What are you doing here? If you've come to try and stop me—"

"I've come to try and protect you."

"Protect me?" Her lips dried. "Don't be silly. I don't need protection. From who? From Daniel?" She shook her head. "Please, step back. Let me greet my...my beloved in private."

Luke's jaw twitched. "All right. I'll be standing right over here, by the stationhouse, if you need me."

She watched him plant himself ten feet away. Trying to regain some control over her careening pulse, she tried not to think of last night. The moonlight in his room...his white, gleaming backside...

Wheels screeched behind her.

She spun toward the train and snatched a breath of air. Dozens of people descended. Jenny looked hungrily at the faces. No Daniel. He must be on the last car. She began walking, faster and faster, her pulse mimicking her steps. Finally, at the last car, a man stepped out with a face she recognized.

Harley Cobbs, the quiet, polite guard at Daniel's office. Daniel must have brought him to help, as part of the team of men he'd brought to rescue her.

"Harley! Over here!" She knew Daniel would be right behind him. Through a throng of people, Jenny raced to the car and watched the huge hairy man step off the train. His boots were so big he couldn't seem to maneuver the stairs, so he leaped down. Jenny waved a handkerchief in the air, beaming at him. "We're over here!"

Olivia appeared beside her.

Harley jolted back in surprise. He stared at them, his mouth open. Then, recovering quickly, he nodded and removed his hat politely.

"Miss Jenny, Miss Olivia, howdy. I didn't expect to see you so soon, let alone you'd be waitin' for me when the train arrived." His cheek twitched. "McLintock released you?"

"Yes," Jenny gulped. "We're free to go."

"But how did you know I was comin'?"

She flushed with excitement. "It's the only train you could have taken, Luke said—"

"Luke?"

Jenny's smile faded with embarrassment. Perhaps she sounded a little too friendly about Luke. She glanced toward Olivia, shifted uncomfortably, then said with renewed vigor, "Where's Daniel? How many men did he bring?"

Harley frowned. He studied Jenny's face, then caught sight of Luke out the corner of his eye. His head jerked in astonishment, and Jenny decided that Harley knew who Luke was.

Where was Daniel?

"I'm sorry to fluster you, Harley. I'm just so excited. Why, you must be tired from your journey." She glanced up at the trickle of people still descending from the train, searching for her black-bearded fiancé. "Daniel, too. For a moment, I was beginning to think he wasn't coming." She laughed. "See how silly I am?"

She peered around his thick shoulders. "Where is he?"

"Ma'am, you're expectin' Mr. Daniel?"

She paused. "He did come, didn't he?"

"Well, ma'am," Harley began to explain, giving Luke a dead-cold stare, "your father came in yesterday, and Mr. Daniel was detained at the office, you see, something he couldn't avoid. Your father wanted him to check prices—"

"Daniel didn't come for me?"

There was a moment of awkward silence.

Daniel didn't come.

The words beat into her mind.

How could that be true?

Jenny tried to brace herself but stumbled backward, unable to keep her wretched disappointment from showing.

Luke stepped up to her side to support her. He reached out, but she spurned his help. Seeing him here, having him witness her humiliation, was even worse.

Olivia cupped Jenny's shoulder. It took Jenny a few seconds to compose herself. Finally, she addressed Harley. "Doesn't he wonder if I'm safe and alive?"

"Believe me, he wanted to come."

"What on earth did he tell my father?" Jenny blurted. "What reason did he give for our disappearance?"

Harley shuffled on the platform. He hooked his traveling bag around his shoulder. "He told them you were visiting his elderly relations. Let's see now…their names… Daisy and…I can't remember…."

"Nathaniel."

"That's right." Harley s broad face spread into a grin.

Jenny shook her head in disbelief.

Luke folded his arms across his chest, and he and Harley scrutinized each other, like two angry bulls trapped in the same corral, searching for each other's soft spot.

Luke's face grew drawn. Jenny trembled at the stifled fury she saw in his eyes.

"Once a coward," Luke said evenly, "always a coward."

"Now, you listen!" Harley's crimson neck bulged. His face clouded over. He looked a lot angrier and meaner than Jenny'd ever seen him. "I know who you are. You've got some damn nerve, showin' your face after what you've done."

Luke spoke through tight lips. "Why isn't Daniel here?"

"I don't think I have to explain it to you."

"Then explain it to *me*," Jenny said.

Harley ignored her, and his dismissive attitude caused her a fresh surge of anger. Whose side was Harley on? Why, she felt closer to Luke than she did to Daniel's guard. And how ridiculous was that!

"Frankly," Harley snarled at Luke, "I'm mighty surprised to see you out here in the open, after the robbery."

"There was no robbery and you know it."

"We'll see what the sheriff has to say—"

"I don't know how much Daniel told you about

this delicate situation," Luke snarled, "but I think the sheriff's the last place you want to be heading. Not with all the attention and publicity it'll bring to Daniel's business, and his new engagement."

Harley groped for words. He floundered for a moment, then looked Jenny in the eye. "Daniel sent you a message. That he...cares for you."

She laughed without humor. "Is that what you think I want to hear? Daniel would never send a message like that through you. You're bluffing. Daniel took the coward's way out, just like Luke said." She swallowed her despair. "Daniel sent you alone because he didn't want to face Luke. Why not? Why doesn't he want to face him? What's Daniel hiding?"

One possibility pounded through her mind. *Was Daniel the boy's father?* She nearly crumpled with the image of the little boy waiting to hear word from a father who wouldn't give it.

Harley was silent.

"What if I'd been injured?" Her voice quivered.

Harley's dark eyes flashed with lightning speed. "Are you?" Incensed, he glared at Luke, stepping closer, clenching his drawn fists. Ready to fight.

"No," she said, stepping in front of Luke. It was a protective gesture, but she was unsure of why she did it. "But Daniel doesn't know that."

Nudging her back by her shoulder, Luke stepped forward. "I don't hide from anyone."

Jenny shook her head and glanced at a very solemn Olivia. Her poor friend, another innocent person trapped in the middle of this.

Daniel was treating Jenny like a nobody. Well, she deserved to be acknowledged. She shivered with apprehension. Adam deserved to be acknowledged. Hadn't Luke told her that?

"When this train turns around," Jenny declared to Harley, "I want you to take a message back to Daniel."

"But you're comin' back with me, aren't you?"

"No."

Harley gritted his teeth. "My orders are to take you back."

"I don't follow orders."

Harley's face was stone. Jenny's gaze lingered on his crooked nose, and she suddenly recalled how proudly Daniel had spoken of Harley's boxing championships in New York. Did she have anything to fear from the man?

No. That was ridiculous.

"What's the message?" Harley asked.

"This." She twisted the engagement ring off her finger and shoved it into Harley's thick hand. "Give him this. And tell him if he wants to talk to me, the next time he can come himself."

Luke nudged her. His eyes widened in alarm. "Wait a second—"

"Go home, Harley," Jenny interrupted.

With drawn features, Luke insisted, "I think you better get on the train. For your own good. For your own safety."

Her eyes narrowed. "You're worried about my safety? Isn't that a hoot?"

His jaw clenched. "Listen, I know you're angry. But take your anger out on me. Hate my guts if you want to—we never have to see each other again. But get back on that train. It's turning around and heading back to Denver in just over an hour. Go on with your life. I'll figure out what to do with Adam.''

Adam. She cringed at what this whole mess implied for little Adam.

But she would not take advice from Luke McLintock. ''If Daniel wants me, he can come and get me.''

Luke stepped closer, looking as if he wanted to shake her. ''You've got to return. You can't stay here. I'll send two men to escort you and make sure you return safely to your father.'' His voice sharpened. ''Take Olivia, and get back on the train.''

Who in blazes did he think he was? Tossing her like a ball, back and forth between Daniel and himself. Well, she was darned tired of always giving in to people who thought they knew what was best for her. And what was best for her at this moment was not going back.

Jenny glanced at Olivia to see if she had any objections, but Olivia only shrugged in confusion.

Jenny turned back to Luke and chose her words very deliberately, very carefully. ''Thank you kindly,'' she said, ''but no.''

Harley took a deep breath and stared at all of them. An artery throbbed at his temple.

''Go home, Harley,'' Jenny repeated.

The boxer peered over her shoulder at the stationhouse. He gave a cold smile that was more frightening than any display of anger. ''First I think I need a drink. It's been a long night.''

With that, he hiked up his bag and walked away.

In stony silence, Luke, Jenny and Olivia watched him go.

What now? Jenny wondered. What had started as

a beautiful morning turned out to be one of the most devastating of her life.

She swallowed the bitterness in her mouth, slowly spun on her heel and turned to face the man responsible.

Luke.

"I still think you should get back on the train. Go back to your father. And Daniel if you want to," Luke said, desperately trying to convince her ten minutes later, but still not having any luck. Why wouldn't the dang woman listen?

The three of them stood near the ticket booth as he tried to calm his frazzled nerves. Daniel hadn't bothered to show up. Luke still couldn't believe it.

"Not on your life," Jenny challenged. "I'll make my own decisions from here on in."

Adjusting the brim of his hat, Luke wavered, watching the animated expression on Jenny's face. She clearly cared for Daniel a great deal, arranged marriage or not. Why had it deflated him, seeing the eagerness on her face as she'd greeted Harley, then seeing it shatter at Daniel's betrayal?

Daniel was a son of a bitch, treating his woman like this. If she were Luke's, he'd never desert her. Come hell or high water, he'd have swum across the ocean for a woman he intended to marry.

"I don't have a good feeling about this," he warned her. "I know your feelings are hurt—"

Jenny spun around to face him. "My feelings are hurt? That's your summation?"

He took a step back and raised his palms. "Look, I'm sorry I brought you into this mess, but we're here now, and I'm telling you, Daniel sent Harley for a reason."

"I know," she snapped. "To take us back. But since we're not going back, Harley will have to return alone. Right, Olivia?"

Olivia nodded. The poor woman looked close to tears.

"I suppose," he answered. But personally, he didn't think it'd be that easy to appease Harley.

Jenny peered down the train tracks to the horizon. "It seems Daniel's not interested in Adam or me."

Luke sighed. "Oh, he's plenty interested in you. He's scared to lose you—that's why he didn't come. He's stalling, hoping you won't learn the truth about the boy. That you won't believe my version of the story."

She assessed him coolly. "Just because I'm staying doesn't mean I'm any closer to believing you. I still don't know who to believe."

Pushing back his Stetson, he met her piercing eyes. He was in her poor graces. Well, why the hell wouldn't he be? He'd gotten them all into this bloody mess, hadn't he?

"And just so you know," Jenny added hastily, deflating him even further, "my decision to stay has nothing to do with you. What you did to me was just as despicable as what Daniel's doing. You took me against my will. I don't trust either one of you. What this little lesson has taught me is that I'm on my own."

Luke shrank and rubbed a hand over his clean-shaven jaw. He deserved every word of what he got. Trouble was, what was he going to do to get them out of this?

He peered up at the train. The conductor was already ushering new passengers aboard. In another fifty minutes, twelve o'clock sharp, the train would pull out of the station. Without Jenny.

Jenny watched the hopper of coal being shoveled into the engine. ''Olivia and I are going to stand on our own two feet from here on in.'' With a final scathing glance at Luke, she pulled her shoulders back, grabbed Olivia by the elbow and sailed off the platform.

He watched her go. Nothing he could say would stop her.

How could he right this wrong? Who would care for Adam? Who would stand up for an innocent five-year-old boy?

It was clear to Luke that Daniel felt no connection to the child. Adam would be better off without him.

Luke's heart ached with the knowledge. Adam would have no father to share his life with. No mother, either. Whatever Luke's problems with Daniel might be, they were nothing compared to Adam's.

What should Luke do with the boy?

He could put him in an orphanage. Another new one had started up last week.

Or he could ask Reverend Thomas to help find a loving home for the boy.

One thing was sure, Luke definitely couldn't take him. He had no place in his life for a boy. He didn't even have a proper home.

Most of all, Luke wasn't sure he had anything deep down to give. In his soul. In his heart.

What did he know about raising a child? He'd never been around them much. At least not paying any attention. Children needed clothes and boots and little beds. Luke couldn't take care of a kid. He didn't even know what little kids ate.

His life was too sporadic, too unscheduled, too wild—just as he liked it. But not the settled type of life a child needed.

And even if he did choose to give Adam a roof over his head, where was the boy supposed to sleep? In the saloon next to Luke's room? With the dancing girls and drinkers? Adam would be starting school next year. Would Luke send him off every morning, with his primer and his pencil from the saloon doors?

The townsfolk would curse him. The schoolmarm, the women, the store owners, the ministers, everyone.

So far, the boy was fine at Daisy and Nathaniel's, but Luke couldn't very well accept responsibility for Adam, then send him their way permanently. Besides, the two old folks were in their seventies.

The locomotive hissed beside him, and Luke jumped at the sound. How long had he been standing here?

"All aboooard," shouted the conductor.

With alarm, Luke straightened and searched for Harley. His muscles strained. No sign of the man.

He peered into passenger windows as they rolled by. Heads bobbed up and down, but not the one he was looking for. He ran to the stationhouse and looked in the window. No Harley.

Racing to the platform, Luke felt his gut churn in apprehension. Hoisting himself to the ladder on the boxcar, he scooted between the cars to the other side of the platform. That side was empty, too.

He rubbed the back of his stiff neck. Harley wasn't on the train. Was he staying behind to convince Jenny to return?

My orders are to take you back.

Oh, hell. Would Harley try to force her? Did Harley have orders concerning the boy, too?

Luke shook his head. No, not the boy. Harley didn't seem interested in Adam, only Jenny.

The situation was spinning out of Luke's control. He gulped, watching the train chug out of the station. It picked up speed, and when the whistle blasted, Luke's pulse screamed with it. What kind of danger had he put everyone in?

Chapter Eight

What should she do? The shaded boardwalk kept Jenny cool as she and Olivia strode along in silence. They'd been walking for the better part of an hour with no particular destination. The screams of frustration at the back of Jenny's throat—directed toward Daniel—had peaked and she was finally calming down.

The shopping district of Cheyenne was crammed with Saturday customers. A mule and wagon inched by, a man shouting, "Get your knives sharpened here."

She and Olivia were all alone to fend for themselves.

No money, no clothes, no food, no friends.

Despite her claims about wanting to stand on her own two feet, she admitted she didn't know how. She always had either her father or a brother looking out for her.

Now they'd be at Luke's mercy, as far as food and shelter went. The thought of being beholden to him caused her blood to heat again.

And how could Daniel, the man she planned on devoting her life to, not bother to come and get her?

Was it possible he was Adam's father? *If* he was the boy's father, then in heaven's name, where did this all leave Adam?

How could she live with a man who'd deserted his own child?

And *if* Daniel was the father, then Jenny had misjudged Luke terribly.

On one hand, she praised Luke for trying to help Adam, on the other, she resented him for what he'd done to her life. The end did not justify the means!

Beside her, Olivia wiped at her tears. "Do you think there's any truth to what Luke says? That Daniel is Adam's father?"

Jenny slid an arm around her friend. "I'm ashamed to say it's possible."

"What the poor woman must have gone through."

"I know." It made Jenny nauseous to think of how Maria had suffered in silence. "About Luke...at one time, I thought we were in physical danger, but I don't feel it anymore. Do you?"

The big brown bow in Olivia's hair shook. "No."

"Then we'll be safe to stay—"

"But I wanna leave," Olivia said with a tremor.

"But we've missed the south train, and there won't be another to Denver for six days. Next Friday. The ones going east or west would just take us to San Francisco or Omaha."

"The town must have a stagecoach."

Jenny paused. "How would we pay for it?"

"We could ask Luke for money."

"The trip would take us days. Would you really

put yourself in that danger, crossing the wild land by stagecoach? What about the buffalo hunters, and cutthroat miners and thieves out there? You've read the gruesome stories.''

"We could telegraph your father."

"I'm not even sure Father's in town. You know how often he has to travel." Jenny ran her fingers along her borrowed bonnet. "It's become so muddled. Besides, until I know what to say to Daniel, I think it's best to leave Father out of it. You know how he is—he'd make the decision for me. He'd force me to do what he thought best. This time, I'd like to make my own decision. You and I together."

Jenny added with a tentative smile, "Maybe it won't be so bad. We're safe and sound. The sun is shining. Luke won't hurt us. We'll get home soon enough and everything'll be back to normal. As normal as it can be."

"Back to normal." Olivia's voice choked. "What does it matter?"

Jenny stepped back in surprise. Olivia was troubled by something more, and Jenny felt ashamed for not noticing sooner. "What do you mean, what does it matter?"

Olivia leaned over the boardwalk railing, staring out into the busy street. "Remember the night we were taken?" Olivia sniffed into her hanky. "When Luke was asking me those questions? Remember? He asked who would miss me if I was gone?"

Jenny leaned closer. "I remember."

Olivia swallowed. "He was right. No one would miss me."

"Oh, Olivia, that's not true."

The beautiful brown eyes watered. "Who would miss me?"

"Why...why Father, of course, and the Windsor sisters, and there's—there's... When we get back to Denver, let's take that visit to New Orleans sooner than we planned. We'll visit those new relatives you just discovered, and—"

Olivia flung herself into Jenny's arms and bawled.

"Oh, don't cry. We won't let this diversion in Cheyenne stop us from visiting your family. I heard someone say last night that Travis's family is from New Orleans, too."

For some reason that made Olivia cry louder. "Travis can trace his lineage back for two hundred years, all the way back to the island of Jamaica. I don't know anyone who can go back that far."

"I don't, either. He does seem like a very proud man."

"Travis knows so much more than I do, about Lincoln, and our heritage and slavery. I'm so involved with myself and finding my family, I haven't even bothered to look around since we moved West." Olivia blew her nose. "Travis told me nearly thirty percent of the cowboys driving cattle here are black men, and nearly the same percentage of people crossing and settling the territories are black families. I don't know anything. He knows it all."

"Well, you might not be able to trace your lineage as far back as he can, but maybe he can give us some pointers when we go searching in New Orleans."

"I don't have family there," Olivia sobbed. "I made it all up!"

"Oh, Olivia…" Jenny sank back into her heels. "Why?"

"I wanted to be from somewhere."

Jenny's throat clenched. "You are from somewhere. You're from Boston. You grew up with me and we…we might not be blood related, but I love you like a sister. We'll look again for your relatives. If Travis knows so much and so many people, maybe he can help us. Point us in some direction."

Olivia blew her nose. "Travis didn't treat me bad at all. He treated me like a princess. Especially when he found out I'm from New Orleans, or thinks I am. All I am is a big fat liar. I can't go to him now for help. He'll know I was lyin'."

Jenny tried to comfort her friend. "We'll be out of this place soon, and we'll never have to face Travis or Luke again."

That seemed to settle Olivia. She mopped her tears.

How long had Jenny known her dearest friend? Twenty years? And she hadn't been able to pick up on Olivia's turmoil of the past few months before today?

What had happened to Jenny's accurate judge of character, the one she prided herself on? She thought she knew people. What did she know at all?

Nothing, she scoffed.

What was it Luke had said to her, the night he'd first met her? *People aren't always what they appear to be.*

Daniel wasn't. Luke wasn't. And neither was dear Olivia.

And what did *Jenny* appear to be, when others looked at her? Why did she keep parts of herself hidden—the part that had ached to go to college, the part that ached to start a business of her own choosing, the part that ached to stand up and disagree with her father?

She gave a weary sigh. If she thought more about it, her head would crack. They needed a diversion. "Let's go get some lunch. It'll make us feel better. Are you hungry?"

"Starving." Olivia gave a weak smile. She collected herself and they stepped off the boardwalk and turned the corner. A line of people stood outside Annie's Café.

"Oh, dear," said Olivia, rummaging through her borrowed satchel, "I don't have any money. I spent my last copper at the train station for gumdrops." She yanked out a coin. "Hey, here's a bit. It was stuck in the bottom."

"Good, because all I have is a dime."

"Uh-oh. My coin's bent." Olivia held it up. "You know what that means."

"Olivia, that's an old wives' tale."

"A bent coin brings years of good luck for as long as you hang on to it. I can't spend this."

"But we're *starving.*"

Headstrong, Olivia folded her arms. "I will not forfeit heaven knows how many years of future good luck for a bowl of soup now." She paused. "We could go back to Luke's and get a free meal. He'd give us one."

Jenny took a stubborn step forward. "I think it's important we buy our own meal," she said, joining the lineup, "without Luke's help. As a show of independence. I'll spend my ten cents. We can split a bowl."

She could darn well feed herself at least one good meal without Luke McLintock's aid.

Unloading kegs of beer was hard work.

In the shaded alley behind the saloon, in the long afternoon shadows, Luke removed his Stetson, peeled off his shirt, then resettled his hat. Sweat drizzled down the bare skin of his shoulder blades.

Travis removed his own shirt. "You sure you should be lifting something this heavy?" He rolled a barrel off the wagon, his black mustache dripping with perspiration.

"The doc told me this morning that exercise is good for me." Luke groaned with the effort and ignored the twitching in his side.

"Does that include liftin'?"

"As long as I take it easy." It wasn't exactly what the doc had said, but there was no way Luke intended on lying around, useless. Besides, Travis was unloading the full, heavy kegs and Luke was reloading the empty, lighter ones.

"Where do you think the women are? You think it's wise to let them loose like that?"

"I put Beuford and Tom on their trail. No harm'll come to them." Luke took a minute to breathe deeply. Travis already knew the full story about Daniel being Adam's father. Besides the judge, Travis was the only man Luke had confided in. Travis could always be trusted to keep silent.

Travis squinted. "What do you think Daniel told Harley to do?"

"I don't know. I think we shocked Harley, meeting him at the station. He probably thought he'd have to work harder than that to locate Jenny. I'm sure he expected she'd go back with him, no questions asked. But he doesn't look the type to sit and think for long.''

"You think he'd force her to return?"

"I wouldn't put it past him."

Travis stepped inside, and Luke lifted a crate of beer steins and set them on the tailgate.

He rubbed his cheek with a sweaty palm. What if Jenny refused to ever go back?

Highly unlikely. But if something like that were to happen, Daniel would never forgive him. Luke wouldn't have a prayer at getting Daniel to ever sign release papers.

Dammit. Luke hated waiting. But it was what he had to do. He had to wait and see what Jenny would do, and he had to wait for Harley's response, too.

Luke thought of last night with Jenny, and his pulse skipped. He hadn't been so ripped or tired that he didn't remember what'd happened. All that honey and laughter.

What had gotten into him? He never reacted this way with other women, and there'd been a few. Was it just because he couldn't have Jenny, he wanted her all the more?

That was very mature of him, wasn't it?

And in six years, he'd never taken a woman to his room before. He always courted outside the saloon, taking women to restaurants, and long walks, and visiting in their homes. What had prompted him to haul Jenny up to his room?

At the sound of crunching footsteps, he looked up. Jenny and Olivia had turned into the alley. His heart thudded at seeing her again.

"Luke," said Jenny stiffly, adjusting her large

bonnet. "We'd like to talk with you." Her eyes skimmed down his bare chest. With a feverish intake of breath, she blew a lock of hair out of her eyes.

Beuford and Tom passed on the boardwalk behind them. Luke nodded to the men. He'd take care of the women now.

At seeing his men, Jenny flushed, then turned her eyes to him. Pools of blue, he remembered, as deep as the Rio Grande.

"You can tell them we're not going anywhere," she said. "They've done their good deed for the day. They can go in and have…have a drink, or whatever it is they do."

He broke into a smile. So she knew she was being tagged.

"Is it necessary to have us followed? I told you we wouldn't try to escape. We're staying put until Daniel comes to get us."

"You still think he will?"

"I expect him on the next train, in six days, after he gets the message—the engagement ring—I sent along with Harley. We'll stay put, I promise."

"That's not why I had you followed."

"Then why?"

"In case Harley was after you."

"Harley? He got back on the train."

"No, he didn't."

Jenny frowned and glanced at Olivia's stricken face. "Why not?"

"I'm not sure."

"You mean…you think he'd try to *take* us?"

He jumped down off the wagon and stood tall beside her. "I'm going to tell you the truth from now on, as it happens."

She bit her lip and gazed away from his chest. "That would be a refreshing change."

"I think Harley might try to take you back whether you want to go or not."

Olivia stepped forward as Travis came through the door. She met Travis's eyes and her gazed dropped to his chest. Suddenly flustered, Olivia looked back to Luke, and said, "You mean Harley would take us against our will?"

"Yeah."

"We don't like that one bit. You tell him to stop it."

"I don't know where he is. And until I do, I think it's wise for you two ladies to stay close to us. In the saloon. Daniel will wonder what happened when Harley doesn't arrive tonight in Denver. Travis, see if you can catch wind of any telegrams being sent from Denver in the next few days."

Travis nodded, then smiled carefully at Olivia, as if he were on a fishing expedition. But she jerked her glance away. What was that all about? Luke wondered.

Jenny's expression tensed. "Daniel would never lay a hand on me. He's not like you. He'd never force me to go anywhere."

Luke's jaw twitched. He deserved that. He should have thought a lot harder that night in Daniel's office about taking Jenny in the first place. But he never would have guessed how Daniel and Jenny would respond. Luke stepped forward and clamped his fingers under her trembling chin. Her eyes grew wide.

"It's not Daniel we're talking about. It's Harley. And if he takes you, I doubt he'd wait for the train on Friday. He'd risk taking you back by horse and wagon, no matter what the dangers between here and Denver.''

His fingers lingered on her soft skin. His gaze dropped to her lush lips. She yanked free and he dropped his hand cold.

"I'm not sure that Harley's such a nasty person,'' Jenny said. "In Denver, he was always quiet and polite.''

"Are you willing to take that risk?''

"What are we supposed to do? Where are we supposed to stay for the next week? This is what we came to talk to you about.''

"You can stay here.''

"Tongues would wag. It wouldn't be proper.''

"*You* know it's proper, and that's all that matters, isn't it?''

The tensing of her jaw revealed her deep frustration. Their eyes locked. She blushed, and he wondered if she was thinking about last night.

He saw the pulse hammering at the base of her throat. Maybe she was right. Maybe it wouldn't be so proper, after all. Not with the things tumbling through *his* mind.

"Could I have a word with you privately, please?'' she asked.

Luke looked from her to Olivia and Travis. The other couple shifted uncomfortably. Travis grabbed another keg and occupied himself. Olivia leaned back against the wagon and kicked at a stone.

"Sure,'' said Luke, grabbing his shirt from the wagon seat and shoving his arms through the sleeves.

"I'll be right back,'' Jenny said to Olivia.

When Jenny began walking down the alley, he joined her. Her long, graceful stride matched his.

"What is it?" Luke stopped beyond the fenced chicken coop, near the old lean-to where Adam's puppies were barking. Jenny's slender shadow graced the board-and-batten wall of the guns and ammunition depot behind her.

As he buttoned his shirt, she hastily glanced away. "I don't want to worry Olivia, but do you really think we're in danger from Harley?"

When she turned back to face him, he stared at the hard line of her brow. "I hope not, but Daniel hired him as a guard because he reacts first, then thinks. I don't want him forcing his way—"

"I think you're overreacting."

"How well do you know the man? Personally?"

"Not personally, but—"

"Harley can't be trusted. I'm sure he helped set up the false robbery charge against me."

"You don't know that for sure, and I'm still not convinced…"

"Of what?" he asked, feeling himself tense.

"Of your version of events."

He clamped his jaw. After all they'd been through together, after meeting his friends and seeing Adam, she still didn't trust him.

Even though Daniel hadn't had the decency to show up for her, her loyalty was still to that man?

Jenny's expression softened. "What about…what about Adam? What's going to happen to him?"

He could see the change in her, the worry, the concern about a small boy's future. So the child had touched her heart. She wasn't as indifferent as she tried to appear.

He couldn't escape it. Jenny was a warmhearted woman, the same woman who'd taken him in when he'd been standing wounded and bleeding on Daniel's doorstep. If the situation had been reversed, he knew he wouldn't have jumped so quickly to help a stranger.

Would she help him get Daniel to sign the release papers for Adam?

Luke cleared his throat, about to ask. Just then, a familiar voice called out from the saloon doors.

"Yoo-hoo, anybody home?" Daisy popped out the door, followed by Nathaniel and Adam, in freshly pressed clothes.

Another complication he didn't need, Luke thought. More questions he couldn't answer. Jenny wheeled back in dismay.

"Just like we promised," Daisy said, waving at Jenny, "we're here to have dinner with you folks and Daniel."

Jenny and Luke glanced at each other, then down at the subdued little boy. Luke ached to right the wrong for Adam.

With a shy smile, Adam peeked out from behind Nathaniel's leg. "Hi, Luke," he said, with total innocence.

Chapter Nine

Thank goodness the man had put his shirt back on. Jenny tried to concentrate on Adam. At least now she could think.

It was difficult.

The saloon was empty except for their group. After Luke had tenderly taken Adam to see the new puppies, they'd pushed two dining tables together and were sharing an early supper. Jenny sat between Luke and Daisy, with Olivia and Travis and Nathaniel on the other side. Adam squeezed in on Luke's other side.

Every time Luke's shoulder brushed hers, an unwanted tingle surged through her. Good Lord, she was reacting to him as if she were fourteen, not a grown woman. She'd been around men before. He was no different.

Her heart went out to Adam. She shoved a piece of apple cobbler into her mouth. Luke had quietly explained to her that it was Adam's first time visiting the saloon since his mother's death. The boy was overly quiet, but this time as they ate, Jenny noticed Luke let the child press right up against him without shooing him away. He paid attention to the boy's questions, made him eat the boiled carrots on his plate, even let Adam play with his hat.

She tried not to stare at the fragile little boy, but couldn't help herself. Was there any resemblance between Daniel and Adam?

They both had black hair, but that didn't prove much. Daniel had a cowlick above his forehead, but the boy didn't appear to. Adam's skin tone was darker. They both had brown eyes, but brown was a common color. Nothing unusual about Adam's fingers or hands, his body shape or his walk. Nothing that reminded her of Daniel.

She wasn't certain if that pleased her or frustrated her. It'd be easier to hope that the two weren't related than to admit the kind of man Daniel would have to be to ignore his own son.

"I'm sorry Daniel couldn't make it, dear," Daisy whispered to Jenny.

Jenny nodded and stared into Daisy's kind eyes. Something sentimental flickered in them, something warm and understanding, and Jenny had the distinct impression Daisy knew more than she was letting on.

Luke rose and opened one of the front windows. When he propped it open with a stick, a fresh breeze rolled in, and voices carried from the boardwalk.

"The saloon looks different in daylight," said Jenny, glancing around the empty tables.

"There's not much business during the day," Luke replied. "It doesn't start filling till six."

It was more than the missing crowd. The saloon looked respectable in daylight, with its hand-carved pine furniture and gleaming oak bar. The room was spotless and smelled of cleaning vinegar and soap. Even the floor planks, though dented from heels and spurs, and stained with occasional spots of spitting tobacco, shone with polish.

Reflected in the bar mirror, Saturday shoppers were passing by in the streets with colorful bonnets and hats.

While the adults talked about the price of beef and buffalo hide, Adam wiggled higher in his seat and reached into the sugar bowl, which was filled with slivers of sugar chipped from the sugarloaf. Jenny saw him sneak a sliver into his mouth when he thought no one was looking. She stifled a smile.

"Would anyone like a refill on their drinking water?" Travis asked, holding out the jug.

Everyone said yes except Olivia.

"Are you sure? You guzzled the last one so quickly," Travis said politely, bending closer. Jenny was touched by his concern for Olivia. He'd been trying to start a conversation with her the whole meal, but Olivia was ignoring him.

"I'm sure," said Olivia. A look of determination flattened her brows.

"Well," he said, somewhat perturbed by her refusal, "I'll just fill it up and you can leave it behind if you like, or you can take some if you want."

"No, please." Olivia cupped her palm over her water glass at the same time Travis poured. The water poured onto her hand.

Without skipping a beat, she pulled her hand back and shook the water off. "Fine, I'll have some—"

"I'm sorry, I'll take it back—"

"Please, it's all right—"

"No, it's not—"

"I can manage," she insisted.

Luke turned and caught Jenny's eye. When his eyes twinkled with amusement and a grin softened his rugged features, Jenny couldn't help but return his smile. Did Olivia and Travis know they were sweet on each other?

Mona came by and stacked the empty platters. "Coffee for everyone?"

"I think Miss Jenny likes tea," Luke said with a grin.

Mona smiled. "Honey on the side?"

"Coffee," said Jenny, trying to diffuse their laughter, although a smile found its way to her lips.

As Mona left, Adam grew restless. He leaned over the table and propped his head in his hands, staring quietly through the swinging doors to the long hallway that led to the kitchen in the other building, as if he were expecting to see someone.

Was he wondering about his mother? The kitchen was where his mama had worked for years, where Adam had spent hours on a daily basis. Was he hoping that, by some miracle...she might be in the kitchen?

Daisy and Nathaniel and the others continued talking, but all Jenny could do was watch the boy. Luke was awfully quiet beside her, too.

The kitchen door swung open again. Ever watchful, Adam reared up in his seat.

Mona walked through and the boy slumped in disappointment. Jenny felt her throat close up. Luke sighed, and his eyes sought hers. For the first time since she'd known him, his eyes glistened with uncertainty. He looked like he wanted to do something to help Adam, but didn't know what. She understood how he felt.

Jenny reached out and caressed Adam's slim shoulder. She wondered if he'd pull away, but he let her hand rest. When he grew more withdrawn, Luke yanked him onto his lap.

"Hey, Adam," he said softly, "it's been awhile since you've been in the kitchen. Want to go look?"

Adam shrugged.

"Come on," said Luke, rising from his chair, holding out his hand. Jenny was rooting for him with everything she had.

Go on, Adam, she thought, *take his hand.*

"I'll go with you," Luke said. "We'll look at those copper pots your ma used to like. Remember? You liked to look at your face in them."

With a flash of interest, the boy got up and took the large, callused palm. Jenny gave a silent shout of hurrah.

"One time," said Luke, "I remember coming down for breakfast. You were a lot younger then. You couldn't even walk. You had those copper pots pulled out all over the floor and you were pouring the cat's bowl of milk into one."

"I was?" Adam laughed, and Jenny felt a tide of relief.

"Yup." Luke glanced down at the boy and hauled him up onto his shoulders. "The cat was drinking right out of it, and I got so mad. Sorry, Adam, about getting so mad...."

They left, and after a few tense moments, Jenny heard Adam's laughter coming from the hallway.

With a sigh, Daisy turned to Jenny. "Every burden, every blow, Luke takes upon himself to try to fix. He denies it, you know, but even as a boy, he was always trying to fix other people's problems. It was a difficult time for him when his own ma passed. He could never fix things for *her,* no matter how hard he tried. She became a shell of a woman when Luke's father died.''

There was more to Luke than Jenny realized. She tried to imagine him as a little boy. ''What was his mother like?''

Daisy stirred milk into her coffee. ''When they took her husband, she lost her mind a little. She could always remember the day of the week, but never the year. After a while, she forgot she had three sons.''

''Where are the other two sons?''

''No one knows for sure. Travelin' the country somewhere.''

Jenny thought about it. It must have been a horrible time for Luke, and how sad not to know his brothers. How lonely. Was that why Luke lived alone now? Because that was what he was used to? Was that why he never bothered with a regular home of his own, with a wife, with children?

Sipping her coffee, Jenny let the fresh breeze from the open window roll over her. Two older woman strolled by, glanced inside and whispered to each other. Obviously, they didn't realize the windows were open and they could be heard.

''I heard he took the woman up to his room last night.''

''What's her name?''

''Jenny something. Her father's a bigwig for the railroad.''

Jenny stiffened. She wished the floor would open up and swallow her.

The voices continued. "And she's engaged to another man?"

"From what I understand."

The other stranger gasped and then the voices faded.

In the ensuing silence, Daisy reached over and placed a warm palm over Jenny's. "I know those two women back from when I was in my courtin' days. They couldn't get a story straight back then, and I don't imagine they've got it straight now."

Jenny felt suddenly overwhelmed by everything in her life.

"I don't know what's amiss between you and Daniel, but I can see you're upset he didn't show. If you need a shoulder to cry on, I've cried many a tear for Daniel myself."

"Oh, Daisy, it's such a mess. I wouldn't know where to begin. My problems are nothing compared to those of that sweet little boy in the kitchen."

"I know. I know how Daniel's involved there, too."

Jenny looked at her in surprise. "Oh."

"Luke doesn't know it, but I had my suspicions when he left for Denver, saying he was going for Daniel." Daisy smoothed her faded dress. "You know, that makes me related to Adam." Her hand trembled. "I'm ashamed to say I never met Maria. I let my dang-fool fears of this saloon keep me from steppin' inside. I wish I'd been stronger. I wish I hadn't let people like those two women who just walked by interfere with what I should've done. Be guided by your strength, dear, not your weakness like I was.''

Jenny felt her burden lift. Daisy understood.

Luke and Adam stepped out of the kitchen. Adam had a length of rope in his hand. Returning to his seat, he scanned the top of the table. Was he looking for the sugar bowl?

Jenny cupped her hand over his, then opened her palm, revealing half a dozen slivers she'd secretly saved for him. ''Want one?'' She popped one into her mouth. ''They're real good.''

He smiled and took one. She was reminded of her own childhood craving for sweets. There was something about the sheer simplicity of having sugar slivers melt in her mouth that made everything seem brighter.

''I brought the rope for Jenny,'' Luke said to Adam. Luke slid his powerful body into the chair next to hers and captured her attention with that commanding presence of his. She suddenly found it difficult to breathe.

''I thought Jenny could show you a rope trick,'' Luke continued. ''She knows how to tie a good knot.''

Jenny stifled the laugh bubbling up her throat.

Adam pressed his warm body against her knees. ''You do? Who taught you?''

''My granddad, a long time ago. He used to be a sailor.''

''On a ship? In the ocean?''

She laughed and ruffled his hair. ''Of course.''

Luke watched her handle the rope. ''Pay close attention,'' he said with a wicked look in his eye, ''Jenny knows one called the constrictor knot.''

Warmth rushed into her cheeks. "I'm very good at that one."

His voice filled with affectionate humor. "I knew you were laughing at me that night."

"I couldn't help it. You looked so helpless, such a big strapping man all tied up on account of me. My granddad would've been proud."

The boy's eyes lit up. "Show me."

She looped the ends together. "This is the constrictor knot. It's very tight. If there's strain put on the rope, it may have to be cut off rather than untied."

"You don't say," Luke interjected.

Her face softened with pleasure at his reaction. "And this was my granddad's favorite. A figure-eight, used to prevent a rope from slipping through a hole. See if you can tie it."

Adam played with the rope, totally enthralled.

"Here, I'll show you one," Luke said to the boy. "This is the hitch you use to tie your saddlebag to your horse."

Daisy and Nathaniel rose to leave. Luke got up with the others to say goodbye. "I'd like Adam to stay here with me," he said, to everyone's surprise. "Just for a little while. I could keep my eye on—" He cut himself short. "I think he'd like it here. Wouldn't you Adam?"

Adam nodded.

Luke explained, "I thought I could clear out the supply room, off the kitchen in the other building. Move him in there. That's the room his ma used for his naps. And then I'd move into the small room next to him."

Jenny liked the idea. Being here again, near the

kitchen where his mother used to work, would bring Adam comfort. But was that all there was to it? What else was Luke thinking? That he could keep an eye out for Adam in case...in case Harley came around looking for the boy?

"Couldn't you stay a little longer?" Jenny said, stepping forward and slipping her arm under Daisy's.

"That's mighty kind of you. But we have to go home to milk the cows. They'll be gettin' antsy."

Luke walked them to the door. "I'll send a man to your ranch this evening for the rest of Adam's clothes."

Nathaniel shook Luke's hand. "If we don't see you before Tuesday, happy birthday."

Jenny glanced up at Luke's rugged face. His birthday was on Tuesday? Three days away?

Nathaniel continued. "Mona tells me the saloon girls have something special planned."

Luke bristled and ran a hand through his wavy hair. "Thanks for the warning. I'll make sure I'm not around."

"Oh, come on, now," said Daisy, looking to Jenny for assistance. "If you don't show up for the party, they'll blame us for telling you."

Despite herself, Jenny found herself intrigued with the notion. What did the saloon girls have planned?

She flicked imaginary lint off her skirt. Why should she care? Luke meant nothing to her. She hardly knew the man. But when the others left and she stood beside his tall, lean figure, gazing up into his mesmerizing, smoky eyes, she felt her pulse leap again.

More than a little annoyed, she left him standing there. There was no logical reason for her to feel envious of the saloon girls.

As humiliating as it was, Jenny might as well get it over with and ask Luke for a favor. She'd already tried three times to catch him alone, but could never corner him. After Daisy and Nathaniel left, Luke took Adam for a horse ride, then came back and did the banking, taking Adam with him again, and then the two of them disappeared with Travis.

Lord, the man was busy. You'd think he were the president, so many people sought his counsel.

But he was back in the saloon now, busy with Lee, and Jenny braced herself to approach him. He'd understand, she told herself. She'd felt a softening in him after their afternoon spent together, and she was also beginning to see him in a more considerate light.

She took a deep breath and wove her way among the empty tables to where Luke and Lee were discussing bills, schedules and liquor supplies. Up on the stage, the piano player and Lola were practicing songs, gearing up for a busy Saturday night.

"Excuse me, Luke," Jenny interrupted.

He glanced up from his pile of papers. He was wearing a chocolate-colored shirt that brought out the brown flecks in his eyes. She suddenly felt very dowdy, dressed in her ragged clothes. All the more reason to ask him for the favor.

"You never seem to be alone," she said, "and…and before I go for a walk with Olivia, there's something I'd like to ask you."

Luke dismissed Lee with a nod. The bartender

folded their papers and headed to the bar, giving Jenny a friendly smile as he left.

"You won't be staying for the show?" Luke asked.

Her senses spun at the clean scent of him. "No, we'd—we'd like some fresh air," she began. Why did she stutter so much around this man? Couldn't she just talk? "And this isn't really the way we'd choose to entertain ourselves, if we...if we had the choice."

His jaw stiffened as if he'd been slapped. "You do have the choice. My men will escort you anywhere in town you'd like to go. Don't force yourself to stay here if you don't want to." There was an edge to his voice. That wall between them appeared again.

She hadn't meant to insult him. She tried to explain. "It's just that we're bored—"

"Bored?" He furrowed his brow.

She was inadvertently getting in deeper. She wasn't bored at all. The truth be told, after last night's show she had no desire to see any of the people she'd embarrassed herself in front of with the honey and the spilled drink. And no desire to repeat any performances alone in Luke's room. She would stay as far out of reach as possible.

"I'd like to ask a favor, I suppose you'd call it."

He slowly leaned back in his chair and appraised her. "Well now, doesn't that sound interesting? A favor from me."

He straightened his broad shoulders and leaned forward on his elbows to stare at her, making her aware of the blouse she was wearing. Another one of Daisy's, buttoned to the top, but this one was more faded and tighter. The only reason she was wearing it was because she'd rinsed the other two and they were still wet. The faded cloth pulled at her breasts, and if you looked real close, the shadow of her undergarment was visible. Where had she left her shawl?

"What kind of favor do you need from me?" The sensual tone of his voice made her blush.

"It's about money. Olivia and I don't have much with us and we're staying for another week—"

"You know the room is yours for as long as you need. And the staff know you're not to be charged for any food or drink."

"We know."

He frowned.

"Well, the thing is, we need pocket money. We'd like to buy some clothes that fit us properly." It was a mistake for her to look down at her blouse, for when she did, his gaze followed hers, and she felt herself blush all over again. "And we might like to send a telegram to my father, or eat at a *decent*—" Her lashes flew up at the insult she'd unwittingly hurled.

His eyes cooled.

"You know what I mean."

"Yes, I do. You might even want to buy a stage-coach ticket out of here as fast as you can."

"That's right." A smile leaped to her face. "Could we borrow, say, thirty dollars from you? Until we get back to Denver?"

"Oh, there's no need to borrow," he said calmly.

Her smile grew wider. "I knew you'd understand."

"You can have all the extra pocket money you can *earn.*"

Her hands fluttered together. "Pardon me?"

"You can *earn* it. You're always saying how no one'll give you a chance to show how hard you can work. So, I say, work. I'll give you the chance."

The idea startled her. "You expect me to *work* for you?"

That maddening arrogance in him surfaced. "Why not?"

She drew herself taller. What the heck did he expect from her? "Because it wasn't *my* idea to come here."

His gaze roved over her. "You're here now."

The man was unbelievable! She spun away. "Forget I asked. This is humiliating—"

"Hard work often is."

She reeled around once more. Was he goading her? Didn't he think she could work? She could outwork anyone. "What exactly did you have in mind?"

Luke glanced at the bar. "What can you do?"

"Well," she said, lifting her chin proudly, "I can sew."

He paused. "I'm not in the market for a new shirt."

"That's not what I sew." She gulped and glared at him. "I sew...*undergarments.*"

It took several seconds for him to respond. He studied her face, then smiled in such a vexing way she felt like kicking him. "You mean like underwear?"

She placed her hands on her hips. "That's right."

"Let me guess." He leaned back in his chair and

laughed. "It all makes sense now. Lavender corsets?"

"Why do you men always find it necessary to laugh every time a woman brings up the subject of undergarments? Why, between you and the bankers—" She shook her head. "Yes, I sew corsets for women. And for men, nightshirts and long johns and..." she swallowed hard "...and men's drawers."

He inclined his head and smiled. "As tempting as that sounds, I'm not in the market for drawers, either."

She averted her eyes. Why had she ever suggested it?

"What else do you know how to do?"

She did have one other important skill. "I know business. I secretly wrote a college paper for my youngest brother once, on British colonial trade, and I got—I mean *he* got—an A. The highest grade he's ever had."

Luke's expression mellowed. He shook his head. "Your brother did that...? I don't need any papers written," he said gently. She could tell he somehow felt sorry for her, and that angered her more. She didn't want his pity. She had enjoyed writing that paper.

One of the Denver bankers she'd approached for a loan had looked at her with the same dismissal in his eyes, as if she were a child who didn't know how to count, let alone succeed in a business venture. "I'm not talking about writing papers. I'm good with business ideas, and I could figure out a plan, say..." she glanced around at the empty tables "...how to bring in more customers."

"It's packed in here already."

"Not during the day."

He squared his wide shoulders. "You have ideas on that?"

"Not off the top of my head, but I could come up with a few, and you could pay me."

"Hmm. How soon could I have your plan?"

"Well, it'd take me a few days. You could give me the money now, and I'll come up with the plan later."

He paused for a moment and stared at her. Then he smiled that charming, irritating smile again. "Sorry, I don't give credit to people I don't know. If you want the money now, you'll have to do the work now."

She tightened her mouth in exasperation. People he didn't know? He'd brought her here to a place *she* didn't know! Was he kidding?

"Thirty dollars is a lot of cash. It might not be in the household you grew up in, but it takes one of my men an entire month to earn that much."

She stiffened at the insult. She knew thirty dollars was a lot of money. Hadn't she and her grandmother worked hard for every bit they'd earned sewing? Why did everyone out West assume she came from a privileged class? Why, her father had worked his way up from loading coal on the railroad to his position now. And each of her brothers had worked at manual labor, saving for their college tuitions.

Yes, they had more than many families, but every penny earned came from sheer hard work, not from sitting on their behinds. But pride made her hold her tongue.

His eyes sparkled with a dangerous gleam. "Do

you know how to wait tables? Do you know how to pour a drink?''

She shot him a cold-eyed glare, spun on her heel and left. He was out of his mind! The man hadn't changed at all!

Chapter Ten

"Are you sure I can have it? You'll sell me this blue velvet gown?" Lola stood beside Jenny in the saloon, above the crate of fabrics Lola's sister from back East had shipped her. The two had spent hours together in the past two days, and Jenny liked Lola's easygoing style. It was early afternoon and the dancing girls were kicking up their heels, practicing their leg raises and taps in preparation for Luke's birthday party tomorrow.

With a burst of determination, Jenny took out a spindle of thread. "I'll mend the torn waistline and replace the missing button. I've already taken it out at the side seams, just like we measured, then it's all yours. Fifty dollars, right?" Jenny gulped at the amount of money Lola was willing to pay. But then again, the fabric alone had cost forty.

Jenny would show Luke she could strike her own business deals without having to grovel to him.

"Worth every penny." Dressed in a simple polka-dot frock for practice, Lola stroked the velvet. Distracted by the girls on stage, she shouted, "Raise your legs higher, girls, at precisely the same time. That's how they do the can-can in New York City.''

Glancing down at the gown, Jenny thought of Daniel. She'd sewn this gown for him, for the night of their engagement. Just last week, she never could have imagined parting with it, but after all that'd happened… Back in Denver, was Daniel missing her terribly? Had he gotten a telegram from Harley, saying she'd given back his ring? Would he come to her on Friday's train, eager to make amends and explain that it was all a mistake?

She sighed, threaded her needle and began stitching the torn pleats. Would she accept any of his explanations?

How would her father manage his speech tomorrow at the podium? He'd given her his rough notes to write up, and she'd stuffed them into the hall desk. Lord knew if he'd even find those without her.

She frowned. Why didn't her broken engagement bother her more? Was it for the best?

Adam's future was more affected than her own. The affectionate hours she'd spent with him eased her own time here. Yesterday, she'd quizzed him on simple addition and the spelling of his name, and discovered how smart he was. She'd repeated the rope tricks for him, then it was back to his puppies.

Luke had given Adam one of the rooms off the huge kitchen and moved his own things into the room beside Adam's. They had their own back door to come and go. Adam could slip out anytime, with the supervision of Beuford and Tom, and play with his friends down the street.

Lola waved toward the stage. "Higher, higher!" When she stepped back beside Jenny, the older woman eyed Jenny's worn dress. "You're not going to wear that tomorrow night, are you?"

Jenny's hand fluttered to the chipped button at her throat. "There's nothing wrong with these clothes."

"There's no life left in them." Lola yanked on the fabrics inside the crate, pulling out an apricot lace. "If you have time, I'd say help yourself to these and make yourself something pretty." She narrowed her green eyes thoughtfully. "Hey, I'll bet one of the girls could lend you something."

"No, thank you, these are fine."

"Oh, wear something pretty. For Luke. It's his birthday."

Jenny knotted the thread and didn't answer.

"Don't ignore the suggestion. I see the way he looks at you."

Jenny felt herself color.

"I know they're Daisy's dresses, but they don't do you justice. They're certainly not up to the standard of clothing you're wearing underneath—"

Jenny's lashes flew up. "I beg your pardon?"

Lola's round cheeks dimpled. "Your purple corset and bloomers. Remember? You got honey on them the first night. When you rinsed them, Olivia hung them by the kitchen fire to dry. They're pretty."

"You...looked at my corset while I was sleeping?"

"Sure, we all did. Olivia told us you sewed them."

Jenny's mouth fell open.

"You know, my girls and I haven't toured the East for three years, and I'd be mighty obliged if you'd tell us about the latest fashions."

"The latest fashions in…in burlesque?"

Lola stared at her for a moment, then tilted her head back and roared with laughter. The troop of dancers had disbanded and two black-haired women hopped off the stage to join them.

"Darlin'," said Lola, catching her breath, her earbobs dangling with her movements, "we know you don't know anything about burlesque. Tell us what the latest fashions are in *normal* clothing. Believe it or not, we go to restaurants just like normal women. And we go to the bank, and we shop at the mercantile. All we are is dancers and entertainers, nothing more, if you catch my meaning. I'd love to get the latest fashions from a high society woman like yourself."

When Lola draped a plump arm around her, Jenny was enveloped in the woman's natural warmth and found herself unable to be insulted by the blunt words.

An idea occurred to her. Was it possible?

Sure. If Lola was really this interested, then the others might be, too. When Olivia burst through the kitchen doors, Jenny hauled her over.

As Jenny gathered the girls around, she sorted through the fabrics, proudly giving suggestions on stylish suits and blouses. "We only have a few days left here, but Olivia and I could sew you anything you like. Lola, how about a day suit with the latest bustle, made from this green linen? It'll match the color of your eyes. The rage in Boston is fingerless gloves, and smaller bonnets. We could make them all to match."

Lola pursed her lips in an expression of satisfaction.

Jenny smiled. "And this bright red bobbin lace, such a delicate pattern of leaves and flowers, why, I could make you the prettiest boned corset."

Lola nodded and Jenny launched into more suggestions.

She'd show Luke McLintock—and all those bankers who'd turned her down—that *her* ideas were nothing to laugh at. She had a good head on her shoulders, and she'd darn well prove it.

The next morning, Adam joined Jenny and the cook in the bright kitchen. He crawled out of his room in his nightshirt, shivering and crying. "Jenny…"

"Adam, what is it?"

Standing there, suddenly looking very young, he didn't answer. He had a short new haircut she'd never seen before.

"Another bad dream?"

He nodded.

Jenny wiped her palms on her faded skirt and glanced down the hall to Luke's door. It was open a crack. He was gone.

She entered Adam's room, came back with his blanket and scooped him up. "Shh, everything's going to be all right. Have you had breakfast yet?"

He shook his head.

"Let's have honey and porridge together."

As they were finishing up, voices carried through the kitchen door. They were coming from the hallway. Luke's voice, and a couple she didn't recognize.

Jenny hadn't seen or heard from Luke in three days, and she had an urge to bolt out the alley door.

The voices got louder. She heard a woman say, "The reverend sent us to look at the boy."

Jenny looked at Adam, but he was talking to the cook and hadn't heard. She burst from her seat. "Adam, grab your hat."

"Where we goin'?"

"Out the door. Come, show me your puppies." Jenny didn't know why, but she didn't feel like facing the couple.

"Oh, yeah, the puppies." Adam raced for the door. He grabbed the pot of fresh water for the dogs, which the cook had already set out for him. Adam could barely lift it. She stifled the urge to take it from him to help. He seemed to get such pleasure caring for the stray animals on his own.

When they dashed out the door, the warm sun greeted them. With a nod to Beuford and Tom, Jenny turned the corner at the old chicken coop, under the shade of the big pine.

Beuford and Tom were being extra careful since they'd spotted Harley poking around yesterday. Apparently he'd disappeared before they got a chance to confront him, but she refused to dwell on it.

Adam tiptoed through the dirt behind a lean-to, bending down when he reached the crate with the pile of straw. "Here they are," he whispered. Three little puppies squirmed in greeting, two of them yellow-haired, one of them black. Adam scooped up a yellow one and placed it in her open palms.

"Oh, he's so sweet," she said, marveling at the feel of warm fur. "No wonder you like them so much."

Adam smiled proudly and lifted the black one into his own arms. "I like Blackie. He likes me, too."

Jenny smiled. "I like your new haircut, Adam."

"Luke took me to the barber and made me cut it. He says I'll get lice if I don't take care of it."

"Well, Luke is right."

"He says I gotta go to school next year, too, but I don't want to."

"He's right there, too. You need an education."

"Yesterday, he got mad at me for takin' off on my pony. He says I can't do that anymore. I'm supposed to tell him first."

Her puppy squirmed. She fought to keep him in her arms. "You took off on your own?"

Adam nodded.

Her eyes widened. "You're only five years old."

"You sound like Luke again. Why do you have to agree with him on everything?"

She reared back in surprise. Now *there* was a different perspective. She thought she and Luke couldn't agree on anything.

Adam held the pup close to his face. "How you doin' this mornin', Blackie? Wanna hear a song?" Jenny stood mesmerized as Adam sang a loving version of "Pop Goes the Weasel." "Do you like weasels, Blackie? Cook says there's a few of them around here, on account of the chickens, but he says they won't hurt you."

As Adam turned his head to rub his face against Blackie's, Jenny got a good look at his profile. Now that Adam's hair was cut, his entire face was visible.

Oh, no. Alarmed, she stepped back. He looked just like... She swallowed. His jaw, his ears. *Daniel.*

Sweat broke on her brow. Even his forehead slanted back the same. His new haircut gave him a cowlick at his forehead—just like Daniel's.

She gulped at the shocking revelation.

He was Daniel's son.

And Daniel didn't want him.

Her throat closed tight.

Adam stroked the puppy. "Jenny, did you ever fly a kite?"

Still reeling, she shook her head and knotted her fingers into her skirt.

"Luke made me one yesterday. Wanna come with me and Blackie to the big hill?" He motioned westward toward the rugged mountains, to the hill that overlooked the valley and the ranches below. She stumbled back to look. Tall golden grass covered the slopes.

Her gaze clouded with tears for Adam. Daniel had lied.

Luke had told her the truth.

She'd been so horribly wrong about Luke.

Although she didn't agree with his method of bringing her here, what desperation he must have felt to seek justice for Adam. Jenny found her composure, slid her puppy next to its mother, then put her arm around Adam's shoulders. "You get the kite and we'll go."

Minutes later, standing under a clump of trees, Jenny watched Adam and his dog race the wind. Three little children, Adam's longtime friends from the boardinghouse, joined him. Their laughter filled the air.

The weeds crunched behind her. She turned and swallowed when she saw who it was. All over again, a hot ache burned in her throat.

Hands in his pockets, Luke stood there, looking dark and rugged.

His galvanizing gaze sent a tremor through her. "Took me awhile to find you. I thought I heard you in the kitchen, but funny thing, when I stepped in to introduce you and Adam to a nice couple the reverend sent by, you disappeared." He lowered the brim of his hat to shield his face from the sun.

Standing this close to his long, lean body made her breasts tingle against the soft cloth of her blouse. In haste, she glanced away.

In one smooth motion, he drew closer. He put his fingers under her chin, bringing her face back up to his. Her blood rushed to where his fingers touched her. She shivered as she met his inquisitive gaze. "Did you disappear on purpose?"

"Yes," she whispered.

Laughter creased his eyes and softened his mouth. "Can't tell a lie. You're the most honest person I've ever met." His fingers slid down her arm and dropped. Her skin felt cool where his fingers had trailed. Why did her body yearn for more of his touch?

They stood there, wrapped in each other's gaze. Why didn't she move? Why didn't she say something? How could he have the power to hold her with his eyes alone?

She twisted away. "I notice you gave Adam a haircut."

"It was about time."

With a moan of distress, she shook her head. "Now he looks like…" She couldn't finish the sentence.

Luke inclined his dark head and glanced at Adam, running in the distance. He swallowed hard. "I know."

When Adam came racing over, Luke reached out for the boy. Although he didn't say anything, she sensed a bonding between him and Adam. She'd misjudged this man so terribly.

Adam's friends called him away, and he and the puppy tore off.

Jenny saw the pain linger on Luke's face, and her heart squeezed. "If there's anything I can do to help," she said quietly, "please let me know."

"You mean that?"

"Yes."

He sighed and removed his hat, stroking the brim. "Thank you."

A quiet understanding passed between them. After a few moments of watching the children, she took a step closer. "That night on the train, when I first asked you what this was all about, you said truth and honor. And doing what you know is right." She took a deep breath. "You weren't talking about Daniel, were you? You were talking about yourself. Your own truth and honor. Reuniting Adam with his father was the only honorable thing you thought you could do."

He stood so close she could feel the heat pounding in his body. He nodded casually, but there was a catch in his husky voice. "I'm not sure anymore if that would be the best thing to do."

"I don't think it is, either. You can't force a man to love his son—" She broke off with a sob.

He reached out and swept her into his arms. Crushed against him, she buried her face in his chest. She breathed him in. He felt like home.

"Oh, Jenny, I'm so sorry."

After a minute, she stepped back and composed

herself. "Who exactly are those people the reverend sent to meet Adam?"

"They're a nice couple. They're interested in adoption."

She glanced toward the buildings. Her nose dripped and she rubbed it with the back of her hand. "Are they still in the saloon waiting for us?"

"No, I sent them away."

"Does Adam know them?"

He shook his head. "Not yet. Thomas told me they can't have children of their own. They arrived last week on their way through to Montana. They plan on homesteading when the new land's released."

"Adam will have to leave this town?"

He paused. "If they take him, yes."

Her eyes stung. "Oh, Luke, isn't there some way to keep him here? Look at him, how much he enjoys his friends. He's peaceful here with you, I sense it. Here with *you*," she repeated, wondering if he'd understand. Was there any hope that Adam could stay here permanently?

Luke turned his gentle, handsome face to the boy and smiled. "Sometimes I almost wish…"

She paused and waited for him to finish, sensing he'd almost let her in. "You wish what?"

"Nothing. I'm just dreaming."

What was he about to say? She turned and looked into his deep eyes, exploring and wondering.

"I don't know what it is about you," he said, "but being around you makes me want to be a better man."

Her stomach knotted. She tried to ignore it, but could no longer deny the intense attraction she felt for him. "You're already a good man. You're the most noble man I know."

His gaze darkened and flickered. With a sharp exclamation, he swung her into his arms and slanted his lips over hers. Sweet, tender lips.

Sensations rippled along her mouth, down her spine and right to her very toes. Her body came alive. He was kissing her. This was what a kiss was supposed to feel like. Like a night sky with a thousand twinkling stars. Her fingers curled into his shirt. With a moan, he wove his hands into her hair. Her skin tingled everywhere he touched her. Their tongues twined and pleasure pounded through her. She pressed her body tighter to his, never wanting to let go. He put a large hand to her waist and drew her closer, his body responding.

Children's voices in the distance interrupted them. She tore away, breathless. His broad shoulders heaved with his troubled breathing.

Adam barreled toward them. The other children followed, chanting for lemonade. Jenny glanced at Luke and they laughed.

"Sure, we got lemonade in the kitchen," he said to the youngsters, rubbing his mouth with the back of his hand. Then, looking at her, he smiled in that tender, almost unbearable way that sent her heart racing again.

"You'll come tonight, won't you?" Luke asked above the children's heads. "To the party?" He suddenly seemed very vulnerable.

Vulnerable? Luke? "Oh," she said, caught off guard. "I don't know—"

"Come with me. Please. Say you'll accompany me."

What harm could come of it? Every harm, she told herself. These were new sensations she was feeling, and where could they possibly lead? The situation was already complicated, and Luke and his drugging kisses would only complicate things further.

With a tremulous smile at the children yanking on her skirts, Jenny met his awaiting gaze. "I'd like that."

Blazes, the woman could kiss.

Despite trying to convince himself otherwise all afternoon and well into the evening, Luke thirsted for more of her.

He *should* push away. But even as he thought the words, he didn't feel them. He wanted her. With every aching muscle in his body. He'd be meeting her in half an hour, and his gut tightened at the prospect.

A tapping sound broke through his thoughts. What was that? As he walked down the dark alley behind the saloon, Luke turned and glanced over his shoulder. He had the uncomfortable feeling he was being watched.

No one there. He was imagining things.

He straightened his shoulders. He was too caught up in Jenny and that powerful kiss. More than just a kiss. A closeness he couldn't describe, one he'd never felt before.

All the more reason to walk away. Why had he invited her tonight? It scared him to think he could become dependent on a woman. He rubbed his jaw. Or…was he more scared to think someone might become dependent on him?

Right now in his life, he wasn't shackled by obligation and sentiment. No wife. No children. He'd always lived alone and been alone. He liked it that way. Sentiment, in the long run, only caused you trouble. Wasn't that what he'd learned as a child in his own family?

Besides, how far could this go between him and Jenny without jeopardizing Adam's situation? If Daniel were to discover anything going on between them, then Luke's carefully drawn out plan with the judge might collapse.

Stones crunched on the boardwalk. His senses went on alert. Two women with ribbons on their bonnets walked by, carrying satchels and packages.

What would Daniel's next move be? Luke had new plans of his own, now that Jenny had agreed to help.

"Evening," he said to the two guards posted at the saloon's back door.

Stepping past them, Luke filled his lungs with air and told himself he had things under control. Harley wouldn't try anything in a busy saloon. All of Luke's men were on alert. So tonight he wouldn't worry about it more than necessary.

Inside, beside the wall of drying herbs and garlic, the tin clock read nine-fifteen. He nodded to his men, the cook and the waitresses, and then looked in on Adam, who was fast asleep. The boy had no problems sleeping in his room.

But the saloon was no place for a boy to live permanently.

Luke ran a hand over his clean white shirt, and that same disquieting thought popped into his head.

Was this a place for *him* to live permanently? Is this what *he* wanted for the rest of his life?

Ever since Jenny came into his life, he'd been raising all sorts of questions he thought were long buried.

Despite the hum of the crowd down the hall, a lonely silence engulfed him. Trying to avoid it, Luke shoved the kitchen doors open and stepped through.

The bar was packed. The smell of leather and cigars and perfumed dancing girls hit his nostrils. Something within him sprang to life.

Hell.

What was going on with him lately? The saloon had always been good enough and it always would be. He liked his life. He liked this place, just the way it was.

He removed his guns and checked them behind the counter, keeping the derringer in his boot.

Never mind the lonely silence.

No woman would *ever* change his mind.

Tonight, he'd enjoy a friendly conversation with Jenny. That's all. He'd just have to restrain himself. How difficult could that be?

He accepted an ale at the crowded bar. Leaning against the oak counter, waiting for her to arrive, he scanned the room.

The dentist was here, Luke noted with a groan.

And Mona, inching her stout body taller, was shouting at the regulars. "If I hear one more person call me by that name, I swear you can get your own drinks! You know my name's not Mona Lisa!"

In the round of ensuing laughter, she caught Luke's amused eye, saluted and mouthed, "Happy birthday."

He nodded and tilted his hat. Mona was a good woman.

A guitar strummed below the stage. The piano player got into position, and Lola, all dolled up in a frilly gown, began singing in that low, melodic voice.

Luke leaned back and planted one booted foot over the other. Then he made the mistake of looking up the stairs to the balcony. Jenny was making her way down.

The vision hit him full force. He shot up and with a taut jerk of his body, knocked his ale onto the counter. "Oh, hell," he said, trying to mop it up. One of the bartenders took over, and Luke glanced up again at the vibrant woman who stole his breath.

How was he supposed to restrain himself when Jenny looked like this?

Chapter Eleven

Several minutes later, Luke was still staring.

Where did Jenny get that gown? A dusty rose color that brought out the rose stain in her cheeks, its small capped sleeves exposing her creamy shoulders and bare arms. A black velvet cameo necklace drew his eyes to the hollow curves at the base of her throat, the most erotic throat he'd ever kissed, one he'd love to kiss again.

Her glistening, long hair danced around her shoulders, free and spirited, just like her. His eyes traveled down her body. Rose fabric cinched her waist and billowed at her hips, making him imagine what was underneath.

He'd never hungered more for a woman.

When she sought him out in the crowd and her deep blue eyes met his, the sparks electrified him.

Restrain himself? He gulped and swiped his mouth. Right.

Despite the crowd that engulfed them, Luke took three strides toward her and held out his hand. ''You look beautiful.''

She took the hand he offered. Her skin glowed

and the pulse quickened in her throat. That crooked, captivating smile of hers quivered. Was she affected by him, too?

"Thank you." When she clasped her fingers around his and he yanked her closer, directing her to two empty bar stools, he felt that pounding in his chest again. He wondered what he'd gotten himself into. Maybe if he didn't look at her, he wouldn't get caught up in her charms.

Kerosene lamps flickered above them, a circle of lights dancing on the polished bar. He pretended to study a floorboard, the only safe place to look. But Jenny lifted her skirts to sit down, and he found himself staring at her shapely calves and ankles instead. It was torture to look at such an intimate part of her. With a soft groan, he removed his hat, checked it behind the bar and tunneled his fingers through his hair.

He loomed above her slender frame. Ordering her a lemonade, he sat down. Dammit, the group of men next to him shifted, accidentally jostling him in her direction. He clenched his muscles and tried not to touch her. It was impossible to hold the strained position for long. Another jarring and Luke's arm and thigh brushed hers. Her heat melded with his and his belly tightened. There was no way he was looking into her eyes, though. He had no control when he did that.

"Where'd you get..." He muttered his question into his ale, finishing in a nervous mumble.

"Pardon? Are you talking to me?"

He turned to look at her. She leaned closer to hear him. The top of her dress dipped open and he got an unexpected eyeful. He blinked and wrenched away. Blood leaped to his loins. He was being ridiculous. For cripes sake, couldn't he handle talking to her, looking at her? Of course he could, and he'd prove it.

In a rash decision, he swiveled to face her. Big mistake. Those velvet blue eyes ensnared him. "Yes," he repeated, "I wondered where..." he gulped "...you got the pretty dress."

Glancing down at her skirts, she smoothed the silky fabric, stroking it over her thigh. Stroking and stroking... He swallowed and snapped himself out of his daydream.

"I bought it from one of the girls," she said with a proud lift of her chin.

"Bought it?" He was too surprised to remember to look away. "With what? I thought you didn't have any money."

She hesitated for a moment, watching him, then her soft lips curved into a smile. "So far, since yesterday, I've earned fifty-one dollars and thirty-five cents. No thanks to you."

His jaw slackened. "*What?* How'd you do that?"

"Sewing."

"You made all that money sewing?"

"Yes. Well, one dollar and thirty-five cents of it, and fifty dollars for selling my blue gown."

A strange sensation of pride filled him. He had no reason to be proud of a woman he had no ties to, but he felt it all the same. "A dollar thirty-five in two days? That's amazing. People pay that kind of money for underwear?"

"It wasn't just underwear." With a haughty flick of her head that made him laugh, she leaned her arms on the bar. Her bare arms… He shook his head to clear the enticing vision.

"Yoo-hoo, Luke!" Lola hollered, popping out from behind the red stage curtains. Her skirts were ruffled and her slinky corsetlike thing shimmered under the lamplight. "We've got a dance planned in your honor. Happy birthday, sonny boy!"

Oh, thank God. Rescued. He nodded and waved. Normally, he hated when anyone made a fuss over him, but tonight he was grateful for the distraction.

The accordion and piano played a ballad from Kentucky, then began rowdier tunes. Forming a line on stage, the dancing girls pulled up their skirts and kicked up their legs. He'd never seen this dance before. Apparently, neither had the other men, for the place got suddenly boisterous.

Even Jenny seemed to take it with a smile. Across the saloon, seated at a table covered with a checkered cloth, Olivia and Travis were talking softly to each other. Luke wondered what they were so serious about. They nodded and glanced in Jenny's direction, then rose and joined them at the bar. Luke saw to it they were seated and comfortable, Olivia next to Jenny.

One of the Texan drovers tossed his hat in the air. "Give us a limerick, Franklin!"

"Oh, no," groaned Luke. "Not Franklin."

Mona was passing by, and Jenny leaned across to ask her, "What's a limerick?"

"It's a party game," Mona answered, arranging the empty glasses on her cork tray. "It's popular in London. Franklin taught us how to play, didn't he, Luke?"

Luke grimaced. He knew it was Franklin's ploy

to somehow get to Jenny. Luke had seen him eyeing her ever since she walked in. Wait a second. Why did Luke always get the urge to prove himself to Jenny when Franklin was around? She was free to court anyone she pleased.

Mona wiped her hands on her apron. "It's a poetry game. Be warned, though. They start out tame, but as the drinkin' goes on, the verses get bawdier. Better, in my opinion."

Lola hollered from the stage, bracing her hand on her hips. "I've got one for you first, Luke. The girls and I made it up for your birthday."

Luke waved in friendly response. Lola was honest and straightforward. Everything that came from *her* came from her heart, unlike Franklin.

"If you've come for a drink, and it's laughter
And good friends and cheer you're after,
The best place in town
Is Luke's—hands down,
For singin', and women, and all that comes after."

Luke grinned. The crowd cheered. "And will you come up to Limerick?" They chanted the line they always did, then drank. "You said it, Lola!"

Franklin stood up and patted his parted red hair. He undid a button on his well-fitting wool suit, peered in their direction and smiled. Luke groaned. There were several women in the crowd tonight, some of them married, but all of them gazing warmly at the dentist. The respectable woman seated next to him stared up longingly at his clear, sharp features as his baritone voice filled the air. Franklin's eyes twinkled as he addressed Jenny and Olivia.

"There once was town called Cheyenne
And there, in the eye of every man,
They were honored to find
Two women of such beauty and kind,
They glistened like jewels in the land."

The crowd chanted their line. "And will you come up to Limerick?"

Franklin swept his hat in the air and winked at Jenny.

Luke winced. What the hell was the man doing, winking at the woman seated next to *him?*

Luke peered at her and she was beaming. He sank into his chair. Was she attracted to Franklin? The possibility burned a hole in his gut—another sentiment he was unused to feeling.

"Oh, how sweet," said Olivia, clasping her hands to her face. "Franklin called us jewels. He's such a gentleman. So dashing in his suit. No wonder the women flock to him."

"And the words. Such grace. They roll off the tongue," added Jenny. "A man who appreciates poetry. Of course, he is a well-educated dentist."

Luke scowled. Poetry? Her obvious pleasure disarmed him. He glanced at an equally unamused Travis, and the both of them rolled their eyes.

During the continued cheering, Franklin wove his way toward them. There was nothing Luke could do to stop the man. Luke stood up and wiped his palms on his denim pants, towering above Franklin and the rest of them. Why did he feel so inadequate around the dentist?

He sighed. Because anything he might offer a woman like Jenny, Franklin could offer twofold. A better home. A *normal* home. A better place in society. All the children she might want. Friends and things she was accustomed to. And Luke was darn sure Franklin would give her all the money she wanted, and not make her *earn* it.

As Luke stood there like a useless knot on a log, Franklin bent toward Jenny's ear and whispered something. Smiling up in response, Jenny placed her hand in the dentist's to rise.

Luke's confidence evaporated. He couldn't stomach watching the rest. He needed air. Grabbing his hat from the counter and his duster at the door, he strode out of the saloon.

Nodding to the men guarding the doors, he hit the boardwalk, weaving past the strolling couples. The cool evening air felt good on his damp skin. A block away, he finally stopped and leaned over the railing.

Horses and carts moved down the street. Light from the lampposts flickered over them. The mercantile windows were dark, but a few taverns and restaurants down the way were open.

Luke took a deep breath of dusty air. What had happened to him back there?

What was Jenny Eriksen doing to him? Why did he want her so badly? Because he couldn't have her?

Quick footsteps raced toward him. Startled, he swung his head up.

Jenny stood there under the lamplight—slender, breathless and beautiful. A soft dew moistened her brow. Her hair tumbled around her satin shoulders.

He leaned his massive body back against the rail, grateful for the support. He was too surprised to do more than nod. Why had she followed him?

She opened her lips, then pressed them closed. Shadows warmed the curves of her heart-shaped face and the silhouette of her bare throat and shoulders. She rubbed her arms in the chill. "You know, it's very rude to just get up and leave."

"I thought Franklin had your attention."

"Well," she said, catching her breath, "he doesn't."

His heart skipped at her words.

"I wanted to say happy birthday before I went up to bed."

"Did you?" He eyed the heightened color of her lips. "Thanks." The thought of her in bed... What would that be like? His gaze riveted on her face, then slowly moved over her body.

Lying naked alongside him, or maybe on top? He shuddered at the thought. Hmm...he'd love to please her. He'd love to show her how he felt about her.

Her heightened color subsided. When she rubbed her arms again, he removed his coat and pressed it around her shoulders. "Here, take this."

She tugged the corners close and he smiled at the baggy fit.

Their eyes met. "You always wind up alone," she said gently.

"That's how I like it."

"Oh," she said humbly, stepping back, "would you prefer I left—"

"No," he responded. He ached to reach out and

touch her, but instead, slid his hands into his pockets.

When she leaned over the railing beside him, he inhaled her musky, womanly scent. How could he resist her?

"You do everything alone," she whispered. "Even with Adam, you're trying to tackle it by yourself."

He didn't answer.

Crickets chirped. The night became still. Then a breeze picked up and lifted strands of her hair. She mesmerized him. "Do you ever accept help from your friends, just because they'd like to give it?"

"I try not to."

"Why?"

"It's simpler that way."

"Is simpler always better?" Her voice caught. Her eyes glistened and her mouth beckoned.

"Not always." Unable to stop himself, he reached up with one hand and untangled her hair. He felt her tremble at his touch. His fingers grazed the soft spot at the back of her neck, and at the contact, fire raced along his skin. His voice was raw and husky. "It would be simpler to walk away from you right now."

He heard her breath hitch. Looking down into her big, deep eyes, he felt like he was gazing into the midnight sky. Like he was dreaming a runaway dream. She was temptation.

He leaned in close and kissed her.

It was a full, sensual kiss on the mouth. First a tantalizing persuasion, then a mutual, deepening need. He slipped his arms around her waist and tugged her body to his. His coat shielded them. She belonged here. Like she was made just for him. Her warmth melded into his until he didn't know where his body ended and hers began.

She responded with a hunger that drove him wild.

His lips searched lower and deeper, tugging at her earlobe, at the hollow curves of her throat and her bare lush shoulders. There wasn't a spot on her he didn't yearn to kiss. He cupped a supple breast, then traced his lips down her throat, over her blouse, over the cloth covering her nipple. He kissed there until he felt the round swell and harden. She quivered beneath his touch. Oh, she felt good.

Heat seeped through his muscles, through his legs and through his groin. His limbs felt heavy. He knew he was defenseless. He couldn't get enough of her, her skin, her mouth, her taste, her scent. If this continued—

They tore apart. She brought a trembling hand to her mouth. He could only stare, trying to regain his composure, calm the beating of his heart and the pounding of his blood.

With a tender moan, Jenny drew herself together and disappeared into the night.

Luke tried to work off his frustration by walking. His boots pounded the dusty, deserted street. For the last hour, it hadn't helped. He still felt restless. Under the lamplight, by the guns and ammunition depot, he kicked at a pebble. It ricocheted off the boardwalk, hit the water trough with a ping.

Alone again. Just like he liked it. He scoffed at his own words.

Voices carried from a nearby tavern and shadows moved at the lighted windows.

The chill air seeped through his shirt.

Could he ever have Jenny? Did he have a hope in hell?

She'd responded to him tonight. He'd felt the ache in her, too. She wouldn't have kissed him back like that if she didn't feel something powerful.

But did he have any right to court her? How could Luke interfere in her life more than he had already? It wouldn't be fair to her, and his pride stood in the way.

With a sigh of frustration, Luke swore and rubbed a hand over his raspy jaw. And what about Adam? How could he commit to Adam for all the years that lay ahead of them?

He snorted in disbelief at his foolish dreams. How could he possibly imagine...

He heard a tapping sound behind him. He flinched, but before he could turn around, someone shoved his shoulder and drove a steel fist into his back.

Luke doubled over, the wind knocked out of him. "Uhhh."

Pain exploded. Panic seized him. A fist hammered on his neck. He stumbled to the ground.

His gun—the derringer tucked in his boot. His left hand was closest. He grabbed for it. The stranger's heavy foot came down ruthlessly, again and again, crunching Luke's fingers. Broken.

"Uhhh..." Warm liquid seeped into his mouth. Slipping toward oblivion, he tasted blood.

"Message from Daniel," said a raspy voice. In his unconscious haze, Luke heard the words echo in his ears. "Stay away from the girl. Oh, and," the man growled as he swung his fist at Luke's jaw, "happy goddamn birthday."

"Has anyone seen Luke?" Jenny asked for the tenth time, pacing the saloon floor.

The bartenders shook their heads one by one. It was almost midnight. Olivia had convinced her to stay and enjoy the music a little longer, and Jenny had spent the last two hours by her side. Half the crowd had left—the ones who had to rise early for chores, or open their stores in the morning.

Where was Luke? Didn't he want to face her?

Jenny hadn't seen him since...since the kiss outside, and she wanted to return his duster. She fidgeted restlessly. What she really wanted was to tell him she couldn't see him anymore.

Even now, her mouth felt bruised from his kisses. She'd never reacted to a man like she had in Luke's arms, and her intensity confused her. She was stuck at a crossroads, not knowing which direction to take. Should she follow the fearsome path of letting this continue with Luke, facing a future she didn't know, or go back to Denver, to a life she no longer wanted to be a part of?

Jenny plopped down beside Olivia and the group playing twenty-one, and strummed her fingers nervously on the arm of the Windsor chair. Potato pudding and fried apples scented the air.

"I'll stick."

"I'll fold."

"I'll raise ya."

Olivia fanned out her cards. She adjusted the yellow sleeve of her leg-of-mutton blouse and shot a warm smile at Jenny. "You know, I told him," she whispered.

"Told who what?"

"I told Travis." Olivia lowered her lashes and watched Travis at the bar, rolling out the empty kegs from behind the counter. "I told him the truth about me not being from New Orleans."

A smile rushed to Jenny's lips, her own concerns temporarily forgotten. "What did he say?"

Olivia's face creased with laughter. "He said he doesn't care. Isn't that sweet?"

"Oh, it is."

"He said he was only talking about New Orleans because he thought he could impress *me,* knowing I was from there."

Jenny basked in her friend's good news.

"And then he said," Olivia lowered her voice to a whisper, "he'd like to visit me in Denver. He says he visits for saloon business at times. I don't really believe that—but I'm so delighted."

"Oh, Olivia, Travis seems like a good man." Genuine warmth filled Jenny as she shared the private moment.

Olivia was lucky. Travis would visit her in Denver.

That's what men did when they cared deeply for a woman. They committed themselves. Jenny sighed. Luke hadn't even mentioned the possibility of visiting *her.*

"Travis," Jenny called as he walked by with a keg, "have you seen Luke?"

"No, not for a while." He placed the keg by the kitchen door and came back. He frowned and stroked his mustache. "What's the matter? Why are you worried?"

"A nagging feeling. And because I know Harley's lurking around..."

"When's the last time you saw him?"

"Just after Franklin recited his limerick."

Travis looked around the almost empty saloon. "Sometimes Luke goes out."

"Where does he go?"

When Travis avoided her question and her inquisitive stare, she got a sinking feeling in her stomach. He stepped over to Tom and two other guards. "Check Miss Penelope's house," Travis told them.

Jenny glanced away in embarrassment. A woman?

Luke might be with a woman?

Travis continued his orders. "He hasn't seen Miss Linda for months, but I saw him talking to her this evening, too. Go check her house, as well. He used to spend all his nights—" Travis looked in Jenny's direction, must have seen her startled expression, and cut his words short.

Humiliation flooded her. She was concerned about Luke, while he might be spending the night with another woman? How gullible could she be?

With a squeezing in her throat she didn't care to analyze, she rose from her chair. "Good night, everyone."

A door slammed and she jumped.

A commotion started in the kitchen, then loud voices carried down the hallway. The alley door slammed. A heavy thump sounded on the floorboards.

"Get the doctor!" Beuford shouted from the kitchen.

The terror in his voice cut the air. "Someone run for the doctor!"

In the quiet midnight hours, they huddled around Luke in the saloon's kitchen. Adam had woken up briefly, Jenny had resettled him, and by the time the old doctor came in, she was standing with the others, horrified by the sight of Luke.

The left side of his face was a bloody mess. His left hand was mangled, the fingers twisted in an unnatural position.

"He might look awful, but he'll be fine," said the doctor, squinting through his spectacles. "He's got three broken fingers, a chipped back tooth and one hell of long cut on his face. But twelve stitches should do it."

Jenny closed her eyes as the doctor knotted a suture. She felt the comforting pressure of Olivia's hand on her shoulder.

"I've seen him a lot worse," the doctor grumbled. His bushy gray sideburns moved up and down as he spoke.

Luke moaned, in obvious agony.

The doctor swore. "I wish you'd let me give you something for pain, dammit. I can't work like this."

Jenny closed her eyes again. Luke had allowed himself only two shots of whiskey before the stitching, demanding he wanted to keep his mind clear.

Travis knelt beside him as the doctor tied the final knot. "Who did this to you, Luke?"

Luke moaned again as the doctor mopped his cheek with a cleansing solution. The older man finished and Luke sat up. His white shirt was stiff with dried blood and dirt, and half his hair was matted. When he looked up at Jenny, her stomach knotted in distress. Oh, God, he looked so sore.

His eyes never wavered as he stated, "It was Harley."

Jenny gasped. The group grew still.

"Are you sure?" Travis asked.

Luke tried to open his mouth to answer, then winced at the movement. He groaned and nodded.

"Son of a bitch," Travis muttered.

As if disturbed by a new thought, Luke bolted up from his seat. "Where's Adam?"

"He's all right," replied Travis. "Safe and asleep."

Calmed by the words, Luke sank back. "Harley got me in the alley behind the gun depot." He talked slowly, his speech slurred from the swelling of his face.

Jenny dug her fingers into her skirt. "You were lying in the alley for all these hours? Unconscious?"

"Yeah."

She cringed and lowered her lashes. "And here I thought…" Her stomach felt like a hard ball. She pressed a hand to her waist, hoping to relieve her tension. "Why would Harley do this to you?"

"It's obvious, isn't it?" Luke took a deep breath and waited for his broken hand to stop shaking. The doctor began splinting fingers. "Daniel's ticked off you didn't go back to him on the train."

Jenny rubbed her temples, then dropped her face into her hands. "I never thought it would come to this. What are we going to do?"

"First, I have to ask—do you want to go back to Denver?"

She fidgeted and didn't reply.

"Or," he said, gulping, "do you want to stay with me until this is settled?"

She quivered at his stare. There was no doubt in her mind. "I'd rather stay with you."

He swallowed and looked to Olivia for her own answer.

"Me, too," she said, glancing at Travis.

"Okay, then we're leaving town. After what Harley did to me, I don't want to leave you women and Adam in jeopardy. Pack your bags. Travis, get ahold of Winslowe. There's a favor I need to ask him." Luke stopped for a breath. They waited for him to recover.

He gritted his teeth, trying to overcome the pain. "Beuford, wake up the judge and ask him for those papers we've been working on. I'll tell you what to do with them. Tom, go to the jailhouse and tell the sheriff to swing by here as soon as he can. I want him to see what Harley did."

The doctor prodded Luke's hand and he recoiled. "Watch out there, that stings!"

Jenny winced and watched from beneath half-closed lids, wishing there was something she could do to relieve Luke's suffering. How could she ever have gotten involved with a man like Daniel?

She pulled herself together. "Where are we going?"

Luke swung his tender gaze to her. She grew weak at the anguish she saw there.

"I'll tell you on the way," he murmured. "The fewer people who know, the better. Now, go pack your bags, and hurry."

Chapter Twelve

The cabin was bathed in moonlight. Built into a hillside, it overlooked shimmering grasslands. In the gully below, a river gushed past their horses and wagon. The pine-scented breeze wrapped around Jenny, and owls cooed from the trees.

It'd taken them three-quarters of an hour to reach it. The place belonged to Winslowe, Luke had told her, although Winslowe never used it much since his wife's passing.

Tumbleweeds rolled past Jenny's feet as she dismounted. She pulled her shawl tighter. Concern for Luke welled in her throat, although he'd finally accepted morphine and his pain had eased.

Jenny glanced at the others. Travis and Olivia stood nearby. Luke was seated in the wagon, the moonlight glimmering on his handsome features and bandaged cheek. Behind him, Adam slept on a makeshift bed of straw and blankets. Luke's four guards surrounded them.

Who was he expecting to fight? A battalion of men?

It shook her to her core to know how brutal Daniel had been to Luke. Were she and Adam in equal danger?

They'd soon find out. Luke had sent two sets of papers to Daniel by stagecoach. Daniel's response, if he used the quickest method, would come by train, in four to five days. Another waiting game.

Which set of papers would Daniel choose to sign?

The set that released the boy from Daniel's custody, so the child could be adopted, or the set that claimed Daniel wasn't Adam's father at all? At this point, Luke had told her, he didn't rightly care which route Daniel chose, as long as he left the boy alone.

Of her own decision, Jenny had written a note, too, one that said she wouldn't discuss her own situation with Daniel until Adam's future was settled. She knew she'd never go back to him, but she was not about to tell him at this crucial moment.

Would her note appease him? Or would it anger him more?

The horses neighed. Luke stumbled off the wagon, and Travis reached out to steady his friend. Exhausted and in pain, Luke could barely keep his eyes open, but Jenny marveled at his stamina. Most men would have collapsed. She thanked heaven he was alive at all. She blinked away her hot, stinging tears.

She cared a great deal for the tough man protecting her. How many fights had he been in, and how many times had he been the last man standing? Would this be one of those times?

Every time she looked at Luke, her breathing grew uneven. Sometimes, searching his warm seductive eyes, she believed the moon and stars were possible between them. Other times, she wondered if he cared for her only as someone he had to guard, a means to an end for Adam's happiness.

Why wouldn't Luke let her into his thoughts and into his heart? Why wouldn't he lower the stone wall he'd built around himself? Always, always, he shouldered things alone.

Yes, she cared deeply for him. And for the first time since she'd met him, she admitted something else. She feared she was falling in love with him.

Her heart tripped with the realization. What she felt for Luke went beyond anything she'd felt for any man. She ached to be beside him. She ached to talk to him, to touch him, to hold him, to soothe away his worry.

But it was too fast and too soon. Wasn't it? Even if it felt like she'd known him a lifetime.

She clasped her hands. The most wrenching, painful question remained: what did Luke McLintock feel for her?

"Anyone up for a stroll by the river?" Luke asked Jenny and Adam, two days later.

Seated on the grass under a willow tree, Jenny cupped a palm over her eyes to shield them from the afternoon sun, and gazed up at Luke, hovering above her. His face was slightly swollen, he had one bruised eye and bandages covered his cheek. It still hurt when he smiled, he said.

He'd removed his shirt due to the warm chinook winds, and she was doing everything she could to avoid looking at his sultry, sinuous body. A sheen of perspiration glistened over his skin, highlighting the muscles of his arms and darkly matted chest.

With his shirt in his hand, she was reminded of another time she'd seen him this way—that first night in his hotel room. Unabashedly naked and boldly staring at her.

Those same eyes twinkled now, and Jenny hastily glanced around the cabin, seeking protection. Everyone else had left, and she was alone with Adam and Luke for the first time since they'd arrived. How had that happened? She'd been so careful to avoid it. "I'll see if Olivia—"

"Olivia and Travis already tore off around the riverbend." His slow grin made her flush. "Seems they can't get enough of one another." His brows lowered and he searched her eyes.

Like *she* couldn't get enough of *him?*

Was it obvious when she gazed at him? Suddenly self-conscious, Jenny tried to rise off the grass. Luke held out his hand. She swallowed and took it. A tingle of excitement warmed her flesh.

Thankfully, Adam was here to prevent whatever might have happened if they'd been alone. And thankfully, Luke had found a weathered pigskin ball behind the cabin and began kicking it back and forth with the boy as they walked.

How much punishment could one woman take? Standing this close to the man she loved, unable to step forward and touch him. She'd already gone through it once earlier, when Luke had shown Adam how to stack the firewood he'd chopped. All those bronzed muscles, bending and stretching and flexing, were enough to drive a woman insane.

Watching Luke with Adam, she realized he had come a long way with the boy since she'd first met them. Adam held Luke's attention as if…as if the boy were his own son.

What would it be like to share a son with Luke? To carry his child? To be his wife?

Now she was being absurd. Luke wasn't interested in children or marriage. He never pretended to be.

Gazing out at the horizon, Jenny thought of how much she, too, had changed since she'd met Luke. Had it only been a week? Was it possible to fall in love in a week?

The intensity of her emotions overwhelmed her. No, she told herself with dismay, it wasn't. And she should squelch those thoughts before she got carried away.

But she did admit she'd changed since being here. She looked toward the old corral, where the horses grazed. Even in horseback riding, she'd improved. She and Olivia had ridden every morning, and Jenny was starting to feel at ease with the animals. She felt at ease with the saloon, too, and the people around her there. She'd misjudged them all.

Most of all, being with Luke, she felt more at ease with herself, more comfortable in her own skin than she had in Denver, or Boston. Why was that? Why did he evoke that in her? And when he gazed at her, Lord, his eyes said so much. The one thing she'd always wanted most from a man was the respect she saw in Luke's eyes.

She wasn't in love, though, she chided herself. She wasn't.

The river gurgled. Luke stopped, raised a muscular arm and pointed in the water. "Hey, Adam, you ever been fishing?"

"No," said the boy, nuzzling close to Luke's long thigh. Adam's overalls were covered with stains. How on earth did he get so dirty so fast? She would wash his clothes again tonight, and set out his others tomorrow.

"How about it?"

When Adam gleefully nodded, Luke strode back to the cabin and returned with fishing wire. He cut three branches off a tree, strung the wires and fastened on hooks. Adam raced to a large stone, rolled it over and grabbed at the dew worms exposed.

With an amused giggle, Jenny removed her stockings, hiked up her skirts and dangled her feet over the mossy, cool bank. When she hooked a fish, she whooped in delight. Luke leaned in close and showed her how to remove it. Was he trying to keep his eyes off her wet ankles and legs, or was she imagining things?

All in all, she thought wistfully, the last three days at the cabin had been the most pleasurable ones she'd ever spent with any man. She pushed the thought away, but it came back when she was helping to fry the trout for supper that evening.

After coffee, Olivia and Travis took Adam outside, and Beuford and Tom, with the two other guards, left to exercise the horses. Jenny had promised to help Luke remove his facial bandage, but now that they were alone, her nerves fluttered.

"How're you feeling?" Jenny asked him. They were in a small bedroom off the main room. She'd made sure the door was left open. Light from the sunset filtered through the small window, setting everything aglow.

Luke couldn't maneuver well with the use of only

one hand, and she didn't want his splintered hand to get wet. He stretched out on the bed, straightening his shoulders on the pillow. He'd already washed up some. He'd managed to put on his denim pants, but not his shirt. "Like I got run over in a stampede."

"You're doing too much. You should slow down."

"Hmm." When one side of his mouth curved, Jenny knew he'd be all right. The swelling had subsided enough that he could smile. Her eyes strayed to his muscled chest, and that hum in her pulse began again. She hastily glanced back at her washcloth.

Sliding to the bedside, she dipped the cloth in the basin of cool water, wrung it out, then ran it along his forehead, leaving damp strands of black hair at his temples. The strong, bronzed cheekbones grew taut. She drew a deep breath to brace herself and gently removed the gauze bandage.

Luke closed his eyes, but didn't flinch. She fought an almost uncontrollable urge to kiss his eyelids, place her hands along his jaw and press her mouth to his.

Swallowing hard, she concentrated on her work and peered at his cut. "It looks good. The stitches are closed. It's still swollen, but not as much. The doctor said the redness will go away if we apply this ointment."

"Hmm." The low sound vibrated at the back of his throat, turning her insides to jelly.

She carried on, her stomach queasy every time her thigh brushed his. She couldn't escape the dewy scent of his skin. Or the sight of his broad, matted chest, the muscular biceps and arms, which tapered to beautiful, large hands.

Her eyes trailed lower, to the scars crisscrossing his flat stomach. She yearned to press her lips to them, to ease the hurt. One of the scars snaked lower, below his belt, below the waist of his pants, and she wondered where it ended. The room seemed suddenly hot. She blew out a breath of moist air.

His warm charcoal eyes flickered open and caught hers. His gaze was like a soft caress. She felt herself flush with heat. With a gentle, playful hand, he reached up and tugged at the washcloth, so they were both holding it, his fingers brushing hers.

Amusement curved her lips. She tried to tug the cloth back, but he wouldn't release it. She lowered her soft voice. "If you don't let go, how can I help you?" When she yanked again, his heated hand clasped over hers. Her eyes flew up at the contact.

"Maybe I like your hand just where it is."

It was now resting on his hard stomach. Trembling, she slid it free and rubbed her palm against her skirt, trying to erase the undeniable effect of his touch.

After a hushed moment, he cleared his throat. "I'm sorry about having to bring you to the cabin. What's this situation with Daniel doing to you?"

She turned and dipped the washcloth into the basin again. "I'll be fine. It's you I'm concerned about. And Adam."

"Yeah," he murmured, "you would be concerned about everyone but yourself. But what kind of life are you going to go back to in Denver?"

She shrugged, floundering inside, but trying to appear casual.

"How's your broken engagement going to affect you? What will your friends say, and your father? And what about the store Daniel promised you?"

"It doesn't matter."

He trailed his fingers along her arm. Heavens have mercy, he could seduce her with a simple touch. "It matters to me."

She gulped. "It's not important, compared to everything else. I'm sorry you got beaten on account of me."

"You didn't do that. That's Daniel's doing."

Regret choked her voice. "How could I get mixed up with a man like him?"

"Because Daniel used to be a good man once."

Lips parted, she could only stare at Luke. After all Daniel had done to him, he still found it in his heart to say a kind thing.

Luke's inquisitive eyes dropped to her lips. Reaching out, he stroked her jawline. Pleasure rippled through her. "I don't think you realize how pretty you are. I think it's got something to do with that crooked smile," he whispered. "Show me again."

She laughed gently, unable to resist his charm, unable to pull away.

And then, before she could resist, his fingers brushed her throat, his other arm slipped behind her back and he pulled her to the bed on top of him— six foot four inches of lean, muscular male.

Her breath became trapped as she met his misty gaze.

He moved his head until his mouth was against her ear, tugging on her earlobe, making her moan and shudder with primal excitement.

"I can't stay away from you," he said with a groan.

His words sent her spirits soaring. With a rhythmic pulse hammering at his temples, he flipped her over so she was lying beneath him. His warm breath caressed her throat, then his lips found hers. She exploded with desire and kissed him back with all the built-up tension within her. It came pouring out of her, surprising her with its intensity. She followed his lead. Their tongues touched, gentle, then passionate. Wildly exciting. Heat throbbed in her limbs, down her breasts and between her legs.

When he unbuttoned her blouse and slipped his hand inside, then under her soft chemise, she arched to meet him.

His hand stroked and kneaded her bare breast, tugging at her nipple until she felt like molten liquid in his arms. When his hot mouth pressed against her flesh, she gasped at the sensation.

He sucked again and again, his velvety tongue tracing little circles around her nipple. When his mouth moved to her other breast, she knotted her fingers in his hair.

More. She wanted more of him. She wanted everything he could give.

She'd never lost control like this, but he was making love to her with every inch of his body, every touch of his tongue.

Her skirts had somehow hiked up her thighs. She planted her boots on the bed, then daringly raised her legs and wrapped them around his waist. He moaned.

He was hard. Knowing she'd done that to him filled her with pleasure.

She responded with sensual abandon. She wanted him. How could he affect her so? Where would this lead them?

She didn't care, didn't think.

When his hand dipped to her bare thigh and trailed up to forbidden places, she let him.

He suddenly bolted upright, sliding from her grasp. His boots hit the plank floor. Her eyes widened as if a bucket of ice water had been dumped on her head. Why had he pushed her away?

"I think you'd better get dressed. This is not..." He gulped. "I don't want to..."

He didn't want to what? Make love to her?

She looked toward the door. No one was there. But they'd be back soon. She tried to calm her bounding pulse.

Color flushed Luke's face. He was breathing hard. He ran a hand through his ruffled hair, gazed down at her parted blouse and exposed breasts, and turned away from her.

His cold shoulder hurt Jenny more than words could express. She didn't give herself lightly to any man! What a blunder she'd made. She thought he cared for her!

Heaving with emotion, trying to catch her breath, she rose and straightened her clothing. Unable to look at him, she turned and buttoned her blouse.

"It's getting late," she said with a trembling voice.

"Yes, it is."

"The others will be coming back soon."

His voice hardened. "Yes, they will."

"I should go."

With a ragged catch to his breath, he responded, "Yes, you should."

He didn't stop her. And he didn't say one word about what had just happened between them.

She tried not to run out of the room, even though she wanted to. Oh, how amused he must be, thinking of how she'd returned his kisses! With a shiver of remorse, she dashed out of the room and raced into her own.

Rage clawed at Daniel Kincaid's gut. He shoved back his chair and swung his booted feet onto his desk. He ignored the man lurking in the doorway, who was waiting for a response to the papers and ring he'd brought. Outside the house, the windows and streets of Denver were quiet and dark. Daniel puffed on his cigar, trying to temper his hostility.

Staring at his clenched fist, he turned Jenny's engagement ring around on his baby finger, watching how the large diamond glistened in the blazing light of the fireplace. The ring was a fine piece of jewelry, bought for a fine woman. And she'd just spat in his face.

He'd been waiting for days to get wind of what was happening in Cheyenne, and he finally had an answer.

Son of a bitch.

He jerked forward and banged his fist on the desk. The diamond punctured his skin, and he hurled the ring across the room. He wouldn't take this treatment from anyone.

His breath burned his throat. Harley, still in Cheyenne, had sent back word he'd seen McLintock *kiss-*

ing her? Just outside the saloon? And on her first night there, McLintock had taken her to his *room?*

Daniel muttered a curse. What kind of a tramp was she? And here he was, suppressing his own sexual urges with all sorts of beautiful, inviting women, vowing to be faithful. Hah! This is what Jenny did to him? Damn her!

She made him look like a fool! Pretending she was an innocent young virgin…

And that smooth son of a bitch, McLintock. He always had been jealous of what Daniel owned.

Well, Daniel hadn't suffered through years of hard work and kissing ass at the railroad just to have her screw it up. Trying to fit in with folks like Jenny and her father. Always believing *he* was the one who came from less, who had to work harder to escape his inferior background.

Hellfire! Daniel snarled and bit into his cigar. Who would have thought the quiet little kitten would be so hard to tame?

His features hardened. Doing so would be his pleasure.

Oh, yeah, he'd have her back and he'd keep her down. And McLintock would pay tenfold for what he'd started. Daniel wasn't going to waste his precious time worrying about any orphaned kid. This kid wasn't his. Daniel had slept with the Mexican woman only once. What were the chances? How many other men had slept with her, even though she'd denied it?

The only thing the kid was to Daniel was a means to get Jenny back. He crumpled up her note and hurled it into the fire, groaning with satisfaction as the edges caught and blazed.

Daniel ground his teeth. Picking up a quill pen, he replied to the messages. Then he turned to the dark shadow in the doorway. "Tell Harley to deliver these and to keep his eyes on the paper trail. They'll lead him to McLintock. Tell Harley not to touch the woman." Daniel knew Jenny had to come back to him of her own free will, if he were to salvage the situation with her father. With a few diplomatic tactics, he'd have her back. Especially with McLintock out of the way.

"Tell Harley to corner that son of a bitch, McLintock. And then," Daniel growled with contempt, "tell him to finish the bloody job."

Chapter Thirteen

It was awful trying to keep his distance.

Luke studied Jenny as she maneuvered between the others around the outdoor fire, stacking the lunch plates. Locks of her rich, honey-colored hair brushed her supple breasts, and her hips swayed seductively as she walked. When he thought of how she'd looked in his arms yesterday, with her blouse unbuttoned, the tips of her satiny breasts exposed, he grew hot all over again.

He shouldn't have taken advantage of her like that. He knew she was a virgin, for cripes sake, and he had no right to lead her on, to the point where she trusted him.

She shouldn't trust him. Ever.

He was the one who'd brought her here and interfered in her life. And what was he supposed to give her in return for her sweet affection?

She hadn't talked to him since last night, and he didn't blame her. The situation between them was complicated and difficult. And waiting for word from Daniel was even tougher. Today was day four. Friday. The first day the legal papers Luke had sent might have a chance of returning. Everyone was jumping at the slightest noise in the bushes, scouring the horizon for signs of riders. For word of any kind.

Luke ran a hand through his damp hair. He hated arguing with Jenny. If he judged her correctly, he knew what'd get her speaking again. Adam would. She could never remain silent when Luke talked about the little boy. Another thing Luke admired about her—her devotion to the child.

Luke eased himself closer. Jenny passed the plates to Adam, who disappeared toward the river to wash them with Olivia. His men rose and left for their lookout points.

Luke sat on the log beside her. The smell of junipers wafted through the balmy air. "I've come to a decision about Adam."

Just as he expected, Jenny turned her startled face up to his. She was so slender compared to him. Her femininity made him feel more masculine, strong and virile. Her sharp blue eyes sparkled with curiosity and the stiffness in her shoulders eased. "What is it?"

"I've given it a lot of thought. I thought about what you said, watching him that day with the kite." Luke hiked a booted foot across his leg. "How happy he is in town, at the saloon. Much happier than he was alone at Daisy and Nathaniel's ranch."

Her pink mouth softened. "Go on." She slid her fingers along her faded skirt. "I'd...I'd like to hear your thoughts. I have high hopes for Adam."

Luke craved the touch of her soft skin. "I know you do." His voice lowered. "At first, I thought what Adam needed most was a regular home. Like a ranch, with two parents and a big yard for him to play in. Not that I wouldn't like to give him that, but I see how happy he is with the simpler things. Being at the saloon, surrounded by people he knows, the memory of his mother, and the little friends he grew up with down the street.''

She hugged her knees.

"He likes the saloon," Luke said with an easy smile. Then, pausing for a moment, he swallowed and glanced down at his boots. "I like him, and he likes me.''

Why did those words come with such difficulty? It was true. And he felt more than "like," Luke silently admitted. With a long sigh of deep contentment, Luke knew he loved Adam.

Jenny reached out and touched Luke's hand. His pulse surged at her tender brush. "Adam adores you. He mimics everything you do, right down to the way you loop your belt buckle. He asks for scrambled eggs for breakfast, just like you, and tries to match the color of shirt you wear each day.''

Pride made Luke grin. "I see it, too.''

"He loves to hum that tune you do. That ballad about the Wild West, and horses and cowboys.''

Luke stared into her eyes. She'd noticed an awful lot. But then, she was a perceptive woman.

"I'm thinking of taking the chance with Adam,'' he said slowly, "to raise him as my own.''

Her eyes moistened. "Oh, Luke.''

"I want to see him grow up healthy and strong. I'd like to give him a home. I want to adopt Adam.''

She was silent for a long time. Her voice came out as a soft whisper. "That would be wonderful. You'll make a fine father.''

He filled with pride again. Her opinion meant more to him than anyone else's.

Why was that? Was there any hope for him and Jenny? Maybe when this was over, he'd dare to ask. But it was all coming so fast—his feelings and this decision about Adam, his awakening feelings for Jenny. He had to take his time and not rush into making a promise he wasn't able to keep. First, he'd see how it worked out with Adam. Then maybe he'd be ready for another step.... Until then, he had to keep his hands off Jenny.

"Have you told Adam yet?"

"Not yet. I'm waiting to see—"

She finished for him. "What Daniel does."

Luke nodded slowly. When it was settled, he'd discuss the adoption with Adam. Luke might even consider buying a property in town, a house maybe, or a small ranch just outside the limits, a place for him to raise his son. Luke smiled at the thought. His *son.*

Olivia came back from the river, with Adam skipping at her side. The boy never stopped moving, Luke noted tenderly. When Adam plopped into his lap, Luke ruffled the boy's hair. He swallowed nervously. Would Adam accept him as a father?

Travis hollered from the riverbank and came running. "Some whittlin' sticks for Adam." He joined the group, unfolded his pocketknife and handed it to the boy. Adam became absorbed in the craft, sitting by the crackling fire.

Olivia made her way to Jenny's side and sat down. Her brown muslin dress caught the sunshine. "To pass the time, Jenny, why don't you tell Luke the ideas you've been kicking around for the saloon?''

Jenny's brows dipped. Luke thought he saw her blush, but she turned away so quickly he couldn't be sure. ''Oh, no.'' She fiddled nervously with her sleeve.

Luke pulled out a pocketknife from his pants, opened it and picked up a chunk of wood. He began slicing, trying to sound casual. ''What ideas?''

''Oh,'' said Olivia, ''ideas for drawing a crowd into the place. Go on now, tell him, Jenny. And make sure you charge him. He can surely afford it.''

Amusement tugged at the corner of Luke's mouth. Jenny bit her pretty lip, then jumped to her feet. Before she could escape, he grabbed her hand. Her fingers were always warm, her touch always arousing. She pulled her hand from his.

''Tell me,'' he urged, ''I'd like to hear your ideas.''

Her earnest eyes held his for a moment, then, with a slight hesitation, she sat back down. ''I've noticed how busy it is in town on Saturdays.''

He nodded. ''Ranchers, farmers and miners work during the week. They come in on Saturdays to sell their goods at the market, and to buy supplies. Maybe catch up on some gossip.''

''And I've also noticed the saloon has a different feel to it during the day.''

''That's right,'' Olivia interjected. ''It's full of sunshine and the smell of soap.''

''And gleaming polished oak,'' Jenny added. She flushed with enthusiasm, totally capturing his attention. ''And the girls aren't dancing.'' Her forehead creased. "You really ought to get some entertainment that isn't quite so...burlesque."

"I'm tryin', but it's hard to come by. Lola and the girls are only here till the end of the month as it is, then they're booked for the winter in California. But what's all this talk got to do with more business?"

"Have you ever thought, in addition to drawing a crowd of men, you might try to draw a crowd of women?"

"Women?" Luke looked up from his wood.

With a soft gasp, Travis inclined his dark head in their direction and shook it. Luke knew Travis's mustache was hiding a stunned expression.

"That's right." Olivia glanced at Travis with a sharp look of irritation. "Women."

"Why would I want more women in my saloon?"

"Well, women draw men, don't they?" Jenny asked.

"True enough," Travis muttered. "True enough."

They certainly do, Luke thought. Just like she drew him.

"And you want more customers, don't you? And with women around, there'd be less violence, don't you think? Less fighting. More of a calming effect on the men."

Well, she did have a point. "Yeah...?"

"Getting women in for the evening, now that might take some doing. I think you should try to draw them in at lunchtime first."

"Lunchtime?"

"Why, Annie's Café is packed on Saturdays. Breakfast, lunch and dinner. There's always a lineup. At first I thought it was just the clam chowder, but Daisy told me no. I'm sure some of the women shopping would love to get off their feet and come in for a bite."

"That might be so. But convincing them to dine in a saloon is more difficult than getting them to a café."

"That's why you can't charge them."

His knife froze in midair. "Beg your pardon?"

"You can't charge them." She shook her head, her hair tumbling around her high collar and stiffly buttoned blouse. She was serious. "You can call it the Ladies' Luncheon. Free lunches on Saturday. But not their drinks. Charge them for drinks—coffee, tea, whatever they like."

"Are you sure you read your brothers' commerce books correctly? How are we supposed to stay in business if we don't charge them?"

Jenny laughed with excitement. "The women will bring in their husbands. You charge the men regular price for their meals. And the husbands are bound to order an ale or two. It'll catch on, and maybe the women will come in for lunch on other days, too, when it's not free."

Luke thought about it for a moment, not quite sure what to say to her. She'd obviously spent some time thinking up this plan, but it was *his* saloon. He glanced at Travis, who was rolling his eyes in disbelief at the very prospect. Luke frowned. "That's a mighty big risk. I've been in business a lot of years."

Jenny's smile faded. She looked away. He felt a twinge of guilt. Still, it was his saloon, and he wasn't sure....

"You're right," said Jenny. "I don't know why I thought... Let's forget about it."

He didn't want to forget about it. Her ideas were important—

"Rider comin'!" Beuford hollered from the crest of the hill. "Rider!"

Luke jumped in alarm. So did the others. They turned toward the grassy slopes, Luke stepping protectively in front of the women. "Ladies, get inside, please, until I see it's safe. You too, Adam."

"It's only Tom," Beuford screeched, waving his hat. "It's Tom, and he's alone."

Luke let the ladies stay where they were as Tom raced in on his black gelding. Panting, he slid to the ground, removed a large square envelope from his saddlebag and dumped it in Luke's hands.

Luke's heart began to race. The moment of truth. Daniel's reply.

"What's that?" Adam peered around Luke's leg, squinting in the sun. His nose was streaked with dirt and his lips stained with sugar.

Luke crouched down low and met Adam's inquisitive gaze. "Some papers from town I've got to look at. Why don't you go for a walk with Travis?"

Travis and Olivia left with Adam. Beuford, Tom and the three other men watched from a distance.

Jenny stepped closer to Luke as he opened the package.

Perspiration collected at his temples. His eyes raced down the page. Nothing. He flipped through the sheets, one by one, then the second set. "No signature," he muttered to Jenny. "Daniel didn't sign a thing."

"Nothing? He didn't sign either set?"

The tension stretched tighter. Luke shook his head. "No. But he sent a note."

Jenny stepped beside him as Luke unfolded the creamy linen paper. His chest felt like it would burst, half from anticipation, half from dread.

I'll sign what you want when you return Jenny Eriksen to me in Denver.

The coldhearted bastard.

Jenny took loud, deep breaths beside him.

Luke shook with anguish at the possibility of losing either Adam or Jenny. There was no way he would trade either one. Dammit, he wanted them both.

It had never been clearer than it was at this moment.

He wanted Adam *and* he wanted Jenny.

He couldn't bear to meet her eyes. She deserved better than this.

As he struggled for control, the words tore from his mouth. "*No deal.* Blackmail doesn't work with me."

"But Luke—"

"*No.* I won't even consider it." Fury gripped him, and until he calmed down and figured out what he had to do, he couldn't face her. He needed time to think. Alone. He stalked off to his horse.

Jenny couldn't let him make that sacrifice.

She watched Luke ride over the hills at full speed, the wind billowing his shirt, his head bent.

He wanted to adopt Adam. Her breath hitched when she thought of Luke's tender admission. She gloried in the knowledge that Adam would have such a fine father.

How could she risk that powerful bond of love by ignoring Daniel's demands?

She glanced down at the ground, to Daniel's crumpled note.

Oh, she didn't trust Daniel one bit. There was no telling what he was capable of, since he'd proved himself to be a coward. She'd stay as far away from him as possible.

But was there a way to get to him without risking herself?

There might be if her father were involved. With the railroad deals hanging over Daniel's head, her father had a colossal amount of influence over Daniel. More than anyone else. Certainly, she'd come to realize with a pang of remorse and shame, more influence than her.

There was a morning train leaving for Denver. If she took the adoption papers with her, to her father, she was certain he'd get Daniel to release Adam. If her father wasn't home, she'd wait for him without alerting Daniel that she was back.

Then, when Daniel signed the papers, he'd get his land deal. And she'd insist on her freedom.

Most importantly, Adam and Luke could be together.

There was no sense arguing with Luke, though; he wasn't about to let her go anywhere.

The notepaper trembled in her fingers. So how could she sneak out of camp and catch the train tomorrow without anyone stopping her?

The train whistle blasted and Jenny's heart lurched at the sound. As the steam locomotive rumbled out of the station, she stared out the smudged window. On the platform, people waved goodbye to friends and loved ones. No one waved to her.

She was finally leaving Cheyenne.

How long had she hoped for this day of escape from Luke McLintock? Now that it was here, she wished she weren't going.

Adjusting her bonnet, she sighed and glanced ahead, at the half-filled wooden benches of the railcar. Folks were chattering, some with crates of rabbits and roosters and ducks on their knees, and worn, scarred luggage pushed beneath their feet.

She'd made the right decision. Wrapping her sweaty fingers around her satchel's leather handle, she told herself again. *She had.*

Then why did her stomach feel so queasy? She pressed it and tried to calm her flutters. Would she ever see Luke again?

It didn't matter. It didn't matter to anyone except her.

Escaping the cabin hadn't been that difficult. Last night, she'd packed her satchel, and when the others were occupied with supper, she hid it behind the junipers over the first rise. At dawn, she had Beuford saddle her mare, as he had the four other mornings when she and Olivia had gone for their ride. Except this time, she'd told him, Olivia wasn't joining her, and she wouldn't go far. Poor Beuford. She hoped he wouldn't catch too much trouble from Luke for letting her slip away.

Two gray-haired, well-to-do women slid into the seats ahead of her. Jenny found herself amused by their conversation and happy to be distracted by their Boston accents. Their husbands, carrying crisp shiny baggage, slid in across the aisle. The women complained about the dust on their seats. Then they complained about the ticket prices. When the train rounded a bend and the sun streamed through the window, they complained about the heat.

"I'll have to write my sister back home," said the big-bosomed lady with the clustered diamond ear-bobs and smart red hat. "At how inferior and *dull* everything is here."

Her thin friend nodded. "The sister who married the surgeon?"

"No, the one who married the juggler in P.T. Barnum's Circus."

One of the gents leaned forward to the women. "You know, there's Indians out here," he said, then elbowed the man beside him, stifling a laugh. "A pretty head of hair like yours, I think they'd be mighty interested."

The big-bosomed woman snickered. "If they grab my scalp, they'll just get a handful of wig."

Her friend giggled and winked at her husband. "My Wilbur has a fine head of long gray hair. Maybe they'd be interested in his scalp."

The group laughed. "Sometimes they got train robbers, too," said the big-bosomed lady.

The thin lady sniffed. "Those are stories people make up."

"No, my sister told me. She showed me a newspaper article." The feathered red hat turned to the window. "Oh, my heavens, what in tarnation is that?"

"It's a man on horseback."

"Oh, my God, it's a train robber!"

Jenny spun to look. A large man on horseback. White shirt, black denims and black vest. A black bandana around his throat and black felt Stetson. No, it couldn't be.

Luke. Her pulse beat erratically. What was he doing here?

Luke was barreling across the golden wheat fields, giving it all he had.

Jenny sank back in the seat. He was coming to get her. Why didn't he stay out of it? Her plan was a good one.

The old folks panicked. The big-bosomed one yanked off her diamond ear-bobs and shoved them into the crevice of her blouse. "Someone get that ticket man! We need help! We're getting robbed!"

Wilbur sprang from his seat with something shiny in his hand. "Don't worry, I've got a gun!"

The crowd screamed.

Jenny gasped and sprang to her feet. "Don't shoot him! He's not a robber!"

"How do you know?" Wilbur pointed his derringer out the open window. His thick gray mane billowed in the wind.

"No, don't shoot! He's my friend! His name is Luke McLintock and he owns a saloon in Cheyenne. Doesn't anyone here recognize him?"

A lone man with a baritone voice spoke up, the Texan who often drank at the bar. "Yup, it's Luke."

Wilbur lowered his gun and Jenny sagged with relief.

Luke and his horse were almost at the railcar's door. "Don't anyone tell him I'm here. Please!" She crouched to the floor behind her bench, feeling dirt and grit beneath her fingertips.

Two seconds later, heavy boots hit the wooden floor. "Everyone remain calm," Luke boomed. "I'm looking for a woman."

"So am I," the baritone said, and the crowd laughed.

"Anyone seen a pretty blond lady, about so high?"

"In the back," they shouted with no hesitation. "She's over there."

Jenny groaned. So much for neighborly assistance.

The steady thud of his approaching footsteps echoed the pounding in her chest. She clamped her eyes shut, and when she opened them again, she was staring at two tan leather cowboy boots.

"Drop something?" Luke whispered with amusement, above her bonnet.

In a huff, she raised herself to her full height and confronted the exasperating man. "Lose someone?"

He looked flushed and overheated. Perspiration trickled down his dark temples. With a provocative twinkle in his eye, he replied, "Matter of fact, I did." He grabbed her wrist and pulled her down the aisle. "You're coming with me."

"*Again?*" She pried her hand free from his sweaty grasp. "Just like that, you're going to take me again?"

With a guttural moan, he stepped closer and peered down, inches from her face. "All right, this time I won't force you. I don't know what kind of scheme you've hatched in that pretty little head of yours, but I'm not letting you face him alone. We'll do it together." His voice softened. "Now, please, I'm asking you to jump with me."

She swallowed. "Jump?"

He fingered the brim of his hat. "Please."

She hesitated and looked out the door at the swirling field below.

"I'd go with him," the big-bosomed lady shouted amid the laughter.

"After you," Luke said to Jenny. With a challenging grin, he removed his hat and made a sweeping gesture.

Despite her apprehension, her heart squeezed with delight.

He'd come for her. Luke had come for her.

The train was rounding a curve and slowing down. Now was a good time to jump.

Jenny pitched her satchel first. It careened down the grassy bank and spilled open. With a final study of the moving ground, she took a deep breath and flung herself through the air.

Chapter Fourteen

"**Y**ou all right?" Luke asked.

Jenny looked fine to him. Matter of fact, how could a woman look so good, dressed in someone else's old blouse and skirt, covered with sweat and bits of grass?

Surrounded by wheat up to her luscious behind, Jenny stood up and beat dust from her skirt. Her lips tightened in response, and he smiled to himself, knowing she was fine. Hurt pride, maybe, but that was easier to mend than a broken bone.

In the field, Luke whistled to his horse, and it cantered toward them. The train careened around the curve and sped off, steam billowing from its engine.

He took three long strides and reached for his fallen hat. "What did you plan on doing in Denver? What exactly did you think you'd say to Daniel?"

"I wasn't planning on going to Daniel. I was going to go directly to my father." She stalked through the wheat, heading for her satchel, yards ahead. He followed, helping to gather her strewn clothing along the way.

"It's not your father's problem. It's my problem and I'll solve it." He handed her a thin white blouse.

She yanked it from him and shoved it into her satchel. "Why do you always have to do everything alone?"

"Don't get mad all over again."

"It's not all over again. It's a continuation!"

"Why? I saved your behind back there." He reached for one long black stocking, impaled on a shaft of wheat, blowing in the breeze. "If you went to Denver, God knows what Daniel might have done to you. You should be thanking me—"

"You should be the one thanking *me*." With an angry puff, she blew the hair from her eyes and tore the stocking out of his fingers before he'd barely touched the silky thing. "I saved *your* behind. The passengers had a gun trained on you."

"They did?"

"One of these days you're going to get your head blown off. Do you know you're severely unbalanced? Chasing a train like that?"

She picked up—what was it? A set of white drawers? His body tingled with interest as he watched her jam it into her bag. The lady could make anything look seductive. Even jamming. With the movement, her hair spilled from its clasp, her gentle hips rocked and her breasts swayed.

"Well, then—" he gulped "—I'm glad you saved me. Much obliged."

She tossed her head in that maddening, alluring way and glanced at his blood bay. "Now what are we going to do?"

He spotted a lacy rose chemise just behind her and stepped toward it. "We'll get on the horse and we'll return to town. Everyone else will be there by now.''

"You packed up the camp?"

He reached the chemise and picked it up. It was very soft and feminine. It didn't look worn, couldn't possibly be something Daisy would wear. Had Jenny bought it or made it? He envisioned her in it, her rosy nipples peeking through.

"I'll take that." Slightly flushed, she yanked it from his hold. "I said, did you pack up camp?"

Was she talking? "Yeah," he answered. A trickle of moisture dribbled down his spine. The sun was hot. And those warm chinook winds seemed warmer than usual. "I've had enough of hiding. I'm going to bring this into the open. The sheriff's involved. Especially since—"

"Since what?"

Luke slid the bandana from his throat and dabbed his wet brow. "While I was getting to town this morning, Harley took some shots at me. At least I think it was him. Tom was with me. While I tore south for your train, he went north to chase Harley."

Jenny's shapely body slumped onto the grass. As she lowered herself to the ground, the anger on her proud face faded.

He slid down next to her. His broken fingers hit the ground and he was unable to stifle his moan.

"What's wrong?" she asked with concern.

"On the way here, I think I rebusted my little finger." It began to throb again. Everything in him was throbbing, but for different reasons.

"Oh, Luke, let me see."

He groaned at her soft touch. "That's the one."

She put her light hand on his bruised shoulder and he groaned again.

"That hurts, too?"

"A little."

She whispered, "Well, you're just a mess, aren't you?"

Her breath felt warm at his throat. He turned and peered into her deep blue eyes and his pulse skittered. Must every look and touch from Jenny send him reeling, in full sexual alert?

"What about you? You sure you didn't get hurt from the jump?"

"My leg's a little sore, but it'll be fine."

He dipped toward her. His large muscular shoulder brushed her slender one. "Truce?" he murmured, captivated by her smooth skin and full pink lips.

Something seemed to awaken in her. Her eyes shimmered, staring at him. "Truce," she whispered.

Abruptly, she jumped up, went to the horse and returned with his canteen. "Drink some water," she urged, standing above him.

Water? What he wanted from her was more than water. And he'd never be able to quench that thirst. "After you," he offered. She sipped, then he drank. "The horse needs water, too. I rode it hard." He gazed out to the fields. "There's a creek half a mile back. We'll ride there and give the horse a chance to rest."

She agreed, and after he anchored her satchel to the horse, he pulled her up and eased her into the saddle.

As they rode, her womanly body stretched in front of him and contact was inevitable. The back of her hot, moist thighs slid against the muscular front of his own. It reminded him of another time. The first time he rode with her, where every graze of her flesh aroused him. Now, inches from her neck, he inhaled the clean, sweaty scent of her and tried not to dwell on her sensual curves.

With every little jostle of the horse, their bodies crushed together and she jolted forward, as if touched by lightning. Did he have that affect on her, or was his imagination running wild?

Thank God the ride was short. Luke hitched the horse under a brilliant gold cottonwood. While it drank the flowing water, Luke removed his duster from his saddlebag and laid it out in the shade of several quaking aspens.

Still silent, Jenny didn't meet his gaze.

She slid down to his coat, sitting with legs stretched before her. God, those shapely calves. Twining her fingers through her long, loose hair, she twirled it behind her neck and replaced the clasp. Luke wished she'd leave it down. He loved the way her straight hair tumbled down her supple shoulders.

He gulped and slid down beside her, gazing out toward the distant mountains. Cool mountain air reached them in the gentle breeze. The smell of moss and damp earth and dry leaves filled his nostrils.

"Taking the train back to Denver like that, you put yourself in a lot of danger."

She smoothed her hair with her slender hands, then flattened them in her lap. The buttons of her blouse strained from the pressure of her breasts, and he ached to release them. "I suppose."

He sucked in his breath sharply and, unable to

stop himself, reached out and cupped her shoulder. He felt her shudder beneath his touch. "You did that for me?"

The warmth of her soft flesh was intoxicating. His hand trailed to her hair clasp. He undid it, heard her soft moan and wrapped his fingers around the satiny strands.

She stilled but didn't move away. "I did it for Adam."

She wouldn't admit she'd done it for him, too. Lord, she was stubborn.

"Why did you come after me?" Her voice trembled, and its vibration strummed through his body.

His hand left her hair and moved down her spine, searching out the hollow curve. Her lips parted with a soft gasp.

Could he admit *his* true feelings? Or was he just as stubborn? "Because I couldn't believe what you did for me. Because when I woke up this morning and found out you'd disappeared, I was terrified I'd never see you again."

He gazed at her face, so beautiful and vulnerable. His muscles went tight with the effort to avoid her. To avoid this.

"I want you, Jenny, in every sense of the word. I'm so damn attracted to you I don't know which end is up."

"Oh," she moaned aloud.

Dazed and aching with frustration, he couldn't breathe. This woman controlled him, body and mind. With her raspy breathing, her chest rose and fell. His pulse bounded as he eyed the swell of her breasts.

"You're irresistible." In one swift movement, he

pulled her close and pressed his mouth to hers. She opened gently for him, like a spring flower opening its petals to accept the welcome rain. Their tongues met, and with every soft caress, his blood rushed faster and he grew harder with arousal.

"You're all wrong for me," she said gently, laughing into his mouth, kissing his throat until he went weak, being very careful to avoid the stitches on his face.

"I know." He pressed her down onto his duster and stretched out his long legs, half on top of her.

She quivered. "You're much too controlling."

He grinned softly. "That I am."

She wound her arms around his neck and returned his kiss with the same scorching passion. "And much too preoccupied with yourself, always wanting to be alone."

"Umm," he murmured, pressing his face to her throat, which was soft and warm and fresh.

"And," she said, lightly tracing her fingertips down the buttons of his shirt, driving him wild with the pleasurable sensation, "you have a way of turning my life upside down."

"I know I do." His hands slid to the curve of her waist and over the fabric of her sleek, graceful hips.

"I'm wrong for you, too," she said. "I'm much too judgmental."

He was lost now, and he'd agree to anything she said. "Yes, you are."

Her eager touch matched his own as she stroked his thigh. He groaned. If she continued that for long...

"*I* like to have my life mapped out in front of

me," she continued earnestly, "but *you* seem to go wherever life leads you."

He loved the sound of her soft voice, even if she analyzed all day.

He ravaged her sweet lips and worked his way down her throat, letting his tongue wet the cloth over her nipple, listening to her moan in pleasure. Trailing his hands down to her waist, he eased himself between her knees and grasped her buttocks, filling his large hands with her rumpled skirts and silky mounds, and pressing her to him.

"Oh, Luke," she said, flushing with the heat of arousal, "what am I going to do with you?"

"Well, let's take this off."

Laughter caught at the back of her throat. Her eyes glistened with joy. What a beauty. With smooth, easy movements, he unbuttoned her blouse and untucked it from her waistband.

"Oh, no," he groaned, "you're wearing that purple corset."

He dipped his head to her bosom. She grasped his head and guided his lips to her nipple. When it popped out of her corset, a silky brown circle, he slid his mouth over it and suckled. She gasped with pleasure. He wanted to please her. He never wanted to stop. He tugged at the laces that bound her corset until he'd slid it off.

Gazing at her, he couldn't breathe. A slow, sweet ache spread through his muscles. How had he come to deserve such a kindhearted, generous woman? "You're like a sculpture, you're so beautiful."

Shadows from the leaves above them played on her ivory breasts. Sunlight shimmered in her hair and the sweet scent of the breeze wove between them. He looked into the blue depths of her eyes and couldn't move. She gazed at him with such pent-up emotion and expectation he desperately hoped he could live up to it. He never ever wanted to hurt her.

She began undoing his shirt buttons with increased fervor.

"Are you sure?" he murmured against her lips, suspecting, knowing, she was a virgin.

"I'm sure," she said in a whisper, helping him to release the buttons of his pants.

"Then I'll try to please you slowly." He tugged off his boots, then unbuckled his belt. When he slid out of his pants, her eyes dropped to his arousal and her cheeks flushed. He lifted her chin to meet his eyes, and kissed her deeply. "You have nothing to be afraid of."

"I'm not afraid."

He hiked up her skirt, then her petticoats, and tugged at the drawstring of her drawers. When she helped glide them over her bountiful hips, he gently slid his fingers up her legs to her soft, feminine center. She moaned into his mouth and he gasped with the thrill of pleasing her.

He nibbled at her bottom lip, then trailed his mouth along her jaw and throat. Her breathing grew more rushed, her heart racing beneath his own. A sheen of dewy perspiration glittered on her skin. When she reached her peak, he kissed her face, yearning to give her everything, every part of him. A feeling of deep peace engulfed him. After years of being alone, he felt like he'd finally come home.

When his kisses reached the soft rise of her belly, she shivered, and he ached to fill her. He needed her. His Jenny. She'd always be his Jenny. "I've never felt this way, about anyone," he offered tenderly.

She nodded, stroking his cheek, her face radiant. "Make love to me, Luke, I want to feel you."

"I want to feel you, too."

Consumed with desire, he covered her with his body.

She wrapped her arms around his neck, welcoming his touch. His swollen shaft entered, and exquisite pleasure rippled through him. He started to deepen their contact, feeling her stretch around him.

He arched against her, with a slow tender pressure. How long had he yearned to hold her like this? To show her how much he cared for her?

His lips grazed her temple. "Are you all right?"

"Yes," she murmured.

She pulsated where they joined. She moaned in sweet agony. With a quick thrust, he was inside her. A frown flashed across her brow, then it was gone, and he felt her tension easing beneath him.

"I want this to last forever," she said.

He nodded, overwhelmed with the sensations, hypnotized by her touch. By her soul. He wanted it to last forever, too.

When she flattened her hot palms on his waist, then ran them up his back, he groaned and submitted to his need for her. They clung to each other, his hips rocking faster and faster until he cried out, gasping with fulfillment, dismayed at how much he loved her.

He loved her.

Jenny lost track of time, surrendering to Luke. To the passion he aroused and the need she saw in his burning eyes. Had an hour passed? A beam of sunlight broke through the branches of the aspen, skimming his bronzed, matted chest. Clasped in his arms, both of them naked and standing up, she gazed up at Luke's dark, handsome face. Her back was pressed against the smooth bark of a tree, her bare legs wrapped around his hips, and he was making love to her again. For this moment, no one existed beyond their world, and she was drunk with sweet emotion.

Her fingers traced a path down his spine.

He moaned into her mouth. "This is some truce."

She arched her neck and laughed. He nuzzled his face into the crook of her neck and shoulder. Could anyone be happier than she was at this moment? Luke filled the empty hollow in her heart. He made her feel whole, with his strength, his sense of honor, his easygoing manner. Although he never said the words, she understood the intensity of his feelings.

How lucky she was to know him. She could learn from him about letting life lead her, wherever it took her. Wasn't that what she'd always wanted? Freedom and adventure? It was right here all the time, waiting to be released. All she had to do was give herself permission to live her life.

Luke stroked the tips of her breasts with his languid fingers, and she welcomed every touch. With wild abandon, she rode him until her muscles ached and waves of ecstasy rolled through her. Contentment and peace flowed between them, like a river in springtime. As if they'd flow together for all time. She felt it with every breath, every pulsing of her heart.

When they were spent and weak, they slid to the grass and let the warm wind caress their bodies. Jenny whispered in his ear, "You're better than I ever dreamed."

"I am?" he said with a lazy grin. "You've been dreaming about me?" He turned on an elbow and faced her. When he stroked her brow, desire glazed his eyes and her heart rang with joy. "Well, I'm honored, then. You shook my world," Luke whispered. His full mouth curved with tenderness. "You're like a dream. You walked into my life and challenged everything I thought I knew about myself. I don't know if I deserve you."

He pulled her closer, almost roughly, looking as if he wanted to say more, something else. But as he grappled with his thoughts, he grew silent. She understood intuitively, without the need for words. He'd always been alone, but now they'd found each other. He needed more time, and she accepted that.

She put her arms around his neck and kissed him. As she pressed her slender form against his muscled body, the silky hairs of his chest tickled her nipples.

Luke stirred. His voice rippled with humor. "You think the horse has had enough rest?"

Her gentle laughter floated through the air. "Never mind the horse, it's my turn for a nap. You've exhausted me."

Her skin tingled where he stroked her arm, then the muscles of her back. "You can nap when we reach town." He slapped her behind with an affectionate smack.

Sighing in utter contentment, she unwound her legs from his, sorry to see the moment end but

knowing it would be etched in her memory forever.
The day she'd made love with Luke McLintock.

"Let's discuss our plans," Luke told her as they
reached the outskirts of town.

He slid off the horse, kissing Jenny's shoulder as
he descended, twisting her stomach in delicious
knots. The sawmill loomed behind him, and the livery stables beyond that.

Luke let her remain on the horse while he
wrapped a gloved hand around the reins and strode
beside the bay. She was riding sidesaddle to ease
her soreness from their afternoon's activities, and
even now blushed when she thought of it. Had she
really done all that with him?

Her face shaded by her calico bonnet, she tried to
smooth her wrinkled cotton skirt. She was proud to
be with Luke and prouder still to discuss plans with
him. What plans did he wish to talk about? Her heart
fluttered with the possibilities.

Plans about their future?

Well, she wouldn't press him. "What did you
have in mind?"

"Let's decide what we're going to do about this
whole situation with Daniel."

"Oh," she said, surprised at his answer. Of
course. *Those* plans. A cold dash of reality doused
her.

His leather boots thudded across the dry, cracked
earth. "I don't want to hide out in a cabin anymore.
Do you?"

"No. I can't live like that, either. That was part
of the reason I decided to go to my father. To end
it."

"For safety, I think we should stick together.

You, Olivia, Adam, me and my men. Let's not split up again, it's too dangerous. Agreed?''

She nodded. "I never meant to put you in danger by leaving. I didn't know Harley was waiting for you." She gripped the saddle horn as she swayed on top of the horse. "Funny, Harley never bothered with me when I left the cabin this morning. Luckily."

"I've been thinking about that, wondering why he didn't take you back when he had the chance. I've come to the conclusion Daniel doesn't want you back by force. But he still wants you, otherwise he wouldn't be trying to get rid of me."

She listened, watching and admiring how Luke's shirt tugged on his powerful shoulders while he walked.

He turned his bristly cheek to look in her direction. "We've got the sheriff and his deputies looking for Harley now. If he's still in the area, they'll find him. But I won't cower in some corner, hoping Harley doesn't attack me, or the people I care for." When he eyed her with open pride, her body felt warm and heavy. "You and Adam."

Warmed by his words, Jenny smiled. There was nothing more touching in a man than to see his tenderness for a child. A child soon to be his son.

He continued. "If we could think of a way to haul Daniel here to my territory, where I'm surrounded by my men and the help of the sheriff, then we can settle this." Luke kicked at the dirt and swore. "Everything I've tried so far to get him here hasn't worked. Now he's got Harley on my tail, and I can't move for fear of what might happen to Adam or you." Readjusting the brim of his hat, he snorted in disgust and peered at the livery corral, where men were exercising horses and ponies. "Wait a minute, maybe there is a way. I could send him a telegram and tell him we're asking the sheriff to press charges. Assault and attempted murder, unless he comes up here to settle."

"We can't prove those charges. It was Harley, not Daniel, who beat you up and took shots at you. And you said you didn't see Harley for certain this morning. You couldn't identify him."

"I know, but maybe just the threat of charges will lure Daniel here."

Her mind fluttered in anxiety. "What's to stop him from getting even with you *after* he signs the papers and releases Adam?" She couldn't mask the fear in her voice. "He could still try to..." she gulped "...try to shoot you then."

"The threat that we'll—that'll *you'll* expose him, and that he'll lose his business with your father." Luke rubbed his raspy jaw.

In the background, behind the board-and-batten mercantile building, the buzz of people on the boardwalk grew louder. They'd reached town.

Luke was right. They had to lure Daniel here. She needed to help end this situation for Adam's sake.

And for her own dignity. This was something she needed to do for herself. As difficult as it was for her to say the word *no,* she needed to say it loud and clear, straight to Daniel's face. To stand up and say what was on her mind. *No, I won't marry you.*

They continued along Central Avenue, heading to the telegraph office. When they reached it, Luke helped her from the saddle. Sliding down his sinewy body, she gazed at him with respect and basked in his unwavering strength and grit. He gave her courage.

Adjusting her skirts, Jenny stepped ahead of Luke and they boldly walked in.

"Don't worry," Luke reassured Jenny the next morning, sitting at the dining table finishing breakfast. His large, callused hand touched her face gently. "We're safe and all together. I've got six men protecting the saloon, two to follow us wherever we go, and the sheriff's got his own arsenal of deputies."

Luke draped his arm around her shoulders. She was trembling again. She'd been jumping at every sound. The sputtering coffeepot had just jarred her.

His warm hold seemed to calm her. It was wonderful to touch her. He couldn't get enough. He wished he could just concentrate on her and his recent decision to adopt Adam, and not have to worry about the dangers that lay ahead.

But he had to protect them, and every muscle in his body was primed for that. There was little time to think of anything else than being on guard, wondering if Harley was waiting around the corner. And wondering how Daniel had reacted to the telegram. If and when he'd appear.

A smile softened Jenny's strained face. "I know you're right. It's just difficult to sit here and wait." She glanced around the empty saloon. "I'll go wake Adam. It's a windy day. Maybe he'd like to fly his kite. Or practice his knots. Yesterday, he couldn't get enough of that."

They entered the kitchen. Travis was standing in

the middle of the room. Olivia was crouched at his feet, hemming his pants.

Travis groaned when he saw them. "New trousers," he explained.

Luke poured them coffee, watching the two women who'd become his good friends.

Jenny's blue eyes shone with delight at something Olivia was saying, and once again, Luke thought about yesterday.

It warmed his heart to remember her beside him, the sun streaming over her naked body. When this was all over he'd take her into his arms and—

A bell rang in the alley. The four of them whirled at the sound. When they realized it was a cowbell, their jitters eased.

Then the hallway door leading from the saloon thumped. Luke reeled and grabbed at his holster.

"What in tarnation is going on here?" a burly male voice demanded.

With his Colt pointed, Luke cocked the trigger at the older gent standing there.

One Luke didn't recognize. Barrel-chested, wool suit, string tie, bowler hat and thin blond goatee... Before Luke had a chance to open his mouth, Jenny dashed to the man, her cheeks flushed red.

"Father. Wh-what are you doing here?"

Chapter Fifteen

~~~~~~~~

"I know there's no train from Denver today. I didn't come from Denver, I came in on the Omaha express. Been there for four days. They're having problems with the new steam locomotives." Nyland Eriksen removed his black bowler hat, placed it on the table in front of him, then patted his chest and looked at his daughter. He ignored Luke altogether.

Luke knew there were two daily trains from Omaha, and Omaha was the central hub for Midwest connections, running east and west. But still, Nyland's appearance had taken everyone by surprise.

"I made my way here to check on the new junction. And on *you*," Nyland said to Jenny. "Am I suppose to believe all this about Daniel Kincaid?" The man sniffed, then finally peered at Luke.

The blue, Swedish eyes were direct. Luke had seen that cold look on faces before—people sizing him up, thinking they knew all about him because he owned a saloon. The fresh scar on Luke's cheek didn't help his image. He slid a palm over it, then straightened in the slatted wooden chair. "It's the truth, sir."

Jenny had decided to tell her father everything. After she'd introduced him to the others, she took him and Luke to a quiet corner in the dining room. Daniel and Harley were two threatening men on the loose, she explained, and they all could be in danger.

Adam entered the big room and came over to Luke. "Luke, will you come toss the ball around with me?"

"This is Adam," Luke said to Nyland, giving a playful tug at the boy's overalls. With a broad smile, Adam revealed his missing front teeth. What was that? Two new white buds growing in the gums? Luke couldn't help but grin. "You've got two new teeth coming through."

"I do?" said Adam, trying to climb onto Luke's lap.

"I can't come play with you right now," said Luke, "and I want you to stay indoors. I'm talking to Jenny's father here, and you've got to mind your manners. Run along."

Adam looked hurt at the dismissal. As the boy walked away, Luke pulled him back by one of his red suspenders, causing Adam to giggle. "We'll do something together later," Luke whispered in his ear.

Nyland watched the interchange with cool interest. When Adam walked away, Nyland turned to Luke. "And you think Daniel's capable of deserting this boy?"

"Not only capable, but he's doing it."

"How do you know for sure the kid is his? I mean, lots of women..." He paused and looked at Jenny, then continued, "Lots of women have been known to accuse men."

Jenny leaned forward. "I didn't believe it at first, either, but if you spend time with Adam, you can see the resemblance."

"And I knew Adam's mother, Maria," Luke added. "She was a good woman, one who didn't lie."

Nyland narrowed his eyes. "But she was just a waitress in this saloon."

Jenny's face flushed with color. "That doesn't make her *less* than Daniel."

Nyland stared at her. "You're raisin' your voice to me?" His face darkened. "You know how foolish I looked on Tuesday? Standing at the podium with my hands shoved in my pockets? Where the hell did you put those notes I gave you?"

Jenny puckered her lips. She smiled almost imperceptibly. "In the hall desk."

Luke couldn't stand idle and see her take any blame for this. "This was all my idea. I thought we could draw Daniel out."

Nyland's voice grew harsh. "You'd use my daughter as bait to get what you want?"

"Father—"

"No sir," Luke bellowed, shoving away from the table, "I'm using myself as bait."

"You think I'm just going to take my daughter's word that you're a good man?"

"Father!"

"You're still young, Jenny. You haven't seen the world like I have. What do you know about people?"

Though she was obviously hurt, Jenny turned her face to Luke and shook her head in a private gesture.

Luke felt like giving her father a good shaking, but he sat still at Jenny's silent request.

She swallowed. "I know a lot more than you give me credit for. I know that Luke is a good man and Daniel is not."

Nyland's face turned red. He loosened his string tie. "Maybe there's something I'm missin' here. How long have you known this Luke?"

Her hand fluttered to her buttons. "One week."

Nyland whistled sarcastically. "That's a mighty long time. One week." He sprang forward in his chair. "I've known Daniel Kincaid for five years. I corresponded with him from Boston long before moving here. He's like a son to me. I've worked shoulder to shoulder with him, and I can vouch he's a good man. Together, we've closed many crucial business deals."

Jenny's spine grew rigid. "*I'm* not a business deal."

Nyland snorted in disbelief. "Who are you sidin' with? Me and Daniel, or the local barkeep here? The one you've known for a solid week?"

Luke slowly stood up. He'd had enough.

With quiet dignity, Jenny slid out of her chair and stepped beside him. "I'm siding with Luke."

Luke filled with pride.

Nyland shoved back his chair. Staring at his startled face, Luke felt sorry for him. He was just a man who thought he knew best. Luke couldn't blame him. Nyland was only trying to protect Jenny, just as Luke was.

Nyland veered around the table and grabbed Jenny's arm. "Let's go. We're staying down the road at the boardinghouse."

"Mr. Eriksen." Luke stepped in. "I can't have my men guarding so many places. If we all stay in the saloon—"

"I said we're staying at the valley boardinghouse. It's where I always stay when I'm here, and it's where we'll stay tonight."

Jenny wrenched her arm free. "I'm staying here."

Alarmed, her father stepped back. "In the saloon?"

She took a deep breath and nodded.

"It's hardly a place for a woman of...of your stature."

"It's the perfect place for a woman of my stature."

Just at that moment, the sheriff strode in from the boardwalk, accompanied by a deputy. "Luke!"

Just in time, thought Luke. "All right, Mr. Eriksen, if you don't believe me about Daniel, then believe the sheriff here. He's been chasing Harley for two days."

Sheriff McCoy looked uneasy. He came straight at Luke. Behind him, the swinging doors creaked. Cowboy hats and bonnets sailed by on the boardwalk.

"Tell him, McCoy," said Luke.

The sheriff spoke. "Luke, there's been news. I just got wired by the Denver sheriff."

"What is it?" Luke replied. "News about Harley?"

The sheriff shook his head and pushed his hat off his wrinkled forehead. He reached for something in his back pocket. The deputy nervously patted the guns in his holsters, and Luke looked from one to the other in bewilderment.

Taking a deep breath, McCoy avoided Luke's eye, slid out a pair of handcuffs and snapped one on Luke's wrist. "I'm here to arrest you."

Luke stumbled back. The blood drained from his face. "*Arrest me?* What the hell for?"

The other handcuff snapped tight. "The theft of ten thousand dollars. Last Thursday in Denver."

"Like hell!" Luke rattled the cuffs. The deputy stepped forward to help the sheriff calm him.

"What?" cried Jenny.

Nyland cursed. "See, I told you—"

"That's Daniel's answer!" Luke hollered to her as he was led away. "To our telegram and our threat—"

The sheriff interrupted, "Kincaid's got three witnesses—"

"Horseshit!" Luke asserted. "He's making it up."

In desperation, Jenny stepped forward. "I can attest to that, sheriff—"

"No, you can't," her father said, placing his arm on her elbow and yanking her in the other direction. "You're followin' me. We're going to that boardinghouse—"

"I won't go!"

The sheriff added, "Kincaid made other charges. Kidnapping Miss Eriksen—"

"Drop those charges," shouted Jenny in a frenzy, from around her father's shoulders. "I won't agree to those—"

"Kidnapping?" hollered Nyland. "Hellfire!"

"What's going on?" Adam raced into the room, holding his favorite rope, staring at Luke in handcuffs. Why did the boy have to witness this?

"Let him go!" Adam kicked the sheriff. "Let him go!" He bit the arm of the deputy, who hollered and tried to swat back.

"Leave the kid alone!" Luke swung his shackled arms in the air. How could he protect anyone if he was taken away?

Adam wouldn't stop kicking or screaming, shouting the same words Luke had when they'd taken his own father. *"Let him go! Let him go!"*

In the uproar that followed, two of Luke's men ran in from the street, and Beuford and Tom from the alley. Nyland was yanking Jenny's arm in one direction, Adam frantically tugging her in the other. Luke bellowed to be heard, issuing orders to Travis, "Get Judge Green. Bring him to the jailhouse."

His men raced from the saloon, some to find the judge, some chasing after Nyland and Jenny, trying to convince them to stay inside.

Olivia dashed forward and tearfully begged Mr. Eriksen to return. Adam tore free from the deputy's grasp and raced away, alone.

"Jenny!" Dragged by his handcuffs, Luke shouted as he was pulled down the side street. "Jenny, get Adam! Adam...!"

Distraught by Luke's cries for Adam, Jenny yanked free of her father in the dusty street and hollered to Beuford. "Can you check the livery stable for Adam? Sometimes he takes his pony." Her heart raced.

"Got it." Beuford ran off.

"I'll check his room," Olivia blurted.

"I'll keep an eye on your father," Tom said.

"There's no need—" her father yelled in frustration.

Jenny ignored him and dashed into the saloon, then the kitchen, then the alley. "Adam!"

No answer. No guards, either—they were all out front. She heard a bark. *The puppies.*

"Adam!" she shouted again, much louder.

"Yeah, over here!"

Relief washed through her. She ran down the alley. "I know you're upset, but you can't tear off like that."

Turning the corner at the shed, Jenny saw Adam lifting Blackie into his arms, but one more stride revealed the boy was not alone. He was standing beside Harley.

She froze. Harley looked up and tilted his hand in silent greeting. The man weighed three hundred pounds. He held the yellow mutt in his blunt, square palms, stroking softly. Harley grinned at her. Terror crackled up her spine.

"I wasn't takin' off, I'm here with my puppies." Adam wiped his tears with his sleeve and sniffed. "And this man here says he knows a way to free Luke. He's gonna help us."

Harley's leer was sickening. "I reckon the others are busy on the other side of the saloon."

If she so much as quivered, Harley could reach over and snap Adam's neck. What was his intent? His timing was too good to be a coincidence. He must have known the wire was coming in for the sheriff. He must have followed him to the saloon, waiting for Luke to be arrested so he could come after them.

She tried to relax the tension in her body, so that

Harley wouldn't feel challenged in any way. "Okay, Adam, put that one down. Let's go back."

Adam squatted and returned his pup to the crate. Harley did the same.

"Hold on, boy," said Harley, tugging on Adam's rope. "I want to show you a rope trick."

Jenny's heart lurched. She stepped forward. "No."

Recognition seemed to flicker in Adam's eyes as he looked from Jenny's stricken face to Harley's. "Okay, you can show me," said Adam, unwinding his rope. Adam gave Jenny a secret nod.

Harley snickered with amusement.

"Adam," warned Jenny. The boy was no match for this brute.

Adam ignored her. "Do it like this," he said to Harley, picking up the rope. Then, in one mad rush, Adam twisted it around Harley's wrists in a half-formed constrictor knot before Harley realized the boy knew what he was doing.

"What the hell? Get back here!" In a tangle of loose cord, Harley lunged at Adam.

Jenny screamed and threw herself between them. "Run, Adam, run! Go get help!"

Adam escaped.

"You little bitch," said Harley, grabbing her by her hair and painfully yanking. "I don't want the boy. Daniel doesn't want the boy. Don't you know by now no one wants the damn boy?"

With uncontrolled fury, Jenny reached out and slapped his face.

Harley wiped his jaw, barely stung. "Is that the way you like to play?" He slid his dirty hand over her mouth and began dragging her backward. "It's you everyone wants."

"Adam, it's not your fault that Jenny disappeared. It's not your fault." Two hours later, in the livery stables, Luke rocked the boy on his lap and tried to soothe his crying. It was *Luke's* fault. And he'd never forgive himself. He cursed Daniel, too. The son of a bitch would pay.

Luke's horse, breathing hard from the recent ride, snorted beside them. Travis was filling the water trough.

Thank God Judge Green already knew the story between Luke and Daniel, seeing that he was the one who'd drawn up the confidential adoption papers. The judge kept the facts private, but released Luke on bail. And Luke had frantically searched for Jenny, racing down the train tracks, knocking on every door, checking with the sheriff. There was no sign of her. He gulped back his fear.

God, if they so much as touched her...

Daniel had to know Jenny would never go back without being forced to. If Daniel harmed her in any way, he would be jeopardizing his position with Nyland and the railroad. Luke tried to focus on that sobering fact.

Adam turned his tear-streaked face to Luke's. "Will she come back?"

Luke swallowed, trying to sound confident. "Of course she will. I'll find her." The sheriff, his deputies and Jenny's father were already looking everywhere. Where the hell was she? Luke tried not to let his desperation overtake him. He stood up, leaving Adam seated on the straw pile. "If you let me remove the saddle, you can help me wipe my horse down so it's rested again when I need it.''

Luke unbuckled the saddle and hoisted it to its usual spot in the far corner. He'd have Adam oil it, to help the boy take his mind off the situation.

From the racks at the front doors, Luke grabbed a tin of oil and a cloth. He turned around.

Daniel stood in his path.

Luke gasped. The tin slid to the ground as he went for his gun.

''I wouldn't do that,'' said Daniel. He was breathing hard, rubbing his black beard and pointing a six-shooter with his other hand.

Luke's mouth went dry. ''Where is she?''

''I'm meeting Harley somewhere not too far away.''

So Daniel hadn't seen her yet?

After all these years, they just stared coldly at each other. Luke slid his gaze toward Travis. Travis was removing the horse's blanket and peering at them with alarm. Adam must still be lying in the straw. What would Daniel do if he discovered Adam here?

No violence, Luke prayed. No violence in front of the boy. *Lie down, Adam. Don't get up*.

''Friend of yours?'' asked Daniel with a leer at Travis.

''One of my men,'' Luke responded calmly, letting Daniel know he couldn't get away with murder here. If that's why the bastard had come.

A fat drop of perspiration trickled down Luke's temple. To distract Daniel from discovering the boy, Luke bent down and picked up the fallen tin of oil.

Daniel glanced down at the worn rag and tin. "I see you're still a workin' class boy."

Luke's jaw pulsed. *And I see you're still a bastard.* "If you want me, take me. Leave Jenny alone."

Daniel raised his gun higher. "Give me Jenny, and I'll sign those adoption papers you want so bad."

One punch was all Luke wanted. One punch to crack Daniel's jaw. "You sign first."

A sheen of desperation clung to Daniel's skin. "No. Not until she says she's coming back with me. I want you to come with me and convince her."

Luke's hand hovered near his gun. He'd always been a better shot. But how could he shoot in front of the kid? As despicable as Daniel was, Luke couldn't shoot Adam's father right in front of him. The boy would suffer the way Luke had suffered, being a party to his father's hanging.

Luke nodded. "Lead me to her," he said, trying not to sound too eager, hoping like hell they'd leave the stable immediately. "I'll convince Jenny to go back...with you."

"You better say something to your man over there," said Daniel, "so he doesn't follow us. Tell him you'll be back by nightfall. I know you won't try anything funny, because if you shoot me, you'll never find out where she is."

The heartless bastard. Luke nodded, about to turn. Before he could, Daniel slid Luke's guns out of his holsters.

As Luke made his way to the stall, Daniel stepped to the open back doors, guns in hand, standing in a wash of sunshine.

"Travis," Luke ordered when he reached the stall, "you're not to follow me. Take Adam to the saloon where he'll be safe."

With Daniel preoccupied talking to the stableboy, Luke crouched down to Adam's level. "Adam, go back to the saloon with Travis and wait for me there. I'm going to see if I can find Jenny."

Adam placed a stained, chubby hand on Luke's denim-covered thigh. Would this be it between them? Luke's throat ached. He'd do everything in his power to make sure he came back, but if not...

"Will you remember this moment with me?" Luke patted the soft, dimpled hand.

"Sure."

He wanted to give the boy something he'd never had himself: a goodbye from his father. "Adam, I know how you feel about me. I know how much you love me." Luke's voice faltered. "Even though I didn't know it then, with you growing up in the saloon beside me all these years, I loved you all along."

"Really?" The boy gave him a tender grin. Then he leaned forward, dropped his grooming brush in the straw and hugged Luke, his little arms able to reach only so far.

Luke swallowed. "Now look at me, Adam. Look at me and tell me...goodbye."

A puzzled look appeared in Adam's brown eyes. He smiled and spoke in that wonderful, boyish voice Luke would always remember. "'Bye, Luke."

Chapter Sixteen

Hooves pounded beneath Luke as they galloped along the railroad tracks. They were heading west, toward the mountains and the setting sun. Daniel had supplied the horses, likely by arrangement with Harley.

Overgrown brush flicked over Luke's boot. He tilted his hat in the wind and swore. Daniel wouldn't win. Not this time.

The horses slowed, winded from galloping uphill. Daniel removed his gun from his holster and pointed it at Luke. "Quiet now," he threatened.

Luke gritted his teeth.

To their left, a clearing appeared, and a hundred yards farther, three temporary crew sheds. Smoke billowed from the chimneys, and Luke realized there were rail workers inside, finished for the day, preparing for the next. Horses neighed from the makeshift corral. Stacks of ties, rails and rods lined the earth.

When they passed the camp, Daniel lowered his gun. "Not much farther." The dark circles beneath

his eyes were highlighted by the flash of orange sunlight.

"Why'd you bring Jenny here?"

"Isn't it obvious?" Daniel snarled, wiping his
greasy brow with the back of the hand that held the
gun. He adjusted his bowler hat. "I helped build this
place. Through my sweat and negotiation, Nyland
bought this land. The transcontinental's pushing
west because of *me*. Jenny's damn proud of that—
she told me herself. Bringing her here will remind
her who I am. She'll never leave me."

Luke shook his head in disgust. The brush grew
denser, pines and aspens closing in on their path.
They had to ride single file to pass, Luke ahead of
Daniel.

A mile farther, around a bend, three rail cars
gleamed in the dusk—a steam engine, a coal car
behind it and a flatcar loaded with logs.

Was Jenny in one of the cars? Riding closer, he
didn't see her, but they were approaching the edge
of a steep gorge. A temporary wooden bridge
spanned the hundred-foot drop, and those tracks
ended just beyond the other rim. Straight down, in
dugout furrows, the footings were laid for the permanent bridge, with huge rocks and boulders beside
them.

"Luke!" Jenny's soft voice called, sending his
heart careening.

He spun around as Harley stepped out of the
pines.

Harley was dragging Jenny by her arm. Luke
stood up in his stirrups, aching to jump down and
hold her. He flinched at the sight of her. Her skirt
was torn. Oh, hell, the side of her face was swollen.

"You son of a bitch," he roared, starting to spring from his saddle.

"Easy," said Daniel, cocking his gun.

Jenny's face twisted in torment.

When he saw Harley press a gun to her ribs, Luke halted and clamped his mouth shut. With rage building, he slowly eased back into his saddle and twisted toward Daniel. "What happened to you, Kincaid?"

Daniel cleared his voice. "I made something of myself." He tipped his hat at Jenny. "You're a sight for sore eyes, darling. Last time I saw you was the night of our engagement. Remember?"

"Yes," she said, her voice quivering.

"Remember how excited you were? How we waltzed together?"

"I remember, Daniel, but things have changed."

"Nothing's changed, as far as I'm concerned. Whatever Luke might have told you about the boy are false accusations. Let your mind unreel for a moment, Jenny, and remember how it feels to be in my arms."

She shook her head. Her straight, dirty hair tumbled around her shoulders.

Daniel's lips tightened into a grim line. "We're going to find the closest minister, and we'll be married before morning."

She recoiled at his words.

Luke felt his innards heave at the thought.

Jenny knotted her fingers in her skirt with a defiant glare. "No, I don't want to marry you." She turned from Daniel to Luke. Her face softened as he gently shook his head. He'd never be robbed of her. *Never.*

Daniel's face hardened. He turned to Luke with

venom in his eyes. When Daniel began to dismount, Luke abruptly motioned to Jenny, nodding toward the woods. Would she understand?

She did. As Daniel slid off his horse, she yanked free of Harley and lurched for the pines. Luke braced himself, then leaped from his saddle directly on top of Daniel.

"What—" Daniel stumbled to the ground, winded. Luke slammed his muscular body hard into Daniel's and was able to punch the bastard's face twice before Harley jumped him.

Fists hammered Luke's skull. He felt the fresh scar on his face rip open. Pain throbbed in his head.

With a hard kick at Harley's gut, Luke rolled away from the two men, swiping one of Harley's guns in the process. He fired blindly in Harley's direction, but the staggering man ducked and the shot missed him.

Daniel cursed as he recoiled from his beating. "Get him first," he ordered Harley, "then we'll go after the girl."

Luke whirled toward the woods. Jenny had disappeared. Crackling branches and running feet echoed from deep within the forest. She'd made it. A cry of relief broke from his lips.

She needed time to reach the safety of the crew camp, and he'd do what he could to give it to her.

He leaped in the other direction, hitting the hard ground with his shoulder and splinted hand, and rolling beneath the steam engine. Raising his gun, he shot in the direction of the men. No one's body thudded to the ground.

That meant two bullets fired, just four left. He'd have to make them last.

He waited but heard nothing.

"Come out," Daniel finally shouted, somewhere off to Luke's right.

"Over here," Harley yelled from the left.

Luke was surrounded. How could he protect himself from two directions? Unless...

He wriggled over the cold rails and slid to the other side of the steam engine. If he got himself and the cars across the bridge, there'd be only one possible direction to come at him. They'd have to follow him over the bridge. Jenny would be long gone by then.

He unhitched the engine, and the two cars lurched backward. He darted underneath one, gave a sharp glance at the moving axle and mechanisms of the undercarriage and wrapped his legs and arms around a solid bracket.

As silent as ice sliding through water, the cars glided along the shiny rails.

"What in hell's he doin'?" Harley screamed.

"You son of a bitch," Daniel cried. "Come back here and face me."

A bullet zinged past Luke's ear. Another one caught his shoulder, ripped the cloth of his shirt, but barely grazed his flesh.

The railcars gathered speed. As they left the bank and rolled onto the bridge, Luke inched forward to the hitch and managed to climb up between the cars.

The wind slapped his face. Pain hammered his grazed shoulder. If his timing were off, if the cars reached the end of the tracks before he jumped to safety, the train might derail with him beneath it.

Where were the two other men? Had they taken the bait and followed?

Clinging to the wall of the coal car, a hundred feet in the air, Luke inched to the ladder. He heard a scraping sound from above him. In one smooth motion, he lifted his gun, and when Harley's head and shoulders appeared, Luke fired.

The blast knocked Daniel's thug through the air. Blood sprayed from his chest. He fell straight to the bottom of the gorge, to the boulders far below.

No one could survive that fall.

Luke braced himself against the coal car wall. Now what?

Where was Daniel?

Luke listened. The train gathered more speed. He had to jump off soon if he planned on saving his own skin. With his fingertips, Luke grabbed hold of the ladder then scrambled onto the coal pile, which was covered with a tarp. Daniel was standing on the other car, on top of the logs facing him. They stared at each other for one eerie moment.

Then Daniel dove for his gun, at the same time Luke jumped from the train.

The steel wheels screeched as the cars hugged a curve. The dark sky raced by in a blur. The train thudded off the tracks, derailing onto the soft earth, and then, with one deafening rumble, rolled over.

Out of control, Luke careened down the bumpy coal tarp, and when the train creaked to a stop on its side, he found himself dangling from the ladder with his arms above his head. The coal had toppled over his head, and coal dust stung his nostrils.

The air grew still again. He wasn't sure how far down the ground was below him, if he'd cleared the gorge at all. His arm muscles shrieked from holding on so tight.

What had happened to Daniel?

Luke slowly turned his head. Three feet away, Daniel was clawing at the edge of the flatcar. His legs cycled in the air above the gorge.

Ever so gently, Luke tipped his gaze upward, above Daniel's head. Most of the logs had tumbled off, but two remained, wedged above him. Daniel stared at the logs, his mouth twisted with fear.

A moment of compassion surged through Luke. A long time ago, when Daniel was a tenderhearted boy, he and his family had taken Luke and his mother in when they were in desperate need of help. Daniel had helped clothe and feed them. What had gone wrong? Daniel's greed? But he'd been a good man once, just as Luke's father had been a good man in his early years. And no one had ever helped his father.

Luke couldn't end it like this. His voice shook as he held out his hand. "Hold on, Daniel. Reach for my hand!"

Daniel turned with vivid terror in his eyes. He opened his mouth, but words didn't come out.

"Hold on," Luke repeated, inching forward. The train began to rock.

"I'm not gonna make it," Daniel whispered.

Luke gulped. "Yes, you will. You were always good on that rope in the hayloft. Hold on, I'm almost there."

Daniel turned as white as a cloud. "Tell the boy—" he gave a desperate gulp "—tell the boy I didn't mean no harm."

And then Daniel was gone. He lost his grip and fell to the bottom of the gorge, his twisted body landing on the footings below.

Luke turned away in horror.

With a roaring boom, the railcars heaved, the remaining logs let go and everything began to topple downward.

Two days later, they buried Daniel atop the grassy slope of the ranch he'd grown up on, next to the gravesite of his folks.

The sheriff had taken care of Harley's burial.

Jenny's heart was heavy, with a burden she'd never felt before. How could it have ended like this?

Scraped and bruised, she bowed her head as the minister said the parting words. Beside her, Luke, his left hand resplinted and his left shoulder bandaged from the bullet wound, gave a heavy sigh.

She thanked God Luke had made it off the ledge with no more than a gash to his leg. After she'd reached the camp, the rail crew had returned with her to the gorge. Luke had suffered a concussion and he was slow to recover, but he seemed to have regained some strength this morning.

Adam was staying with the cook and his wife while Luke, Jenny, her father, Olivia, Travis, Daisy and Nathaniel paid their last respects.

A shovelful of dirt hit the casket. What a pitiful waste, she thought.

The wind whipped at her ribboned hair. The warm chinooks had finally left, replaced by bitter cold. She wrapped her shawl tighter around her shoulders and leaned her bonnet into the wind.

Afterward, Luke walked with her to the bottom of the hill.

Jenny turned and searched his sober face. "Will you ever tell Adam about his real father?"

"When Adam's old enough to understand, I'll tell him about the fine things I remember. I know this may seem strange, but in the end, Daniel became that childhood friend I once knew."

Her eyes stung with tears. She turned away.

Luke grabbed her arm gently. "Jenny, about what's happened—"

"Don't, Luke. It's too awful to talk about."

"What happened to Daniel is not your fault. He brought it on himself."

"I know, but it's still too awful to talk about. I was a party to it, and coming back with the rail workers, seeing Daniel's body sprawled on the rocks..."

When she looked Luke in the eye, she knew he couldn't deny it. The agony in her heart was reflected in his sorrowful eyes.

She was numb with grief. She didn't know what she felt.

For Daniel or for Luke.

The wind howled around her ears. It was cold here in Cheyenne. The wind never stopped blowing. It was best she stay out of the chill. It was best she return to Denver.

Jenny barely ate for three days, barely paid attention to her surroundings at the saloon, barely noticed Olivia's coming and going.

Clearing up the dishes from their final dinner together in the saloon, knowing she'd be on the morning train, Jenny turned to Olivia with utter astonishment. "You eloped yesterday?" Jenny asked her. "Just two days after the funeral?"

Luke, hands full of cups and saucers, pushed the

kitchen door open with his foot and glanced from Olivia to Travis, equally flabbergasted.

Olivia placed the porcelain cups, which were rattling in her jittery hands, on the kitchen counter. "Oh, I know it was wicked of us, Jenny, it really was."

She twisted her fingers in her apron, but when Travis joined her and placed a large arm around her slim shoulders, Olivia burst into a smile and began to chatter. "But the timing was so perfect. It was such a lucky day to get married. First, in the morning, my apron strings accidentally came untied, and you *know* that means my sweetheart loves me very much. Then I pared an apple whole, without breaking the peel. I know you think it's an old wives' tale, but when I threw it over my shoulder to see in what shape it would land, to discover the first initial of my future husband, well, it was *T*—for Travis! And then the third lucky thing," she said, clasping her hands in delight, her voice gaining speed, "was when Travis tripped and fell over a horseshoe. A horseshoe! And it was still studded with nails, bringing extra good luck."

Olivia gulped and kept going. "I didn't know how to tell you, Jenny, seein' how we're supposed to be leaving tomorrow, but I just can't keep it bottled up any longer. Travis and I got married!"

Jenny was already laughing. So was Luke—for the first time in days.

"Oh, Olivia," Jenny said, stepping forward to hug her dear friend, "I'm so happy for you." She truly was. "And for you, Travis." She shook his hand.

"Thank you," he said.

Luke stood apart from the others for a moment, arms crossed over his broad chest, his black shirt neatly pressed and his black hair slicked back at the sides. Lord, he looked handsome today, thought Jenny. Extra handsome.

Luke stepped closer and clapped Travis on the shoulder, then shook his hand. "When did you decide to ask her?"

"Days ago," said Travis, grinning through his wide mustache. He squeezed Olivia. "One morning before the rest of you were even awake, when the roosters were still crowin'—"

"Travis, watch what you say," Olivia interrupted, squirming beside him, lowering her lashes. "You make it sound like…like we woke up together in the same bed—"

"Oh, no," he said, trying to explain himself. "It happened—it happened…" He turned to Olivia. "When did it happen again?"

Jenny glanced at Luke. His eyes twinkled at her, and she gave him a warm smile, amused at Olivia and Travis's obvious ploy to get their story straight.

Olivia's lashes fluttered. "Why, you asked me during our walk."

"Right," said Travis, nervously, "our walk just before breakfast."

"Just *after* breakfast, remember?"

"Just after breakfast," Travis corrected.

Jenny noted the happy glow on Olivia's face, and every loving touch she gave her beloved Travis, and her own heart ached. "I'll miss you terribly, Olivia." Jenny sniffed into her handkerchief.

Olivia's mouth quivered. She wrapped her arm around Jenny. "That's the only thing I can't bear about this. I can't stand to leave you. Please stay here a little longer.''

''Oh, I don't know.'' Jenny looked at Luke. Other than a few polite comments, they hadn't spoken since the funeral.

He inclined his dark head, waiting for her response. Did he want her to stay? she wondered.

She couldn't read those glimmering, gray eyes.

What did *she* want?

How did she feel about him? After all they'd been through together, where did it leave them?

Two weeks ago, she hadn't even known Luke. She'd been engaged to another man. How could she run into Luke's arms in so short a time?

But what she did know, when she looked at him, was that he was the most honorable, decent man she'd ever known. And he still made her heart flutter and her pulse beat faster. And why was she never able to catch her breath around him?

Jenny grabbed Olivia's hands. ''Will you have lots of babies?''

''We want dozens and dozens,'' Olivia cooed.

''You'll have a long family tree to explain to them. All the way back two hundred years.''

Olivia's tears spilled over. She nodded, unable to speak for a moment. ''Thank you, Jenny, for being my sister.''

The two women hugged, and Jenny knew she'd explode if she thought much longer about being separated from Olivia.

Olivia pleaded, ''Say you'll stay two more weeks. You can help me look for a place to stay, something temporary for me and Travis. Travis said we might even look for a little house.''

"It's all right by me if you stay longer," her father boomed from the doorway.

Jenny straightened. With deep respect, she gazed at her father as he congratulated Olivia and Travis. He'd been through a lot these past three days, and he was quieter than she'd ever seen him.

"I'll—I'll catch the train tomorrow myself," her father stammered. "You can follow in a week or two. I mean, *if* you're askin' me, it's all right."

"Thank you," she said, embracing him.

As for Luke, her sentiments were still a confused tangle, but Jenny took a deep breath and faced the others. "Olivia, I'd love to stay with you for two more weeks."

If Luke paced the floor much longer, he'd wear a hole in the kitchen planks. But he couldn't get his mind off Jenny. Tonight, she'd said she'd love to stay for Olivia's sake. Not his. Olivia's.

Why wouldn't Jenny talk to him? Every time he looked at her, he wanted to snatch her into his arms and carry her off to his bed. But things had cooled between them. She'd grown distant and detached. How could he approach her when she would barely look at him?

And how would the townsfolk react to seeing her with Luke, so soon after they'd buried her fiancé?

Jenny and Luke couldn't, of course, explain about Daniel's true nature and the cause of their fighting, because they wanted to spare Adam's future feelings when he discovered that Daniel was his father. The judge was sworn to secrecy. And Luke and Jenny, with the others, vowed they wouldn't tarnish Daniel's name. His death had been an accident—caused by Harley, the judge had decided to rule. They would let Daniel rest in peace.

Luke was grateful to Judge Green for implying there must have been a business rift between Daniel and Harley, which allowed the townsfolk to mistakenly conclude the fighting had occurred between the two of them.

Meanwhile, the situation was complicated, and Luke knew Jenny needed more time to put her feelings in order. But how much time?

Lord, if she never got over it, he'd crack and crumble into a thousand pieces, wither like a dry weed blowing in the wind. To come this far, to open his heart and make love to her, and then never hold her again, would be the end of him.

He was still recovering from his wounds, and had his hands full trying to get his name cleared of the Denver robbery, not to mention tending and caring for little Adam.

Tired of thinking about it, Luke stepped into the spring room off the kitchen, pumped the well handle and filled the basin with cool water.

Adam burst in. ''Can't I stay up a little longer?''

''No,'' Luke said, grinning, trying to be firm, but always ending up being soft. ''It's time for bed. Here,'' he said, playfully tossing the youngster a washcloth, ''wash your face and hands, then change into your nightshirt.''

Luke drew the boy closer, so grateful Adam had been spared witnessing the ordeal with Daniel. The boy was happy just to be with Luke, and thrilled they'd found Jenny.

''I'm never takin' these clothes off,'' Adam said proudly, ''never.''

Luke laughed. The boy was wearing some new clothes Luke had bought at the mercantile. Nothing fit. While the trousers were a little snug, the shirt billowed and the sleeves hung too long. The new leather shoes flopped on his feet. He'd grow into those, Luke supposed, but he didn't understand it. It seemed Adam needed a size six shirt, but size eight trousers and size one shoes. Who could keep track of all those sizes? Adam, bless his heart, wouldn't let Luke return anything. The boy insisted he loved it all.

Luke sighed in deep contentment.

He smiled to himself at how nervous he'd been in the beginning. But he'd discovered he didn't have to learn how to be a father overnight, he'd learn it one step at a time. Adam would guide him.

Hearing Jenny's voice in the kitchen, Adam jumped up. "Jenny, Jenny, is it true? Are you staying two more weeks?"

Luke's pulse began to hum at the sound of her gentle voice.

Jenny poked her face through the door with a rustle of skirts. She came in only so far and then stopped. She was avoiding Adam, too, Luke noted with disappointment. He knew why. It was as if she were afraid to become attached to the boy, in case...

With an uneasy glance at Luke, she settled her smile on Adam. The contours of her face softened, set off by the creamy apricot color of her new blouse. "Yes, it's true."

Surely, that day in the sunshine by the creek, when they'd joined in union, would be more than just a memory Luke would remember into his old age?

Adam asked her, "Can you help put me to bed tonight?"

"Oh," she murmured, then looked at him brightly. "Sure, I haven't done that for a few days. I miss it."

When the boy was settled in his bed, Jenny and Luke standing above him, tucking him in, Adam whispered, "Tell me, again, Luke, how you're going to adopt me."

In the hazy glow of the lamp, Luke turned to Jenny and they shared a private smile.

Luke's throat tightened. "I'm going to adopt you, Adam. You're going to be my son and I'm going to be your father."

"Do you promise?"

"Yup."

"When?"

Adam already knew when. Luke had told him a dozen times already. "The judge will have the papers drafted tomorrow," Luke said. "I'll sign them as soon as they're ready."

"Promise?"

"Yup."

Luke bent down low and kissed the boy's brow. He ached to tug Jenny down with them, a circle of three, but she stood off to the side.

"Night, Jenny," Adam whispered.

With a soothing murmur, Jenny leaned down and pulled Adam into her arms, looking as if her heart would break.

When Luke turned down the kerosene lamp and they left the room, Jenny spun away with only a simple nod in his direction.

What was she so afraid of? To go near the boy? Or to come near him?

Chapter Seventeen

"**P**a?" asked Adam, scooping Blackie into his arms and feeding him a biscuit.

Luke's hair ruffled in the cool breeze. He crouched down to the boy's level and stroked Blackie's fur. Would Luke ever get used to being called that? In wonder, he drew a hand over the young boy's shoulder. "Yeah, Son?"

"Can I keep Blackie for myself?"

"Are you going to look after him?"

"Sure I will." Adam buried his face in the puppy's soft fur.

The boy had already proved he could look after the strays. "All right, then, I reckon you can keep him."

Beyond the valley, a train whistle blew and echoed off the buildings behind them, giving Luke a jolt. The eleven-twenty was arriving from Denver. It was Saturday morning, and Jenny was leaving today.

Two weeks had passed and they weren't any closer to coming together. He'd kept his distance, giving her time, hoping and waiting for her to come to him, but she never had.

Not once.

She'd spent her time with Olivia and Travis. And after all she'd done to stay away from Adam, it seemed she couldn't. She'd spent hours with him daily for the past two weeks.

"Jenny's not stayin', is she?" Adam's brown eyes pierced Luke's.

"I don't think so."

Adam lost his smile. "Why not?" he asked with such honesty Luke couldn't answer for a minute. "Can't you make her stay? Don't you want her to stay?"

"I do, but it's complicated."

The steam engine blew again. In just over an hour it'd be gone. And Jenny with it. Before she left, he had to show her something, something he'd planned specially for today.

Should he spill his heart to her, as well?

How much longer should he wait? Till she went to Denver and settled in down there? Till she completely forgot about him, that he even existed?

Adam lowered Blackie to the water bowl. The puppy slurped. "Jenny's gonna be all alone when she leaves."

Luke startled at the thought.

It was true. She'd be alone. Like he'd been once in a former life, before he'd found Adam.

Jenny had lost Daniel, and then Olivia, and all her plans for her store.

Most of all, if she left, the two of them would lose each other.

He rose to his feet.

No. He couldn't let that happen. No matter how much more time she thought she needed, or what the townsfolk thought of them, he had to find her.

"Why do you have to go?" sobbed Olivia in their bedroom at the saloon.

Jenny folded a dress into her satchel. "My life's in Denver."

"But I'll miss you so much," her friend wailed. She pulled out her damp hanky and buried her face in it. The brown bow on top of her curls bobbed.

Jenny flopped onto the bed. Her eyes grew misty. "Please don't cry, or I'll start all over again. I'm thrilled it worked out for you and Travis. He's a good man and you deserve happiness and sunshine. Just think of the nice house he bought for you, where you'll raise your family."

Olivia's chest heaved with sobs.

"Be happy for me, too," Jenny said, trying to calm her.

Olivia glanced up. "What do you mean?"

"Well, I'm going back to Denver, and I'm going to work hard to open my lingerie store."

"Oh, well, that is good news."

It wouldn't be so bad in Denver, Jenny told herself. She'd stood up to her father, although he still disapproved of her store and wouldn't back her. But in the spring, her brothers would be joining them, and she was looking forward to that.

She'd do whatever it took to provide capital for her store. In the last two weeks, she'd earned twenty more dollars sewing for the dancing girls. When she returned to Denver, she'd scrub floors and sew fancy dresses until her fingertips were raw. And she'd take pride in every cent she earned.

Denver bankers had turned her down, but there were a number of businesswomen cropping up here and there. Maybe they'd loan her the money for start-up. She'd certainly give it a try.

Jenny heaved her heavy satchel off the bed. Her heart thudded. How would she say goodbye to Luke? To the man she loved with all her heart? She freely admitted it now. In these two longest weeks of her life, he hadn't approached her. Every time she tried to muster her thoughts and words to speak to him, she wound up remaining silent.

Thankfully, her anguish over Daniel's death was fading, and whenever she saw Luke and Adam together, her heart filled with joy, so very pleased Adam had Luke as a father now.

Luke had been the better man all along.

She pressed a hand to her fluttering stomach. But Luke had never promised her a future.

He'd never promised her anything, and anything she might have hoped for was just a wild, runaway dream of her own foolish imagination.

She inhaled a steadying breath of Wyoming air. Well, she'd have to make her own future, then. And she wasn't as scared to do it as she'd been a month ago, before she'd set foot in his saloon.

Taking a final glance in the long mirror, she smoothed her beaver tail, adjusted her blue feathered bonnet and ran a hand down her newly sewn, blue twill dress. The bustle shimmered in the sunlight streaming through the window.

"Do you promise you'll visit often?" Olivia sniffled.

"I do."

"I still can't say goodbye."

"Then please don't follow me to the station. I'll fall apart." Jenny's throat burned with hot tears. "Let's say goodbye at the saloon doors instead."

Olivia nodded in agreement and headed down to the saloon, where they embraced.

Pensively, Jenny dropped her bag by the bar and glanced around for Luke. The moment of reckoning couldn't be postponed forever. Would this be it, then?

The saloon was almost empty, except for the dancing girls moving behind the stage curtains, and the two bartenders polishing and stacking glasses along the mirrored wall.

Jenny didn't see Luke. It was getting late, quarter to twelve.

"I'll look in the kitchen," Olivia said, disappearing in that direction.

"Are you looking for me?"

Jenny's breath caught at the sound of Luke's deep voice behind her. She spun around to face him.

Tall, rugged and dangerous.

Dressed in black from head to toe.

He seemed overwhelmed to see her. His full lips parted slightly. When he grazed her body with his eyes, slowly working his way up from boots to bonnet, over her blue dress and bustles, heat raced through her bloodstream.

She was shocked at the impact of his deep gaze when he finally peered into her face. "You look so different. Did you make that dress yourself?"

She nodded proudly.

"And the bonnet, and the cloth gloves?"

She nodded again. *And the lacy cream corset, and the fleeced petticoat, and the silk stockings with the monogrammed initials, Miss J.E.*

"You are indeed a very talented woman."

He was so good-looking, and she reacted so powerfully to him, that she could barely speak. "Thank you."

Her thoughts filtered back to the day she'd made love to him. How beautiful his body had been beneath hers, how remarkably sensitive those callused palms were. She yearned to reach out and wind her fingers through the soft hair at his temples.

Instead, she glanced away. "I'd like to find... *Adam* to say goodbye."

"Weren't you going to say goodbye to *me?*"

She raised her gaze slowly to look at him. His eyes glistened. Nervously, she ran a hand over her skirt. What was that? Something hard in her pocket. With a frown, she dug it out, staring at a hard black lump. Then she smiled.

"What is it?" Luke asked.

"Olivia must have put this in my pocket. It's a lump of coal...for good luck." She gripped it firmly between her fingers, about to place it on the bar, but changed her mind and slipped it back into her pocket.

"You have a good friend in Olivia."

If he started talking about her dear friend, Jenny would likely start crying again. "Will you keep an eye on her? I know Travis is a good man, but will you just watch out for her?"

He nodded. His voice grew husky. "You'll never change, you know."

If she looked at him much longer, her heart would

burst. He reached out, about to stroke her face, but she stepped to the bar to get her satchel.

Before she could stop him, he yanked it from her grasp.

"Hey, I need that."

He placed it firmly back on the floorboards. "I want you to follow me first. Take a look at this."

"At what?"

"The sign beside the door."

She frowned and slipped out to the breezy boardwalk. A freshly painted sign was nailed to the wall.

Ladies' Luncheon on Saturdays. All Ladies Welcome for Complimentary Meal.

Her mouth gaped open. "Luke, what have you done?"

"I took you up on your business idea."

She'd thought the idea was sound when she'd mentioned it, but putting it into practice made her insides jump. "But are you sure it's wise?"

"I want to show you how much I believe in you."

He grabbed her by the hand and led her back inside. Her skin prickled all the way up her arm; it felt so wonderful to be touched by him. And did she hear him right? He said he believed in her.

"It's true," said Mona, handing her the morning paper. "Winslowe wrote about it in his editorial. Look behind you, there's a few ladies coming in now."

Jenny still couldn't believe it. Luke was actually taking a chance on her idea. That's why the tables were covered with checkered red cloths.

Outside, the train whistle blasted. With a jolt, Jenny dropped the paper. "I'll miss my train."

"Don't you want to see how your idea pans out?" Luke asked.

Sure she did, but she only had about thirty minutes left. Regulars began trickling in, settling at the bar. Franklin tipped his hat to her, then Reverend Thomas and Winslowe. Mona and Olivia. Travis and Lee. The cook and his wife.

"I'm not sure about your idea, myself," Mona complained, leaning closer and wiping her fingers on her apron.

"It'll work," Luke said.

"Anyone comin' in yet?" asked Beuford.

"Well, not too many yet."

"This I gotta see," said one of the stagecoach drivers, ordering an ale.

Women began arriving. Old Mrs. Robins and her granddaughter, then the bank teller and her mother, and then a dozen more women with their daughters and grandmothers. This was not exactly what Jenny had in mind. Where were the men?

Well, at least the women would have to pay for their drinks. Jenny listened to them give Mona their orders, and groaned along with Luke.

"Water, please."

"Just a glass of water."

"Water will be fine, here, too."

"Hey, Luke," said a laughing man. "I see a lot of women, but I don't see no payin' customers."

Jenny looked around in frustration. Only women. Lots and lots of women, but no husbands.

An elderly woman timidly opened the saloon doors and approached Mona. "Can my sisters have free meals, too?"

Mona glanced at Luke in disbelief. Jenny held her breath.

"That's what the sign says," Luke stated. He said it very calmly, but Jenny noted the perspiration collecting at his temples.

Finally men start crowding into the bar, until there was standing room only. "We want to watch this nonsense," they hollered to Luke, putting down their money for drinks and calling out for bacon and eggs and fried cornmeal and roast beef dip.

Luke turned to her with a wide grin on his handsome face. "I think your plan's working. Not quite like we expected—it's the spectators who are buying—but your plan's working."

She smiled back in utter relief.

"I hired two extra cooks today, and Lola's singing," Luke told her.

"Oh, no," said Jenny, "I'm not sure that's a good idea."

"She's wearing one of the costumes you sewed her."

"That's an even worse idea." Jenny hadn't sewn her any costumes, she'd sewn mainly undergarments. And if Lola was wearing one of her corsets for a costume...

Lola came out in the crisp yellow Sunday dress Jenny had sewed for her. She made a very respectable sight.

The women diners settled in, gazing at the menus, listening to Lola sing a beautiful Irish ballad.

Luke turned to Jenny. "Now I've got something to say to you."

"I'll miss my train," she said, striding to the bar and picking up her satchel amid the noisy crowd.

"Where's Adam? I've got to find Adam. Adam!" she hollered.

Jenny was almost at the kitchen door when a black Stetson whirled overhead and landed at her feet. She halted in midstride.

"Come back here," Luke told her.

The crowd around them began to hush.

She turned to face him. What could he possibly want? "You can handle the Ladies' Luncheon all by yourself. You don't need my help."

"I'm not talking about the luncheon. I'm talking about you and me."

Her heart stopped pounding.

Lola finished her song. The crowd grew silent. Jenny wished someone would talk to break the spell that filled the room. What did he mean?

"Uh-oh," said Lola. "Ladies, hang on to your drinks."

Not another public display, thought Jenny. She spun on her heel toward the kitchen.

Behind her, she heard a loud thud and a jangle of spurs. Ladies began to laugh.

Jenny whirled around. Luke was standing on a red-checkered table. "Stay here with me, Jenny."

The crowd gasped. One lady spoke up. "Is this part of the show?"

"I think so," her friend replied.

Jenny met Luke's unwavering gaze and thought she'd melt right there. "Don't say things if you don't mean them," she whispered.

"I never thought I'd be up here saying this, but I don't want to be alone anymore. I never knew what I was missing until I met you. I love you, Jenny. Share my life with me. Be my partner."

"Your partner?"

He swallowed hard. "My wife."

Jenny's satchel dropped to the floor. She gulped and stared at him.

Luke continued earnestly, "I didn't think you'd even consider me until...you were free to do so. I didn't want to put any pressure on you, and that's why I left it so long. Please, Jenny..." His voice strummed through her like a warm welcome breeze. "Please say you'll be my wife."

A proposal from Luke McLintock? Her heart began to race. He loved her just as she loved him? A delicious heat shuddered through her body. His compelling eyes, his stance, his words, riveted her to the floor.

She looked around the room at the wonderful people she'd grown to love and trust, at Olivia, sobbing with anticipation, waiting for her answer, and then back to the ruggedly handsome man who was asking to marry her.

Her pulse hammered wildly at the base of her throat. She'd go with him to the ends of the earth and back.

Her voice crackled with emotion. "I can think of no man I'd rather call my husband."

"Yee-ha!" Luke jumped off the table and closed the distance between them. Her warm laughter filled the air and rippled through her body. When he wrapped his firm arms around her, she opened her heart to all the love they were about to share. She reached up on tiptoe and they kissed with fervent passion.

"Is *this* part of the show, too?" Jenny heard the same woman whisper.

"I think so," her friend replied.

Their kiss ended with laughter.

The men at the bar whooped. "Never thought I'd see the day when Luke McLintock would admit to bein' lonely!" one old cowpoke exclaimed.

The women, on the other hand, nudged each other, chuckling and clapping.

Lola began to sing again. Meals were served, drinks were guzzled.

"Barkeep," said Luke, "a round on the house."

Cheers exploded. "What a great day it is," shouted one man. "Luke shoulda got engaged a lot sooner than this. Free meals *and* free drinks!"

Jenny's heart pealed with joy.

Gazing at the customers, Luke whispered in her ear, his delicious breath warming her throat. "Your plan is working, and you deserve the credit."

She glowed from the pride in his voice.

Luke caressed her shoulders. "You know how I feel, don't you? I love you with everything I have."

"I love you, too. You and Adam."

Luke smiled. "I've got my eye on a small ranch, just outside of town. But I want you two to see it first. What do you think?"

"I think I've never been happier."

"And I'll leave it up to you, but you can open that store if you want to."

"My store?" She stepped back. "You'd help me get on my feet?"

"Sure, I'll help in any way I can."

"Oh, Luke."

"I'll help you earn it."

"*Earn* it?"

He laughed and pulled her tighter. "Sure, the

Ladies' Luncheon is your idea, it's bound to bring you a tidy sum. What else do you know how to do?"

Enraptured, and wrapped in his arms, she smiled up at him. "I do a truce real well."

His charcoal eyes twinkled. "A truce. I like your truces." He yanked her tight against his chest. Her breasts squished against him. His face sobered. "You believed in me as a father before I could even see it myself."

"Where is Adam?"

"He's playing with Blackie. I spoke to him already, about us."

"What did you tell him?"

"That you're going to be my wife."

"Pretty sure of yourself, aren't you, stranger?"

He laughed, then hollered for Adam. "Are you in the kitchen, Adam?"

The boy came barreling into the room and Jenny gazed at him with tenderness. Dear, sweet Adam.

The bottom of his overalls were caked with mud. Adam peered up at Luke. "Did you ask her yet?"

"I did," said Luke.

"What'd you say, Jenny?"

Jenny stooped down and clutched her little boy. He smelled like fresh air. "I said yes." She kissed his cheek. He'd be her son, now, too.

Adam opened his mouth in delight, and Luke embraced them both.

When Jenny straightened, she marveled at the crowd surrounding her—an enchanting mixture of people from all over the country. The warm, adventurous atmosphere filled her with joy and excitement.

Beyond the valley, a train whistled, on its way to Denver without her.

She knew in her heart she'd never leave this place. Never.

"The wild wild West," Jenny murmured with a sigh, as Luke caressed her throat with kisses. "I'm finally here."

* * * * *

KATE BRIDGES

is fascinated by the romantic tales of the spirited men and women who tamed the West. She's thrilled to be writing for Harlequin Historicals.

Growing up in rural Canada, Kate developed a love of people-watching and reading all types of fiction, although romance was her favorite. She embarked on a career as a neonatal intensive-care nurse, then moved on to architecture. Later, working in television production, she began crafting novels of her own. Currently living in the bustling city of Toronto, she and her husband love to go to the movies and travel.

HHIBC626

Cravin' stories of love and adventure set against the backdrop of the Wild West? Then check out these thrilling tales from Harlequin Historicals

ON SALE NOVEMBER 2002

RAFFERTY'S BRIDE
by **Mary Burton**
(West Texas, 1866)

Will revenge evolve into a powerful attraction between a life-hardened military man and a bewitching nurse?

BECKETT'S BIRTHRIGHT
by **Bronwyn Williams**
(North Carolina, 1890s)

Book #2 of *Beckett's Fortune* miniseries

Watch for this prequel in the riveting new cross-line series from Harlequin Historicals and Silhouette Desire!

ON SALE DECEMBER 2002

BOUNTY HUNTER'S BRIDE
by **Carol Finch**
(Arkansas and Texas, 1870s)

Forbidden love ignites when a New Orleans debutante weds a half-breed bounty hunter....

BADLANDS HEART
by **Ruth Langan**
(Dakota Territory, 1888)

Book #3 of the *Badlands* series

A feisty cowgirl falls head over heels for a mysterious stranger!

Harlequin Historicals®
Historical Romantic Adventure!

Princes...Princesses...
London Castles...New York Mansions...
To live the life of a royal!

In 2002, Harlequin Books lets you escape to a world of royalty with these royally themed titles:

Temptation:
January 2002—*A Prince of a Guy* (#861)
February 2002—*A Noble Pursuit* (#865)

American Romance:
The Carradignes: American Royalty (Editorially linked series)
March 2002—*The Improperly Pregnant Princess* (#913)
April 2002—*The Unlawfully Wedded Princess* (#917)
May 2002—*The Simply Scandalous Princess* (#921)
November 2002—*The Inconveniently Engaged Prince* (#945)

Intrigue:
The Carradignes: A Royal Mystery (Editorially linked series)
June 2002—*The Duke's Covert Mission* (#666)

Chicago Confidential
September 2002—*Prince Under Cover* (#678)

The Crown Affair
October 2002—*Royal Target* (#682)
November 2002—*Royal Ransom* (#686)
December 2002—*Royal Pursuit* (#690)

Harlequin Romance:
June 2002—*His Majesty's Marriage* (#3703)
July 2002—*The Prince's Proposal* (#3709)

Harlequin Presents:
August 2002—*Society Weddings* (#2268)
September 2002—*The Prince's Pleasure* (#2274)

Duets:
September 2002—*Once Upon a Tiara/Henry Ever After* (#83)
October 2002—*Natalia's Story/Andrea's Story* (#85)

Celebrate a year of royalty with Harlequin Books!

Available at your favorite retail outlet.

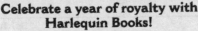

HARLEQUIN®
Makes any time special®

Visit us at www.eHarlequin.com

HSROY02

If you enjoyed what you just read,
then we've got an offer you can't resist!

Take 2 bestselling love stories FREE!

Plus get a FREE surprise gift!

Clip this page and mail it to Harlequin Reader Service®

IN U.S.A.
3010 Walden Ave.
P.O. Box 1867
Buffalo, N.Y. 14240-1867

IN CANADA
P.O. Box 609
Fort Erie, Ontario
L2A 5X3

YES! Please send me 2 free Harlequin Historicals® novels and my free surprise gift. After receiving them, if I don't wish to receive anymore, I can return the shipping statement marked cancel. If I don't cancel, I will receive 6 brand-new novels every month, before they're available in stores! In the U.S.A., bill me at the bargain price of $4.47 plus 25¢ shipping and handling per book and applicable sales tax, if any*. In Canada, bill me at the bargain price of $4.99 plus 25¢ shipping and handling per book and applicable taxes**. That's the complete price and a savings of over 10% off the cover prices—what a great deal! I understand that accepting the 2 free books and gift places me under no obligation ever to buy any books. I can always return a shipment and cancel at any time. Even if I never buy another book from Harlequin, the 2 free books and gift are mine to keep forever.

246 HDN DNUD
349 HDN DNUE

Name	(PLEASE PRINT)	
Address	Apt.#	
City	State/Prov.	Zip/Postal Code

* Terms and prices subject to change without notice. Sales tax applicable in N.Y.
** Canadian residents will be charged applicable provincial taxes and GST.
   All orders subject to approval. Offer limited to one per household and not valid to
   current Harlequin Historicals® subscribers.
   ® are registered trademarks of Harlequin Enterprises Limited.

HIST02   ©1998 Harlequin Enterprises Limited

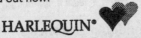

ENJOY THE SPLENDOR OF
Merry Old England

with these spirited stories
from Harlequin Historicals

On Sale November 2002

GIFTS OF THE SEASON
by Miranda Jarrett
Lyn Stone
Anne Gracie

*Three beloved authors come together in this
Regency Christmas collection!*

THE DUMONT BRIDE
by Terri Brisbin

*Will a marriage of convenience between a lovely
English heiress and a dashing French count
blossom into everlasting love?*

On Sale December 2002

NORWYCK'S LADY
by Margo Maguire

*Passion and adventure unfold when an injured
Scottish woman washes up on shore and is
rescued by an embittered lord!*

LORD SEBASTIAN'S WIFE
by Katy Cooper

*Watch the sparks fly when a world-weary nobleman
discovers that his adolescent betrothal to a deceptive
lady from his youth is legal and binding!*

Harlequin Historicals®
Historical Romantic Adventure!

HHMED27